A SHAMWELL TALES NOVEL

PLAYED!

JL MERROW

RIPTIDE
PUBLISHING

Riptide Publishing
PO Box 1537
Burnsville, NC 28714
www.riptidepublishing.com

Played!

Cover art: Natasha Snow, natashasnowdesigns.com
Editor: Carole-ann Galloway
Layout: L.C. Chase, lcchase.com/design.htm

ISBN: 978-1-62649-612-5

Second edition
June, 2017

Also available in ebook:
ISBN: 978-1-62649-611-8

A SHAMWELL TALES NOVEL

PLAYED!

JL MERROW

RIPTIDE
PUBLISHING

This book is dedicated to all those who tread the boards in village halls and community theatres up and down the land, bringing the work of our most famous playwrights to the (usually) grateful masses and seeking no recompense but a round or two of applause. Long may the show go on.
With thanks for their help to Beverley, Pender, Jennifer, Lou Harper, Cleon, Susan Sorrentino, Kristin, and of course, all at Verulam Writers' Circle.

He's usually a good puller—but he couldn't get it up that time.
—Brian Johnston, iconic British cricket commentator

TABLE OF CONTENTS

CHAPTER ONE
A PLAGUE ON BOTH YOUR HOUSES

There was a frog in the kitchen.

Again.

Tristan crouched down to glare at it, quite certain that such incursions would not have been tolerated had Nanna Geary still been alive. And while she had now, at the ridiculously young age of eighty-two, passed on to her reward, he was damned if he'd let her house be invaded on his watch.

The frog stared back at him with an inscrutable amphibian gaze.

"This," he told it firmly, "has got to stop. Do I hop into your pond and frolic among the lily pads? I do not. So why you feel you can make free of my living area, I really cannot imagine."

The frog blinked once. Then, in a series of spring-loaded manoeuvres almost too quick for Tristan's startled eyes to follow, it hopped behind the fridge.

Damn it. This called for desperate measures.

Tristan picked up Nanna Geary's phone and dialled a number he'd had the foresight to memorise.

"Yeah?" The voice was deep in timbre, yet clearly young. Excellent.

"Hello. I perused your advertisement in our local emporium. *All—*"

"You what?"

"I read your card in Tesco," Tristan clarified with a sigh. Some people had no appreciation for the beauties of the English language. "*All household job's*—I assume the apostrophe was ironic?—*done, resonible rates.*"

"Er, yeah." The man on the other end of the phone sounded somewhat nonplussed, possibly due to the way Tristan had stressed the "ibble" at the end of *resonible*. "What's the problem?"

"Biblical."

"What?"

"I have a plague of frogs."

Pause. "Is this a joke?"

"If it is, it's on me. I keep coming down in the morning to find a frog in my kitchen. *Not* something one wants to see before one's first cup of coffee. And let me tell you, I'm something of a connoisseur of unwelcome morning sights." At least, Tristan comforted himself, this one hadn't been in bed with him.

Yet.

He wouldn't put anything past the vile green creature. It was probably hoping for a kiss, and far be it from Tristan to brag, but he had an impressively wide experience of where kisses tended to lead.

Over his dead body, in this particular instance.

"*A* frog," the handyman was saying. There was another pause. "So technically, yeah, that's a plague of *frog*. One of 'em."

"Semantics. The plural, in this case, may be taken to include the singular."

"Right . . . Look, I think you want pest control, anyhow."

"*Finally* we reach agreement. So how soon can you be here?"

"No, I mean you want someone who works in pest control. Um. You're in the village, right?"

Tristan rolled his eyes. "I'm certainly in *a* village. However, there appears to be an elegant sufficiency of villages in this vicinity. Perhaps one might essay a tad more specificity, hmm?"

There was a silence, then the voice on the other end was back. "Well, go on, then. Essay me specific."

Tristan frowned. Unless he was very much mistaken, there had been a soupçon of sarcasm in the handyman's tone. "Shamwell," he said shortly.

"Thought so. Right. I've got this mate. Where are you? I'll send him round."

"Excuse me? I'm sorry, I believe I must have had some kind of catatonic fit and missed the part of the conversation where I told you to feel free to invite all your friends to my house. Perhaps you'd like to create a Facebook event, make it a free-for-all—"

"Look, do you want rid of this frog or not?"

"*Obviously.*"

"Then lemme give Sean a call. He's a professional. What's your address?"

Tristan sighed. "Twenty-two Valley Crescent."

There was a pause. "That's Mrs. Geary's house."

"Was." Tristan's voice came out perhaps a little on the sharp side. He *missed* Nanna Geary. She'd always loved to hear about Tristan's latest triumph on the stage, and she'd certainly never told him to go and get a proper job. "Now it's mine."

"Right." The handyman's tone was equally abrupt. "I'll send Sean over."

"Immediately?"

"Well, he's probably on a job right now, but soon as he can make it, yeah."

"Make it soon. This is an *emergency*." Tristan hung up. It was often best not to give these people a chance to make excuses.

Then he went back to sorting through Nanna Geary's belongings. It was, Tristan had to admit, not proceeding as quickly as it might. He kept getting distracted by memories from his childhood. He'd been set back half an hour already this morning by coming across her old boiled wool jacket, a stiff heavy thing in the vilest shade of green imaginable—really, next to it, this morning's uninvited visitor would be a thing of beauty. The smell of wet dogs and camphor emanating from it had taken Tristan right back to rainy afternoons playing games of rummy in a dripping gazebo, because Nanna Geary thought boys needed fresh air even when the weather was dreadful . . . He sighed and folded it reverently before adding it to the charity shop pile.

Tristan was knee-deep in women's underwear when the doorbell rang. Most of it was of the sturdy thermal variety, but he'd been shocked and delighted to find some black lace nestling at the back of the drawer of, well, drawers.

"Nanna Geary, you saucy little minx," he murmured as he got to his feet, detached a wayward suspender belt from his sleeve, and made his way downstairs.

There was no hall, as such, in Nanna Geary's house. The front door opened directly from what she had liked to call the living room, comprising as it did both lounge area and dining room. Tristan strode along its length and flung the door wide.

The man looming awkwardly on the doormat was *delicious*. Tall, muscular, and delightfully rough around the edges, with dark stubble on his chin and unruly jet-black hair. He was casually dressed in jeans and a singlet, perfectly accessorised with a touch of the grime of honest toil. Things were *definitely* looking up. And up, and up. Actually, the man's height was bordering on the offensive, but Tristan was a forgiving sort. He beamed at the stranger and barely restrained himself from a *Hel-looo gorgeous*. "You must be Sean."

The man's face twisted, and he rubbed the back of his neck, displaying some nicely honed triceps and a tuft of armpit hair. Tristan's inner princess swooned dramatically. "Yeah, about that. Sorry. Sean says he don't do frogs, cos they're not classed as pests. Says they're good for slugs and all. I'm Con."

"Con? Short for Conor? Now you come to mention it, you do have something of the look of the Black Irish about you."

Con frowned. "If you think I'm black, mate, you shoulda gone to Specsavers."

Tristan rolled his eyes with a dramatic air he felt sure, had they been on stage, would have carried right to the back of the gods. "The *hair*, dear child. I was referring to the hair. So is it?"

"What, black? No, it's just sort of dark brown."

Con was now looking at Tristan like *he* was the one spouting nonsense, which Tristan felt, in the circumstances, to be grossly unfair. "I meant, your name. Conor?"

Inexplicably, Con blushed. "No. It's Constantine."

Ah. That explicated that one. "Never mind. There are worse fates. Take me, for instance: a Jewish boy named for a Cornish adulterer made famous by a Nazi composer. God knows what my parents were thinking of. I suppose you'd better come in," Tristan added, stepping back from the door.

"Uh . . . I just came over to explain about Sean not coming." The shuffling of his feet was heading in the wrong direction. Time to nip that *firmly* in the bud.

Of course, thoughts of *nipping*, *firm*, and even *bud* were, with the excellent visual aid standing in front of him, having a predictable effect on Tristan's libido. *Down, boy*, he told himself sternly.

"Now you're here, you can hardly leave me besieged by amphibians. Or even amphibian, singular. Come on, come in." Tristan made impatient beckoning motions. "And wipe your feet, please." Nanna Geary would have a posthumous fit if he let anyone tramp mud onto her living room carpet.

"'S'okay. I'll take my boots off." Con toed off his alarmingly large footwear on the doormat and *finally* stepped inside, looking around him as he did so. In his socks, his height was merely mildly irritating. Tristan could live with that, particularly when coupled with the rest of the package.

Mmm. And there was another Freudian choice of words. Tristan could *definitely* see himself coupled with Con's package . . . Damn. The man was speaking again.

"Just moved in, did you? I didn't even know the place was up for sale yet."

"It wasn't." Tristan supposed he'd have to explain himself or risk finding out just what the police in this area thought of squatters. "Nanna Geary left it to me."

Con blinked—then beamed, his whole face lighting up with the twinkle in those soulful, dark eyes. "You're *Tristan*, aren't you? I thought you looked familiar."

Whilst having his reputation precede him wasn't a totally new experience for Tristan, neither was it always a positive one. Still, he felt reasonably safe in assuming Nanna Geary hadn't said anything *too* terrible about him. "The one and only," he conceded modestly. "But I really think I'd remember if we'd ever met."

Con's smile was a little lopsided, curving up farther on one side than the other. It was annoyingly endearing. "Old Mrs. Geary showed me your picture. She used to talk about you all the time. Reckoned you're the next Laurence Olivier or something."

"Well, I prefer to think of myself as the first Tristan Goldsmith, but—"

"She said it was a real shame, you going to work for your dad's business in New York. Leaving acting behind. Said it was a terrible waste, what with you being all talented and that."

"Yes, well. Talent, sadly, is not noted for paying the bills." Or appeasing paternal figures, alas.

"So, what, you taking a few days off to get the place sorted out?" Con looked around Nanna Geary's living room, which was much as she'd left it aside from the regrettably small stack of boxes by the stairs that was all Tristan had so far managed to pack for the charity shop.

"I haven't actually started yet. At Goldsmith & Klein, that is. That's the firm. In New York. So I'll be here until October." Even Father had grudgingly agreed that settling Nanna Geary's affairs was an acceptable excuse for one last summer of freedom. "Though why that should be any of your concern—"

"I liked her. Your gran, I mean."

Tristan didn't correct him; after all, there were literal truths, and there were essential truths, and while Nanna Geary might not have been a blood relation, she'd been his grandmother in every other way that counted.

"She was a nice old lady," Con went on, his expression engagingly fond. "I did a few jobs for her around the house and the garden—cleared out that pond last year, in fact."

Tristan raised an eyebrow. "So what you're saying is, it's actually your fault I'm suffering from this plague?"

"Uh ..."

"Right. You can sort the wretched thing out, then. Last I saw it, it was behind the fridge. Come on, this way. Chop chop." He sent Con a winning smile.

Con hesitated but nonetheless padded into the kitchen, which, now Tristan came to think about it, really hadn't been designed for people of Con's size. He seemed to fill the space entirely, Alice in Wonderland style, giving the curious impression that it was the kitchen that had shrunk.

Not to mention Tristan, who was starting to get a crick in his neck from looking the man in the eye. "Do you *have* to be so tall?" he asked distractedly, scanning for signs of frog.

"I can kneel down if it'll make you feel better," Con suggested with a smidgeon of surliness.

Well, nobody could be expected to let *that* one go. Tristan sent Con a flirtatious smile. "Maybe later," he purred.

Con blushed and looked away.

Tristan stifled a laugh. He resumed his search, only to give up in frustration a moment later. "Bugger it. The wretched thing's gone into hiding. Or gone out the same way it came in. Whatever the hell *that* was."

"Doubt it," Con said, sounding amused.

Tristan glared at him, suspicion blooming. "Is this some Welsh-style conspiracy to stop newcomers invading the village? Have you been planting vermin in my house? What next, arson?"

"What? You ought to see someone for that paranoia, mate. Nah, it's obvious, innit?" He gestured at the kitchen door.

There *was* a cat flap in it, but surely not? "If you're trying to convince me the frogs around here have learned to use cat flaps . . ."

"Nah, but the cats have. It'll be Meggie, bringing you a housewarming present."

Tristan folded his arms. "Meggie died two years ago." Tristan had very fond memories of Meggie, who, despite the name, had been an overlarge neutered tom who'd strongly reminded Tristan of a less lurid Bagpuss. "If you're trying to tell me I'm being haunted by some kind of feline poltergeist—"

"Doubt it, seeing as she was fine last Tuesday. Must be a different cat—I think Mrs. Geary got her just before I moved to the village, cos she was hardly more than a kitten when I first saw her. So, yeah, not part of a village conspiracy, all right?"

"Nanna Geary got a new Meggie?" Tristan was horrified. Meggie couldn't simply be *replaced*. What had Nanna Geary been thinking of in any case, getting a new pet in her eighties? And why hadn't she mentioned it to *him*?

Tristan *knew* he should have visited more this last year, not just relied on phone calls, letters, and that time she'd flown all the way up to Edinburgh to see him in the Scottish play, bless her. Life with a touring production might not exactly lend itself to taking odd days off here and there, but he could have managed *something*, damn it.

Of course, he'd been meaning to come to see her in the summer. *Properly* meaning to, not just saying he would. He hadn't expected to run out of time so quickly.

"Yeah, but don't worry," Con was saying, as if he thought Tristan gave a damn about a cat he'd never even met. "The neighbours over that side"—he pointed vaguely up the hill towards number twenty—"have been looking after her. S'pose she's just noticed someone's living here again."

"Right, well, that can be the first order of the day—you can nail that bloody cat flap shut." It was hard enough coping with the thought of never seeing Nanna Geary again; Tristan was damned if he'd deal with some feline usurper to boot. And anyway, it wasn't like he was going to be staying here for long. Best not to confuse the wretched animal. "Now I come to think of it, there are quite a few jobs you could be getting on with."

Tristan looked around and grabbed Nanna Geary's shopping-list notepad, with attached pencil, from its hook on the wall. He thrust it at Con, who took it with a strange appearance of reluctance. Hah. Now it was Tristan's turn to regain the upper hand. "Here. Take notes. The ivy along the garden fence is getting *completely* out of control, and the back door keeps sticking. Oh, and the window frames all need painting, and the bathroom—"

"Hang on, hang on. You gotta slow down, yeah?"

"I wasn't talking that quickly. How far have you got?" Tristan peered at the notepad. And frowned.

Con's untidy scrawl extended to one word, and even that was being charitable.

"'Dor'?" Tristan asked, almost spraining his eyebrows in the process.

Con flushed and hung the notepad back on the wall with exaggerated care. One fist, Tristan couldn't help but notice, was clenched by his side. "Look, you want me to do a job—that's *a* job, right," he added pointedly, "the singular don't include the plural—you call me and I'll come do it when I'm free, all right?"

Tristan folded his arms once more and resisted the urge to tap his foot. As he was currently, he realised for the first time with a swiftly stifled pang of embarrassment, wearing a pair of Nanna Geary's tartan slippers, the gesture would in any case have lacked oomph. "You're free now, aren't you?"

"No, as it happens. I'm s'posed to be over in Bishops Langley in ten minutes. I wouldn't have come over at all, 'cept you kept saying it was such a bloody emergency." Con folded *his* arms, and Tristan couldn't help but notice the strength in those uncovered biceps, particularly as compared to any other biceps that might be in the vicinity. Dark brows lowered over stormy eyes, the man a veritable Heathcliff to Tristan's Isabella.

Catherine. He meant Catherine, damn it.

They glared at one another for a long moment.

"Fine," Tristan ground out. "I shall await your leisure."

Con drew a breath, then clearly changed his mind about whatever he'd been about to say. "Yeah. See you." He stomped to the door, jammed his feet into his boots, and left, closing the door softly behind him.

Bastard. Guilt surged anew at having visited Nanna Geary so infrequently in recent months.

Tristan would have been camped out in her living room twenty-four seven if he'd known *this* was the sort of company she'd been keeping.

CHAPTER TWO
ALL THE DEVILS ARE HERE

Con stormed out of Mrs. Geary's house wanting to punch something. Preferably her grandson's face. Poncey, smug, entitled *prick*.

How did someone as nice as Mrs. Geary end up with such a total git of a grandson? She'd had *proper* class, she had. She'd never treated him like he was just the odd-job man. Always brought him his tea in a cup and saucer when he was working round her place. There'd always been a bourbon biscuit or a custard cream to go with it too. He'd used to stop work, and they'd have a bit of a natter while they drank their tea, 'specially after she'd found out his gran had just died and he didn't have any other family. Well, none that counted.

The way she'd talked about this Tristan bastard, Con had expected someone *totally* different. Someone who was actually nice. Course, he was an actor, wasn't he? Probably put on some manners when he was with his gran. Wouldn't have wanted her to leave him out of her will, now would he?

And he'd had to be good-looking, hadn't he? And pretty obviously gay. He looked a bit like Mo, if Con thought about it, which he *didn't*, all right? Mo was ancient history. Tristan was small—well, a good head shorter than Con, at any rate—with a bit of a curl to his dark hair and God, those sharp brown eyes of his . . . Like he'd been laughing at Con inside the whole bloody time, and reckoned even if he'd said the joke out loud, Con would've been too bloody thick to get it.

Con fumed his way up the road to where he'd wedged the van in between a Mini and a Renault with a dent in the side. He wasn't in the mood for *Heart of Darkness* right now, so he changed the CD to Harry Potter book one before he eased the van out into the narrow channel between the rows of parked cars that lined Valley Crescent. Most of the houses were dead old, so driveways weren't exactly a thing.

Stephen Fry's soothing voice did its job of calming him down a bit as he drove. Funny, really, what with him being a posh git and all. Then again, maybe it was just how it always reminded Con of Gran. She'd bought him a Harry Potter audio book a year for Christmas, right up until she died, and they weren't cheap either.

Harry's Aunt Petunia would've loved Tristan, Con reckoned, with his plummy voice and ninja sodding spelling ability. What the bloody hell did it matter if Con had spelt a word or two wrong? The bloke had still known what it meant.

Course, Tristan probably wouldn't have thought much of *her*. Aunt Petunia, that was. Tristan probably didn't think much of *anyone* except himself.

Shit. This wasn't helping. Con wished he still had the latest Terry Pratchett, but it'd gone back to the library. Con got a lot of his audiobooks from the library, always had—they were way too expensive to buy all the time—but it was a pain not being able to listen to them again whenever he wanted. Course, he had all of Gran's old books at home. Trouble was, more than half of them were on cassette tapes, and it was getting harder to find things you could play 'em on. And, well, Mills and Boon romances weren't exactly the sort of thing he'd want to be caught listening to in public. Even if they were actually a lot better than you'd think, as a rule.

He got a few digs for the Harry Potters, come to that, but they could just shove it.

Con was in a much better mood by the time he drove back to Shamwell at the end of the day. The afternoon spent clearing gutters and replacing tiles in the sunshine probably had a lot to do with it. He wasn't a roofer, but that sort of thing was easy enough if you had a head for heights. Con actually liked being up high—you could see stuff, and the air was clearer, somehow.

Harry was at Hogwarts now—Con had skipped ahead a bit—and the descriptions of all the food at the welcoming feast had his stomach rumbling louder than the van's engine.

He parked the van round the back of the post office, and headed up to his flat. It was pretty poky as flats went—just one bedroom, which was also the sitting room; a kitchen that was too small to swing a mouse in, let alone a cat; and a shower room, because there wasn't space in it for a bath. Which would have horrified his gran but was fine by Con—bathtubs were always too small for him to really get comfortable in anyhow. Oh, and there was a small walk-in cupboard, or if you were an estate agent, a "dressing room."

But small as it was, the flat was home. It hadn't been easy making the rent when he'd first moved to the village, but work had picked up steadily since then. Villages like this, people didn't like to look in the yellow pages when they wanted some work done. They'd go round and ask their neighbours who they got in to do such-and-such. And Con would tackle pretty much anything, as long as it wasn't too technical and there weren't any safety issues, and even if he said so himself, he was dirt cheap, so word got around fairly quick.

His mate Heather liked to say it was his looks that got him half his jobs, but Con reckoned people were a bit more savvy with their money than that.

He'd be seeing Heather down the pub tonight, her and Sean. Con smiled as he kicked his boots off and nudged them with his foot until they stood more or less neatly by the door. He'd be able to tell Sean what a narrow escape he'd had, not going round to deal with Tristan bloody Goldsmith and his Plague of Frog.

Con padded into the kitchen to fill the kettle. Maybe he should live down to Tristan's expectations and organise an *actual* plague of frogs. That'd send the bloke screaming for his mummy. Con grinned to himself. He could see it now—Tristan all wide-eyed and panicking, and Mummy, who probably looked *exactly* like him, only smaller and not as pretty—

Shit. Had he just thought Tristan was pretty? Must be time to get some food down him before he got any more light-headed. Con opened up the fridge and pulled out ham, eggs, and cheese. By that time, the kettle had boiled, so he grabbed a mug and bunged in a teabag.

Quarter of an hour later, Con was sitting on the sofa in front of the telly, a plateful of omelette, beans, and toast warming his lap. Nothing like a hearty meal after an honest day's work. He bet that tosser Tristan wouldn't know an honest day's work if it bit him on his well-shaped arse . . .

Oh, *bloody* hell. Con switched over from the news to an old *Top Gear*. If Jeremy Clarkson and his mates being all ultra-blokey couldn't stop him thinking about that poncey git, nothing could.

The Three Lions pub was right on the edge of the village centre, where the high street turned into The Hill and stopped having shops and stuff on it. Con walked past the wine bar, Badgers, on his way. Now *that* was much more the sort of place Mrs. Geary's grandson would meet his mates for a drink. If he had any mates.

Con laughed at himself. Nah, course Tristan would have mates. They'd all be stuck-up posey gits like he was, who thought they owned the world and probably did and all.

He reached the pub just as Sean was getting off his motorbike in the car park, so instead of diving straight in, he wandered over to greet him. "All right, mate?"

Sean pulled off his helmet and ruffled his hair up from where it'd gone a bit flat. It was really short at the mo, so he ended up looking like a ginger hedgehog. "Yeah, I'm good. You?"

"Good, ta. How did your sister's checkup go?"

"Great—still cancer-free and no sign of it coming back. Debs has even got a date tomorrow, actually—she got talking to this bloke in Tesco, and he asked her out. Me and Rob are looking after the lads."

Sean was looking pretty happy about it, which Con didn't reckon was down to the prospect of babysitting his twin nephews. He'd heard they could be a bit of a handful. "Yeah? That's great. So, you know, if it works out, think you and Rob'll move in together?"

Sean laughed. "Bloody hell, it's only the first date. Give 'em a chance! But, well, you know. Might have crossed my mind, yeah." He ducked his head. "Hey, how'd you get on with the bloke with the frog?" he went on as they walked over to the pub door.

Con groaned. "Bloody nightmare, he was."

"Bit of a tosser?" Sean asked, pausing just outside the entrance.

"Too bloody right. Ex public schoolboy who thinks he's too good for this place, and we're all just a bunch of peasants he can order about."

Sean gave him a sidelong look. "He can't help it if he's posh, you know. He didn't ask for his family any more than you asked for yours."

Shit. He'd forgotten Sean's bloke was an ex public schoolboy too. "Yeah, but . . . your Rob. He's posh, right? And educated and all that. But *he* never makes me feel stupid, or . . . or like he thinks I'm common, or anything. Not like this bastard, with his big words and his jokes about my bloody spelling, the git."

"Okay, point taken. He's a dick." Sean grinned.

"Yeah, and would you believe he's old Mrs. Geary's grandson? That nice old lady who used to go to all the Sham-Drams stuff, remember her? She left him the house in her will. Christ, why is it always the bastards who luck out in life? If someone left me a house, I'd think I'd won the bloody lottery." Tristan probably thought it was just his due.

"Yeah, but didn't your gran leave you something when she died?"

"Well, yeah, but she never had much, Gran didn't. The flat was rented from the council, so by the time I'd paid for the funeral, there was just a few hundred quid left from her savings account and some bits of furniture." Con's mouth twisted, the memory still a bitter taste. "Caroline took all her jewellery."

"That's your mum, right?" Sean's tone was cautious. Con hadn't said a *lot* about his family to his mates here—it'd all still been a bit raw when he'd moved to the village—but they knew some of it. Like how he felt about his—about Caroline.

Con nodded. "Turned up to the funeral after three bloody years of us not knowing if she was alive or dead. Said she ought to have Gran's rings and her locket as she was her daughter, 'and it ain't like you're ever gonna 'ave a girl to give them to, you big nance.'" He mimicked her tone, still able to hear her mocking voice in his head.

Sean winced. "Sounds great, your mum."

"Why'd you think I don't call her that anymore?" That, and the fact she'd barely been around since he'd turned three. Con shrugged, feeling a bit bleak. "Doesn't matter. I've got other stuff to remember

Gran by. Bet she never even kept it—the jewellery, I mean. Probably just sold it straight off and spent the money on booze. Only thing I'm ever likely to inherit from *her* is a bill from the off-licence."

"All goes to prove my point, doesn't it? You can't choose your family. Now, are we going in this pub, or are we just going to hang around outside till it gets dark?"

Con gave a sheepish grin. "Sorry. Keeping you out here moaning on about stuff." He pushed the door open, and they stepped inside.

Sean clapped him on the shoulder. "Don't worry about it. What are mates for? Hey, look, Hev's here already."

Heather was sitting at a table by a window, tapping away at her phone. She looked up as they waved, and gave them a smile. Con liked her smile. It was genuine, like the rest of her—not all painted-on eyebrows and bleach-blonde hair extensions like a lot of girls these days. Next to girls like that, Con always felt like he'd just wandered down off a mountain somewhere—all rough and unpolished. Heather kept her hair its natural dark brown, crinkly like her Jamaican dad's and just pulled back into a bouncy ponytail, most of the time. You could relax with someone like that.

Course, it was just possible he was channelling his gran there. She'd had some very firm opinions on modern fashions. Con smiled at himself and made a *do you want a drink?* gesture, but Heather held up her bottle of Beck's and shook her head, then went back to her texting, so he turned to Sean. "What're you drinking?"

"I'll get 'em. Pretty sure it's my round. Pint of bitter?"

Con nodded. "Cheers, mate." He leaned on the bar while Sean ordered the drinks, looking round. The place was pretty full—mostly of men, but the one or two women there besides Heather didn't look uncomfortable or out of place or anything. The Three Lions was a lot friendlier than the town centre pubs he'd been used to in Bedford.

"Here you go, mate."

Con took the pint Sean handed him and took a long, slow swallow, savouring the dry, hoppy taste.

Sean grinned at him. "Better now?"

"Yeah. Well, getting there, anyhow." Con even managed to smile back.

They wandered over to Heather's table. "Won't be a mo. Just gotta . . ." she said without looking up as Con and Sean pulled out a stool each and sat down.

Sean and Heather had had a thing, once upon a time, but they seemed to be fine as just friends now. Con wasn't sure how that worked, so it was probably just as well Sean had been snapped up by Rob before Con could work up the nerve to ask him out. Sean was a good mate, and good mates were hard to find.

Course, in a small place like this, finding blokes who were into blokes *and* who you actually fancied wasn't easy either. Bit of a shame Tristan turned out to be such a total wanker . . .

Con was glad of the interruption to his thoughts when Sean spoke up. "Listened to any good books lately?"

"Having a go with *Heart of Darkness*, but it's a bit grim."

Sean grinned. "Yeah? Who'd have ever thought it from the title, eh?"

"Shut up. Hev recommended it. And it was free on Amazon. It's very . . . I dunno. Literary. 'The word "ivory" rang in the air, was whispered, was sighed. You would think they were praying to it,'" he quoted, laying on the ominous tone a bit thick to get a laugh. "That sort of stuff."

"Yeah? You want to go back to those Discworld books. You had me in stitches with those bits from . . . Which one was it? One of the ones about the city guards."

"Probably *Guards! Guards!* then. I can see why you forgot the title. Nothing to link it with the subject at all."

"Tosser."

"Dick-brain."

Heather stopped tapping at her phone and bunged it away in her bag. "For God's sake, can't I leave you for five minutes before it descends into name-calling? *Men*."

"All right, Hev?" Sean said, straightening his face. "Rehearsals going okay?"

She groaned. "Don't bloody ask. We've barely even *started* rehearsals, and it's already a nightmare." Con smiled, and she gave him a sharp look. "What?"

He shrugged self-consciously. "You know. *Midsummer Night's Dream*, nightmare? Sorry."

"Oh. Yeah, well, it's not funny. Alan's saying he can't do Puck after all, cos he had this big split with his girlfriend and now he can only act in tragedies, which, like, what? And that means Patrick's got to do Puck, cos he's the only one who's even got a hope of not looking stupid. So now we're short a Bottom."

Sean laughed. Heather looked daggers at him, and he straightened his face out quick. "Sorry. Just sounds a bit funny, that's all."

"Yeah, laugh a bloody minute, I am. I'll just go do a gig at the Comedy Store." Heather stared into her Beck's like she wished she could dive in.

Con felt pretty bad for her. Patrick and Alan were two of the society's best young male actors. There wasn't a lot of competition, to be honest. Half the male actors in the society were the wrong side of sixty, let alone thirty.

"Actually, that reminds me of something," he said slowly. "Not the Comedy Store or the . . . Bottom. The other bit. You know old Mrs. Geary's grandson? Tristan, you remember? The one she was always on about like he should be heading up the Royal Shakespeare Company."

Heather perked up a bit. "Ooh, yeah, I remember her talking about him. What about him?"

"Well, he's here. In the village. She left him her house. I was round there today."

"Yeah? You met him? What's he like? Is he staying?" Heather leaned forward, an eager expression on her pretty, dark face.

Con frowned. "Thought you were going out with Chris, now? And anyway, I don't think he's into girls."

"Checking you out, was he?" Sean laughed.

"Nah, nothing like that," Con said quickly. His face was hot, probably because Tristan bloody well *had* been checking him out. Con knew he hadn't meant anything by it, though, so why mention it? "He's just a bit, well . . . Can't really see him with a girlfriend."

Heather *tsk*ed. "I'm not after *that*. I just wondered if he'd be up for some amateur dramatics while he's here." Con and Sean exchanged looks. "What? I'm serious. We're having a crisis at the moment, and it's all on me. I mean, everyone said it was a mistake to do *Dream*, there's just way too many young parts, and there was me being all 'No, it's fine, we can do it.' Should've bloody listened, shouldn't I?"

"Oi, you'd better not be thinking of cancelling it. I've been sweating blood over that forest scenery." Con had got involved with the Sham-Drams fairly early on when he came to live in the village. He liked the challenge of doing the scenery and some of the props—it was a bit more creative than his usual run of work.

Sean laughed. "Literally? Cos I reckon that'd be a whole other play."

Con grinned. "Yeah. *Lord of the Flies* or something. Or what's that Shakespeare one you were telling us about, Hev? The one where everyone gets hacked to pieces?"

Heather flapped a hand in a *don't change the subject* sort of way. "*Titus Andronicus.* So go on," she insisted. "Do you think he'd be up for it?"

"Well . . ." Con took a swallow from his pint. "He's not moving in permanently. He wants to fix the house up—s'pose he's planning to sell it. But he reckoned he'd be staying until October."

"Which is perfect, cos the performances are at the end of September," Heather interrupted. "So go on, do you think he'd do it?"

"S'pose I can imagine him doing Shakespeare." Con shrugged. "He likes big words."

"What's he look like?"

Small and dark and gorgeous. What Gran used to call *fey*. And yeah, like he was going to tell his mates that. "Uh . . . short. Ish."

"That's anyone compared to you."

"And he's, uh, got dark hair. Sort of curly." Con caught her looking at him and shrugged, feeling a bit on the spot. "That's it, really."

"Is he good-looking?"

Con swallowed, wishing he'd never mentioned the bloke. "Uh, yeah? Maybe?"

Heather looked like she'd won the lottery. "Oh my God, you fancy him!"

"I bloody don't." Con's face was getting hot again, which only made him more annoyed. "He's a git, all right? Total poseur."

"Yeah? To hear Mrs. Geary talk, you'd think the sun shone out of his solid-gold bum. Well, we don't have to like him. Just recruit him." She gave Con a sly look. "Course, *you'd* be perfect for a rude mechanical."

"Yeah, well, you know that's not gonna happen. I don't do acting, all right?"

Heather gave him a challenging look. "Have you ever tried it? Seriously. You might like it. Bottom's a great part—he gets the laughs *and* the girl."

Sean laughed at that bit. "Don't reckon the last one's much of a selling point for Con, right, mate?"

Heather carried on like she hadn't heard him. "*And* if we could put you on a poster, we might get a few more young people joining the society."

"Leave it out," Con muttered. He never felt comfortable when she went on about his looks. So he was tall and his job had given him a few muscles? He wasn't anything special.

Sean leaned forward. "Leave him alone, Hev. You know it's not his fault he can't do it."

Which wasn't exactly good for Con's ego, even if he knew Sean meant well.

Heather frowned. "Don't gang up on me. And that's crap, anyway. There's loads of professional actors who're dyslexic. Orlando Bloom, Tom Cruise, Keira Knightley . . . I'm just saying, it doesn't mean he *can't* learn lines."

Con stood up. He was fed up with this. "*He'll* just let you two sort it out between you, all right? Let me know when you've decided if I'll ever make it as a useful member of society, yeah?"

"Oi, mate, sit down. We didn't mean . . ."

"Sorry, Con," Heather said, looking like she meant it.

Con sat down. He sighed. "I just . . . Look, I'm not saying the dyslexia's got nothing to do with it, all right? But I just don't fancy the idea of getting up on stage in front of everyone. Scenery, that's my thing. Anyway, how come you're not hassling Sean about having a go?"

"Oi, don't look at me!" Sean backed his stool off a couple of inches.

Heather rolled her eyes. "Sean's not a member. You are," she said, like that justified it all somehow. Con would've thought twice about signing up to do the scenery if they'd mentioned upfront they'd be press-ganging him into anything else they felt like. "Look, if you don't want to do it, that's fine. Just see if you can get this Tristan to come along tomorrow night to rehearsals."

Con stared. "Me? Why've I got to do it?"

"Because you know him." The way she smiled was worrying. "And if he's gay, he almost certainly fancies you, so it'll be a piece of piss for you to get him to do what you want, won't it?"

Oh God.

He was never going to get away from Tristan bloody Goldsmith.

CHAPTER THREE
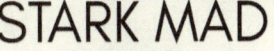
STARK MAD

Sometime after Con had made his stormy exit, and after around a gallon of Nanna Geary's soothing nettle tea, Tristan checked his watch. It was four o'clock now, so that meant it'd be midnight in Hong Kong. *Possibly* a little late to call Amanda, but at least she'd be likely to be in. He opened up his laptop and clicked onto Skype.

Amanda answered immediately, so she'd probably been playing some inane game on Facebook. Or watching gay porn—it was always a bit of a toss-up between those two, for her.

She'd taken the same MA course in classical acting Tristan had, and had been an absolute lifeline for him. He'd somehow managed to rub his fellow students up the wrong way—perhaps it had been because he'd taken his first degree in English, rather than drama like the rest of them, and some of them felt he didn't belong on the course? Then there had been the unfortunate incident in their first term. Tristan still maintained it could have happened to anyone—the tutor involved had been a very attractive man, and surely nobody censored their speech while in the heady grip of postorgasm endorphins? He hadn't *meant* to get anyone thrown off the course, and how was he to know the classmate he'd been babbling on about had lied on their application?

At any rate, Amanda had been pretty much the only one who'd stuck with him after that.

She'd followed him into a job with the Players afterwards—eventually—and had left at the same time as he did, although her descent into wage-slavery had of necessity been rather swifter. Actually, she'd probably been rather more influential than Father in finally persuading him to hang up his greasepaint. For some reason, she'd seemed a tad disillusioned by the life of a professional actor.

"How's Hong Kong, darling?" he asked as her familiar, heart-shaped face hove jerkily into view. She was in bed, he decided, with her laptop actually on her lap—from this angle, she seemed all chin and nose, with two tiny un-made-up eyes squinting at him from above.

"An absolute bloody nightmare. God, the *humidity*. My straighteners burned out last night, so now I'm having to walk around looking like a dandelion stuck in an electric socket." Actually, her dark chestnut hair seemed perfectly sleek to Tristan. "And I hardly get a *minute* to myself. It's all right for *you*. Some of us have to work for a living."

That stung. "I'll be joining the ranks of the gainfully employed soon enough, thank you."

"And in the meantime, spending three months lolling about by Daddy's pool. As I said, it's all right for some."

"Actually, I'm not at home right now. You remember I told you about Nanna Geary?"

"Vaguely. Your old nanny, isn't that right? Older than Moses, keeps sending you those horrid scarves for Hanukkah? Oh—she died, didn't she?" Amanda paused. "Sorry."

Tristan let her shameful lack of appreciation for one of England's national treasures go. She hadn't known Nanna Geary like he had. "She was Mother's nanny first, actually. She was more a sort of honorary grandmother to me. We used to sit and do jigsaw puzzles together, and she'd make boiled sweets and fudge in a vast pan in the kitchen." He smiled at the memory.

"God, it sounds practically medieval. Only less interesting."

Tristan frowned, a little hurt. "Anyway, she's left me her house. I'm there right now. In Shamwell. I went down to look at the house, clear it out a bit—"

"Why on earth don't you just *pay* someone to do that?"

"—and I'm going to spend the summer here."

"*You*? You won't last a week out there in the sticks. You'll die of boredom. Become an unshaven slob. Start talking to yourself."

"Nothing wrong with that, darling. Shakespeare loved a good soliloquy. And, anyway, there are all sorts of things to do in the countryside. *Par example*, I could get an allotment and start growing cannabis."

"Don't expect me to visit you in prison."

"You'd let me pick oakum in solitude? Heartless creature. Anyway, I think I've found something to make the time go a little faster."

"Oh?" Amanda's tone turned arch. "Let me guess: tall, blond, and hung like a stallion?"

"He has dark hair, actually, but one can't have everything. And I'll have to let you know about the stallion part, but initial observations are promising. *Not* overburdened with intellect—or charm, for that matter—but he'll do for a distraction until October."

She laughed. "Now who's heartless?"

There was no disapproval in her tone, nor had Tristan expected any, so he was rather disconcerted to find himself justifying his proposed course of action. After all, it was quite clear Con could do with taking down a peg or two, what with his *essay me specific* and his *obvious, innit?* and his demands Tristan make a bloody appointment every time he needed some work done. "Darling, I'm doing him a favour. It'll be something for him to look back on during those long winter nights. After all, in a place like this, how many opportunities for dalliance can there be?"

"In a place like that, they probably still burn gays in a wicker man on midsummer's eve."

"In which case I shall be fine, seeing as we're already into July."

"Other solstices *are* available."

"And I'll be long gone by the next. No, you shan't dissuade me. Think you a little din can daunt mine ears? I shall woo him with some spirit, and board him before the clouds in autumn crack."

"So certain of yourself, Petruchio? Fifty pounds says you *don't*."

"I'll take your bet. I'm born to tame him."

"A bargain, then. But don't blame me if you end up cursing your wooing."

Tristan spent a peaceful night, his dreams rather magnificently inhabited by a certain member of the labouring classes. He was just in the middle of a sumptuous historical epic, featuring Tristan as Rome's youngest senator and Con as a trouser-clad barbarian envoy in dire need of civilisation, when he was rudely awoken by someone knocking on the door.

Damn it. Tristan had just offered Con a golden platter of freshly peeled grapes—not peeled by him, obviously; his dream-self had people to do these things—and been about to insinuate that there was something else he'd rather have peeled. He tried to drift back into slumber . . . Yes, there they were . . .

The knocking sounded again, louder this time.

Bugger and tarnation. Tristan hurled back the blankets (Nanna Geary hadn't agreed with new-fangled duvets), marched to the window, and flung it open to shout down at the street below. "Whoreson, beetle-headed, flap-ear'd knave!"

Con's face stared up at him, his brow creased in a frown. "*What* did you just call me?"

Tristan gulped. His wooing, it appeared, was *not* getting off to an auspicious start. "Ah. Forgive me. No aspersions intended on the character of your dear mother, which I'm certain is entirely without blemish."

Con looked, if anything, even angrier. His face had taken on the sort of colour that, if seen in the morning sky, would send a prudent shepherd scampering for his crook. "What do you know about my mum?"

"Absolutely nothing," Tristan said quickly. "For all I know, you sprang fully formed from the head of Zeus. Might I ask why you're disturbing my slumbers at the ungodly hour of . . ." he glanced at Nanna Geary's old-fashioned alarm clock, which he'd made damned certain wasn't set to go off after the first morning when he woke up thinking someone had installed a fire alarm inside his skull ". . . ten o'clock in the morning?"

Con's colour subsided to a more normal hue, and his feet performed a rather endearing shuffle on the pavement. "Um. Well, you said you had some jobs for me, so . . ."

"Absolutely! Splendid. Just one moment, and I'll be with you." Tristan closed the window and hastened to his bedroom door. His hand upon the doorknob, he paused. Was opening the door in his current state of nudity advisable? True, it might advance the wooing somewhat, but on the other hand, it might just as easily send Con running for his no doubt tediously virtuous mother. Tristan could picture her now: a solid woman with a plain face and well-rounded hips who fed her son on vast quantities of red meat and boiled vegetables.

The maternal image caused a definite deflation in areas Tristan would much prefer Con see at their best, and that decided it. Clothes it was. Tristan pulled on his trousers and slipped a shirt around his shoulders, then checked his reflection. Yes, that should do it: respectably covered, but with a hint of debauchery. And *nobody* did debauchery like Tristan. He blew his reflection a saucy kiss and hurtled downstairs to open the door.

If anything, Con appeared even larger and more magnificent today. The jeans were the same, but the grimy white singlet had been replaced by a spotless red one. Tristan beamed. "Excellent, excellent. Labouring on a Saturday. My orthodox ancestors would be appalled, but personally, I applaud your work ethic. It must be the Eastern European in you. You *did* say your forebears were of Eastern European extraction, did you not?" Tristan resisted the urge to wipe his palms on his clothing. Why was he nervous? No, no, he couldn't be nervous. That would be ridiculous.

Then again, Con *was* frowning. Possibly because, as Tristan now recalled, all he'd said about his origins yesterday was that he was neither black nor Irish. *Damn* it.

Miraculously, the storm clouds cleared once more. Tristan gave himself a mental pat on the back for having left his shirt unbuttoned. "Uh, can I come in?" Con asked, his voice strangely hesitant.

"Of course! Step this way. Well, you know the way, of course, having been here only yesterday. And upon many other occasions, of course. In fact, now I come to think about it, you've probably been here more times than I have, ahahaha." Tristan cringed internally, but Con actually gave a polite smile at the feeble joke.

Curiouser and curiouser.

Once again, the boat-sized footwear was kicked off on the doormat, and Con padded into Nanna Geary's living room like a miscast understudy who'd carelessly neglected to learn his lines, only to unexpectedly find himself replacing the star on opening night.

"So, um, where did you want me to start?" he asked, looking around him as if for inspiration.

"'Nothing of him that doth fade, but doth suffer a sea-change,'" Tristan murmured to himself. Still, odd though this compliant manner might be after yesterday's belligerence, he'd be a fool not to take advantage of it. "Oh, no hurry," he said in more normal tones. "Coffee? Tea? Bacon and eggs? I was just about to make a spot of breakfast."

Con ran a hand through his unruly dark locks. "Uh, I'm good, thanks."

"Oh, I'm *sure* you are," Tristan purred. "Coffee, then," he decided. "After all, we shouldn't want you falling asleep on the job." He strode to the kitchen and opened up a cupboard.

Nanna Geary having been a confirmed tea drinker, Tristan had taken care to lay in stocks of his preferred brand of instant—he'd used to be a stickler for cafetière coffee, but if there was one thing life on the road with the Players had taught him, it was that one couldn't afford to be a coffee snob. Or, for that matter, a food snob, or an accommodation snob—really, it was remarkable he'd survived at all, with all the roughing it he'd had to put up with.

Actually, Tristan admitted to himself as he filled the kettle, it'd been bloody good fun. He was going to miss all that when he was in New York. Still, duty called—generally with the voice of his father, and often with a reminder of just how much had been spent on Tristan's education. He sighed and grabbed the biscuit tin.

"Choccy biccie?" he asked, proffering it to Con, who was hovering uneasily in the doorway. "If you're sure I can't tempt you with the bacon."

Con frowned but took a biscuit. "You said you were Jewish."

Tristan *tsk*ed. "Secular. Do you see me in kippah and payot? You do not," he added quickly, guessing from Con's look of bafflement that the question was anything but rhetorical to him. "The kippah is a skull cap; the payot, the sidelocks. And I thought religious education was compulsory even in state schools."

"Yeah, well. It was a while ago. And I didn't get on too well at school, all right?"

Tristan bit back the impulse to raise an ironic eyebrow and say something witty about Con's clearly high-flying career path. From the pinkish tinge to the man's cheeks, it probably wouldn't be taken in the spirit in which it was intended.

"Never mind. I'm quite sure you have excellent qualities in other spheres." Tristan allowed his gaze to trail appreciatively over some of Con's excellent qualities. "Milk? Sugar?"

The pink tinge deepened noticeably. "Just milk. Thanks." He took the proffered mug as though it were a lifebelt tossed to him in a stormy sea. "Um."

"Yes?" Tristan looked Con in the eye, all polite attention, which had the not unexpected effect of causing him to drop his gaze and shuffle his sock-clad feet.

"Look, you're an actor, right? I mean, you're a proper actor, yeah? So, um, you probably won't wanna—but I promised her I'd ask—I mean, you'd be really helping us out, but, yeah, there's no reason why you should. But. Um. It's tonight. If you wanted to. Rehearsal, I mean."

Tristan waited, but Con's wellspring of gobbledygook appeared to have run dry. "For?" he enquired politely.

Con stared at him blankly for a moment, then blinked. "Oh. *Midsummer Night's Dream*—you know, Shakespeare."

Tristan nodded gravely. "I believe I have heard of him, yes. And my role in this would be?"

Con was now positively *crimson*. "Bottom." He took an over-hasty gulp of coffee, then made exactly the face one might expect from someone who had just burned their mouth and was trying not to show it.

Two years in rep and an MA in classical acting stood Tristan in good stead. He was—barely—able to keep a straight face. "Hmm. Not my *usual* role, I'd have to say. But what about you? I'd think you'd make an *excellent* Bottom."

"That's what she said," Con muttered.

Tristan laughed politely, then realised the man meant it literally, and not as a rather overused punchline. "'She'?"

"Hev. Heather. She's playing Hermia. And directing."

"'Though she be but little, she is fierce'?" Tristan guessed. "So what part *do* you play in this endeavour?"

"Me? I just make the scenery."

"And I'm guessing this would be some sort of amateur dramatics group?"

"Yeah. Shamwell Amateur Dramatics Society."

"Hm. I'm not entirely sure I'd like to be associated with a group that has the acronym SADS." More to the point, they were undoubtedly an unholy mix of unrepentant scenery-chewers and wooden hacks. Did Tristan really want to cast his metaphorical pearls before such swine?

"Your gran used to go to all their plays," Con said, an accusatory gleam in his eye.

Tristan thought quickly. Certain things were becoming clear to him. Firstly, that Con's curious volte-face in attitude must be due not, as Tristan had hoped, to his charms, but to the rather less flattering explanation of Con wanting Tristan to do him a somewhat unwieldy favour. And, secondly, that in the matter of wooing, refusal to oblige in this respect was likely to be a deal-breaker.

Was it worth it? Tristan eyed Con in assessment. His libido voted an enthusiastic *yes*, but what did his less easily swayed head think?

"She'd have loved to see you on stage in Shamwell," Con added, impressing Tristan with his unsuspected affinity for dirty tactics.

Oh, hang it. It might be a bumbling village production, but it was still acting. And undoubtedly Tristan's last chance to do any before taking on the yoke of wage-slavery. Plus, he could hardly spend the whole summer just wooing. He'd need something else to occupy his mind until October . . . Wait a minute. "When's the production?"

"End of September. So, you know, before your job starts." Con looked pleased with himself, as well he might.

"Hmmm . . ." His mind made up to go for it, Tristan nevertheless didn't want to appear too easy.

"Look, just come along tonight, yeah? And, you know, see if you like it."

"Will you be there?" Tristan asked, his eyes artlessly wide.

"Uh . . ."

"I'd really feel better if there were someone I knew there." Tristan leaned in to place a hand on Con's splendidly muscular forearm, enjoying the little frisson that spread through him at the touch.

Con swallowed. "Yeah, I can be there. Um. It's seven thirty in the village hall."

"Excellent!" Tristan rubbed his hands together. "Now, what shall we get on with first?"

"Uh . . ." Con glanced at the kitchen clock, which was of the old-fashioned china-plate variety, embellished with large, friendly numbers—all the better to be seen by elderly ladies who didn't hold with wearing their spectacles all the time, as it would only encourage their eyes to be lazy. Tristan had given it to Nanna Geary for her seventy-eighth birthday. "I really gotta go. Cheers for the coffee. I'll see you tonight, okay? Up at the hall."

"'Exit, pursued by a bear,'" Tristan muttered, irritated, as Con took his leave with unseemly haste.

He felt he was entitled to feel a little miffed with the man. Having *said* he'd come round to do some work, he'd merely drunk Tristan's coffee, eaten one of Tristan's Belgian chocolate biscuits, press-ganged him into joining the local ragtag band of rude mechanicals, and left.

Tristan stomped back into the kitchen to wash out the mugs, and cursed prolifically.

To add insult to injury, that bloody frog was back.

CHAPTER FOUR
BY THE SCROLL

Con drew in a deep breath as Mrs. Geary's front door closed behind him. That grandson of hers was really messing with his head. Con just wished he knew if the bloke was seriously coming on to him, or if he was just like that with everyone. Nah, Tristan couldn't be serious. Not about wanting Con. He'd made it pretty bloody clear yesterday he thought Con was a complete thicko yob.

Although he'd been different today. Nicer. None of those digs about spelling and stuff. He'd even made him coffee and offered him one of his posh biscuits. It'd been just like when he used to go round to do work with Mrs. Geary. Course, it'd been tea when she'd been alive, and most likely a custard cream, but, well, it was the same sort of thing.

And . . . and it was stupid, anyway, because even if there was anything between them, it obviously wouldn't be going anywhere, not with Tristan buggering off out of the country at the end of September. He had to remember that, or it'd end up just like with Mo, wouldn't it? Just as Con started getting serious—which he *would*, because he always bloody *did*; he always fell too hard and too fast—the other bloke would be packing his bags and leaving him high and dry.

Of course, he wouldn't have to worry about seeing Tristan around town all the time after they split up. If Con was honest, he probably wouldn't have moved out of Bedford after Gran died if it hadn't been for seeing his ex out and about with the new bloke. Well, blokes.

Huh. Some bloody comfort that'd be.

No, he was better off keeping his distance.

Course, when he rang Heather to let her know Tristan would be coming along to rehearsal that night, she practically had the two of them married already. "Well, duh," she said, and he could almost hear her rolling her eyes. "Course he's into you. I *knew* it. He's a professional actor, isn't he? There's only one reason he'd bother doing a village production for free. Oi, you did tell him he's doing it for free, yeah?"

"I . . ." Shit. That hadn't been mentioned. "Nah, he's gotta know," Con reassured her and himself. "I told him it was an amateur dramatics society." He decided not to mention the crack about the name.

"So it's obvious. He fancies the pants off you. I mean, come on, who wouldn't? And it's about time you got some action. That Mo bastard was *ages* ago."

"Leave it out," Con muttered. "And anyway, nothing's gonna happen. Told you, he's a prick." Although he felt a bit bad about saying it, after the way Tristan had been this morning. Then again . . . "I think I woke him up when I went round, and he leaned out the window and started slagging me off."

"What, and he *still* agreed to do it? What did you do—take him back to bed?"

"No!"

"But I thought you *liked* pricks," she teased.

"Har bloody har. Look, nothing's gonna happen, all right? Even if I *did* like him, which I don't, he's going off to New York in October."

"So? You could go with him. Why not? You're young and single— live a bit. Take a chance. It'd be brilliant."

"What the bloody hell would I do in New York? Anyway, I like it here. Feels like home."

"Yeah, but you don't wanna be a village odd-job man all your life, do you? You could do something proper with your life."

"What's wrong with what I'm doing now?" Con demanded. "I make a living at it."

"And you wanna be stuck in that flat over the post office for the rest of your life? What about if you wanna have kids? Gonna keep 'em in the window box?"

"Yeah, like being an office dogsbody pays so much better," Con snapped, hurt.

"Not gonna do that all my life, though, am I? One day I'll be running the place. You gotta have plans, or you never get anywhere in life. Look, I'm only saying this cos I care about you. You know that, right? I just think you need to broaden your horizons a bit. Land of opportunities, America, innit?"

"Yeah, but . . . it's different for you. You've got exams and stuff. Failed all mine, didn't I?"

"You ought to sue that bloody school you went to. I can't believe they didn't get you diagnosed and get you some help. How come your gran didn't push for it? She must have known something was wrong."

"She had a lot on her plate, all right? And I'm fine, anyway. I don't need any bloody bits of paper to prove I'm not thick. When did school ever teach you anything worth knowing, anyhow?" It maybe came out a bit loud, but sod it, nobody got to say stuff about Gran. Nobody. All right, maybe she hadn't ever got round to doing one of those adult literacy courses people kept telling her to try, but she'd managed just fine. Brought up two kids on her own too, including him, after being widowed way younger than was fair.

"Jesus, keep your hair on. Look, I gotta go. I'll see you tonight, okay?"

"Yeah. See you tonight." Con hung up, breathing hard. God, he wanted to punch something again. Blokes like Tristan, yeah, he expected them to look down on him. But not Heather. He'd thought she was on his side.

Maybe he'd go and see if the old bloke up on The Hill wanted his tree stump digging out today, instead of waiting till Monday. Yeah. Bit of hard work, that was what he needed.

Come seven o'clock that evening, Con was grimy, aching—in a good way—and drenched in sweat. And, oh shit, he had just half an hour to get to rehearsal. Digging out that tree stump had gone on a bit longer than he'd expected. 'Specially as he'd noticed a few loose tiles on the roof, so he'd fixed those before he started on the digging. Old Mr. Smith had said it could wait, but Con hadn't liked to leave it like that—the forecast on the radio had said it might rain tonight.

By the time he packed up here, he'd have time to either grab something to eat or shower, but not both. Con looked down at himself and had a go at brushing off some of the dirt. Trouble was, the few slightly cleaner patches that resulted meant the streaks on his T-shirt where he'd used the bottom of it to wipe sweat off his forehead showed up even more.

Sod it. He probably stank too. Shower it was, then, Con decided regretfully as he packed up the last of his kit and went to knock on the kitchen door. He watched through the frosted glass as the old bloke shuffled towards him, a hunched blur that got slowly larger.

It seemed like forever before the door creaked open, letting out a tantalising whiff of meat pie. "All done, Mr. Smith," Con said with a smile.

Watery grey eyes blinked up at him from underneath wispy white hair. "Oh, good, good. How much do I owe you?"

Con named his figure, after mentally adjusting it down a bit because, well, the old bloke couldn't have a lot to live off if the shiny, bagged-out knees of his trousers and the threadbare elbows of his cardigan were any guide.

Mr. Smith nodded. "I'll write you a cheque. Won't be a tick." He shuffled over to the kitchen table, where Con saw chequebook and pen lying ready, and lowered himself into a chair. "Who do I make it out to?"

"C. Izzard, please," Con said.

"Izzard, Izzard . . . I used to know an Izzard. Long time ago now. We were at school together during the war." Con guessed he meant the Second World War, not the Falklands War. God knew the bloke looked almost old enough for it to be the *First* World War. "Bill, that was his name. Bill Izzard."

"Yeah?" Con looked at him with sudden interest. "That was my grandad's name. William Izzard. And, yeah, that sounds about right. He was evacuated here. Didn't know he went to school here, though."

"Oh, life went on, you know. Everything didn't stop just because there was a war on. There was a bomb fell on Shamwell one time, but it didn't explode. Just crashed through the old brewhouse roof and sat there on the stairs . . ." Mr. Smith trailed off, his eyes getting even more out of focus, then seemed to come back to the present. "Well, well.

Bill Izzard's grandson." He shook his head, smiling. "He was a regular rapscallion, was Bill. Always getting into scrapes, as I recall."

"Yeah? Do you remember much about him?" Con asked eagerly, then thought he probably ought to explain. "I never knew him. He died when Ca—when my mum was little. But Gran told me about him being evacuated here. That's why I moved here." Well, it was close enough. He'd come to see the village out of curiosity, one time he'd been in the area, and, well, pretty much fallen in love with the place. "I mean, I haven't got any family here—not that I know of, anyhow—but it's still nice to have the connection, you know?"

The old man rubbed his chin. "Let me think . . . Now, he was a Barnardo's boy, wasn't he? And there was something about a graveyard . . ."

Con nodded. "Yeah, that's right. He was a foundling—the vicar here at St. Saviour's heard a baby crying in the churchyard one morning and found him wrapped up in a blanket on some long-dead bloke's grave. So they called him William Izzard, cos that was the name on the gravestone." Least, that had been what he'd told Gran. And she'd reckoned his birth certificate just had "unknown" on it for his mum and dad. "He got sent to the children's home in Stortford, but when they started sending the kids to the countryside, the vicar took him back in."

"That's right. Yes, I remember, now. We used to play in the vicarage gardens. Lots of apple trees, there were, although we weren't supposed to climb them when they were in fruit. Well, well," the old man said again. "Fancy that. I haven't thought about old Bill in donkey's years. We were thick as thieves at one time," he added wistfully, as he handed Con the cheque, carefully written out in shaky handwriting.

Con thanked him and shoved it in his back pocket. He was trying to work out how to politely grill the old bloke for more information about Bill when his stomach gave a loud rumble. "Sorry," he said, embarrassed.

Mr. Smith chuckled wheezily. "Hungry? Not surprised, after all that hard work. You know, I always cook far too much. Never have got the hang of cooking for one. Why don't you join me? It's almost ready."

Con was seriously torn. He desperately wanted to hear some more about his grandad, but he'd promised Tristan he'd be at rehearsal tonight. "Uh . . . that's really kind, but I'm not sure I've got time to stay."

"Oh, it won't be a minute. And you wouldn't want it to go to waste, now would you? Come and sit down."

"Don't wanna get your furniture dirty . . ."

"We'll only be in the kitchen. I never use the dining room these days. You know, I can't remember the last time I had company with my supper." He blinked hopefully up at Con, who found himself sitting at the tiny kitchen table before he even knew he'd agreed to stay, while Mr. Smith, who told Con to call him Alf, served out boiled potatoes, boiled carrots, and Tesco steak-and-kidney pie. It was just like something Gran might have made. Even down to the bottle of brown sauce on the table.

"So you and Bill Izzard were mates, yeah?" Con prompted, taking a forkful of pie.

"Oh yes." Alf chuckled. "I don't think my parents were too pleased at the time, but, well. They could hardly stop me going to the vicarage."

"They didn't like him? Bill, I mean?"

"I think they thought he was a bad influence. Of course, they were quite right. We used to cut tree branches with a penknife to make bows and arrows, I remember, and we got into terrible trouble for shooting at people's cats."

Er, yeah. Con could understand why that hadn't made them any too popular.

"And there was one time we shot the lady who used to clean the church . . . Now what was her name? We both got a sound thrashing from the reverend for that. My father gave me another when I got home."

Bloody hell. And people got all nostalgic about old-fashioned childhoods? Con had listened to *Lord of the Flies* last year, and he'd reckoned it was a bit far-fetched, all that descending into violence and murder. Now, he wasn't so sure.

After a while, Alf moved on to stories about when he did his National Service in the fifties, half of which Con hoped were made up, because seriously, it did his head in to think of respectable old blokes getting up to all that sort of daft stuff. It was like hearing his gran talk about her old boyfriends.

Con stood up reluctantly at the end of the meal. "Thanks for dinner, that was really great. And for all the stories. Can't believe I've finally found someone who remembers my grandad. But I really gotta get going now, or I'm gonna get in trouble. Got somewhere I need to be in—" He looked at the clock and winced. "Five minutes ago. Heather's gonna kill me. Let me just wash the plates up quick and I'll—"

"No, no, you leave that to me. And you must come again." He ushered Con out of the door with surprising firmness. "Can't keep your young lady waiting." He chuckled again. "They don't like that at all, I can tell you."

Con opened his mouth to tell Alf he'd got the wrong end of the stick, then shut it quick when he remembered he needed to get a shift on. He wasn't sure he wanted to come out to Alf just yet, anyhow. Blokes his age could be a bit, well, old-fashioned about stuff.

He dived into the van and got going. God, he hoped Tristan had actually turned up like he said he would. And not just because Heather was desperate for him to take the role. Con had to admit he was really curious to see just how good an actor the bloke really was. Yeah, his gran had thought he was fantastic, but that didn't mean anything, did it? Neither did the way he was so bloody full of himself.

Con grinned. He might turn out to be a total ham. Which, if it hadn't been for Heather, would probably be the outcome Con was hoping for. Then again, it wasn't all that likely, was it? He'd actually got paid for acting in that touring company of his, the Something-pretentious Players, Mrs. Geary had said, so he couldn't be completely crap.

It was nearly quarter to eight by the time Con pulled up outside the village hall. Shit. Heather really would kill him if Tristan had flounced off in a huff because Con wasn't there. He kicked off his boots at the door and tiptoed through the foyer in his socks.

There was definitely some rehearsing going on. And yeah—that was Tristan's voice, thank God, although it wasn't anything like as plummy as it usually was. He'd put on some kind of ooh-arrr yokel accent that made his *r*'s about three miles long, and was reading out a bit of Bottom's part.

". . . and tharrrr we may rrrrre'earrrrrse most obscenely and courrrageously. Take pains. Be perrrrfec'. Adieu.'"

Con's French wasn't anything to write home about, but he was fairly sure Tristan's pronunciation of *adieu* would have made his old French teacher cry. He crept closer and peeked around the door to see Tristan standing in the middle of the hall, everyone staring at him. He looked like he was enjoying himself.

Con smiled. No surprise there.

Heather looked like Christmas had come early. In fact, she looked like she was only a couple of minutes away from dumping Chris like a ton of bricks and demanding to have Tristan's babies.

"Or," Tristan was saying, "I could ease off on the country bumpkin—how's everyone else on their accents? After all, hamming it up for comic effect is all very well, but we want these men to be plausible as a group of friends."

The others—Chris, Gordon, and the three *N*'s, Neil, Nigel and Norman, who were all older blokes Con didn't know very well—gave each other doubtful looks.

"How about you try it in more of a Hertfordshire accent, then?" Heather suggested quickly. "And we'll all read through together, so you can get a feel for how the others are playing it, yeah?"

Standing around in a rough circle, they started reading through the scene.

Con didn't have to go to rehearsals—it was useful being there sometimes, because Heather would come up with changes she wanted made to the scenery, but most of the time he was just a spare part. It was dead interesting, though, watching how they worked out how to play the roles, and what bits of stage business worked and what didn't. And sometimes they'd ask his opinion as a stand-in audience, and that was pretty good too.

He'd already seen some of the bits with the rude mechanicals a few times, though he was buggered if he knew why they were called that. What with there being six of them in it, plus Heather, they tended to use the hall to go through their scenes. A lot of the other scenes just had a couple of actors, so they could rehearse somewhere smaller.

So, yeah, he had something to compare Tristan's performance to. And Tristan was *amazing*. Mrs. Geary hadn't just been saying it because he was her grandson. And Con had known the rude mechanicals were *supposed* to be funny, but to be honest, he'd had a job seeing why before.

With Tristan, though . . . He was so energetic, for one thing, rather than just standing there and reading off the lines. He moved around the stage and used his arms to make big gestures, all puffed up and pompous one minute, and all ridiculous the next. And it wasn't just him—all the others seemed to up their game or catch the energy or something.

Con felt bad about thinking it, because Patrick was a good bloke, but he hadn't really got that Bottom was supposed to be a *bad* actor, until he saw how Tristan changed from totally believable to, well, really crap, when he was acting the acting bits. He'd put on an accent now that somehow managed to make him sound like someone trying to be posher than they were. The parts where he put on a girly voice or roared like a lion absolutely cracked Con up, and he wasn't the only one. And the words Tristan was speaking, all that weird old-fashioned English, they actually made sense when he said them. It was like Con was watching the film of it again—only better, because he was right there. And, in the film, they'd cut it all down to essentials, whereas Tristan was giving the full speeches. Giving the full effect.

Con wasn't the only one just staring at Tristan in amazement at the end of the scene.

"So . . . you've done this before, yeah?" Heather said at last.

"What, acted in *Dream*? No, no. But I've studied it, obviously, and seen it performed at the Globe, of course."

Yeah, Con thought. Of course.

"Actually, there's a few bits of stage business I rather liked from their production which we could borrow, if you wanted. Concerning Wall's, ahem, hole. Unless you think it'd be too coarse for a provincial audience?" He didn't wait for an answer, just grabbing Nigel's arm. "Now, if you would be so kind as to stand here, legs, as they say, akimbo . . ."

Con felt safe padding into the hall now.

He might have known Tristan wouldn't let him go unnoticed.

"Aha! Better three hours too late than a minute too soon, hmm?" Tristan bounded over to Con, clapped him on the back and beamed at him in a way that, well, did weird stuff to Con's insides. It was the first time he'd seen the bloke smile like that—friendly, and happy, and despite his words, not like he was laughing at a joke and Con was the butt of it.

Trouble was, it didn't last. Just as Con smiled back, Tristan's face changed into an exaggerated expression of disgust. "Ye Gods. I realise you have to grunt and sweat under a weary life, but perhaps a tad less of the latter before going into company, hmm?"

Bugger. He'd never had that shower, had he? "Sorry if a bit of honest sweat offends you," he snapped, hurt.

"It's offending the rest of us and all, Con," Heather put in, wrinkling her nose with a laugh.

"Yeah, well, I ran out of time, din't I? Got talking to the old bloke I was working for. Don't worry, I'm not staying. Wouldn't want to *offend* anyone." Con stomped off the best he could in his socks, knowing he was getting more worked up about it than he should—Heather teased him all the time, and he knew she didn't mean anything by it—but he couldn't seem to help it.

Sodding Tristan. He'd probably never done a day's honest labour in his privileged little life. Closest he ever got to hard work was most likely lugging Fortnum & Mason picnic hampers to the opera at Glyndebourne. Con bet the only time he actually broke into a sweat was when the Oxford/Cambridge Boat Race started looking like it was going to be won by the wrong team. Crew, whatever.

Bastard. Why did he have to keep rubbing it in Con wasn't in his league? Con knew that already.

He might be thick, but he wasn't a total idiot.

CHAPTER FIVE
WOO PEACEABLY

Tristan watched Con's exit in some bemusement. Who'd have expected the man to prove so sensitive? Tristan wouldn't have thought he'd have the imagination. "Perhaps I should . . ." He gestured eloquently into the sudden silence that had fallen.

"Leave him," Heather said firmly. "He's just being a grumpy sod. Right, so what were you saying about Wall?"

Tristan wrenched his attention back to matters merely theatrical rather than overdramatic, but it kept trying to wander back Con-wards. After all, the man had even managed to make stalking off in a huff look rather magnificent. In his socks.

"Tristan?" Heather asked loudly.

"Ah. Sorry. Yes. Where were we?" He forced himself to concentrate on rehearsing, which was, after all, no hardship. Yes, of *course* his fellow cast members were for the most part more wooden than a herd of hobby horses rampaging through a forest, but you couldn't fault their enthusiasm—or Heather's direction, for that matter. And yes, all right, it was exceedingly good for the ego to be looked up to as a professional. And to know that, come the performance, *his* would be the stand-out role everyone talked about. Despite all the self-sabotaging he was doing by helping the others with their interpretations of their parts.

The facilities here, too, were perfectly adequate—indeed, rather better than he'd been expecting. There was a permanent stage, with wings and curtains, at one end of the hall, and proper lighting as well. Tristan could have made do with far less—indeed, had done so more than once in the course of his career, which had encompassed Roman-style outdoor amphitheatres, sports halls, and on one occasion, simply a large rock.

He didn't think of Con again—well, not to the point of having to be told anything twice, at any rate—until Heather looked at the clock and told them it was time to call it a night. Tristan frowned. It was barely ten o'clock. "So soon?"

Gordon (a rather ratlike fellow with greying hair who played Quince in an acceptably downtrodden manner) clapped him on the shoulder. "Some of us have church to get up for in the morning."

"And the hall's only booked till ten," Heather added. "Can you give us a hand putting these chairs back?"

As he set to with the rest of them to accomplish the minimal amount of tidying that was necessary, Tristan finally gave his attention licence to wander back to Con's finer attributes. It promised to take some time. After all, there were so *many* of them. He was, he decided, not the least bit put off by what had passed between them earlier. With hindsight, perhaps Tristan *had* been a little thoughtless in what he'd said. It wasn't even as though he'd particularly objected to the man's rather musky aroma. It had just taken him by surprise, that was all. But, still, he could perhaps have curbed his tongue.

Yes… Going to see Con to apologise would be *entirely* appropriate, he decided. Only to remember he didn't have a clue where the man lived. Still, Heather ought to know. "Heather, darling, a word?"

"Yeah?" Heather looked up from her notes. "Actually, I meant to say, we always go down the pub after rehearsals—you coming? We can talk more there. I wanted to speak to you about Bottom's costume and stuff."

She was clearly taking it as read that he was going to play the part, although he was fairly sure he'd have remembered it if he'd actually agreed to do so. Tristan approved. It was exactly what he'd have done in her stead—never give the buggers a chance to back out. "Ah. While there is, of course, nothing I should like better than quaffing a pint or two of ale"—figuratively speaking, of course, as Tristan couldn't stand the stuff; he much preferred a nice Chablis—"with my fellow mechanicals and your lovely self, I feel it incumbent on me to make amends for my little faux pas earlier. I don't suppose you'd happen to have a certain over-large handyman's address?"

She frowned. "Con? You don't have to apologise to him. He's just in a mood."

Tristan gave her a winning smile and was gratified to see her tan skin tinged ever so slightly pinker as she flushed. "Nevertheless . . . After all, one must have harmony in the ranks."

"Well, if you're sure . . . He lives over the post office. First floor. Flat number's 6a. You know the post office, right?"

Tristan nodded. "Down the hill, over the bridge, on the left. Next to the more bijou of the village's two hairdressing establishments."

"Something like that, yeah. You'll find it. Tell Con to come and join us in the pub when he's got over his grump."

"I shall indeed," Tristan said smoothly. It was, of course, a bald-faced lie. If he was going to beard the lion in his den, he'd be buggered if he'd let said king of beasts get away that easily. This could be the perfect opportunity to put his plans of seduction into action—after all, what better way to show his apology was sincere than by making it very plain he had absolutely no objections to Con's person, sweaty or no?

He took his leave of his fellow players—promising to attend the next pub session without fail—and strode purposefully down the hill. The sun had fully set during rehearsals, and the gentle night breeze was refreshingly cool after the stuffiness of the village hall. Actually, a little *too* cool—Tristan shivered, dressed only in a shirt damp with perspiration from some rather energetic stage business.

Tristan's route took him past the village shops, and for a moment, he entertained the notion of purchasing some sort of placatory gift for Con. Most of the shops, of course, were long closed, but the off-licence was open, as was Tesco. A bottle of something, perhaps? (Not shower gel.) Or a cake?

Did Con even eat cake? From the looks of him, rare steak might be more to his taste. Or cow pie. A bottle, then? Perhaps a nice merlot or malt whisky? They could open it together . . .

No. That might look like he was trying too hard—and possibly, and which was even *less* flattering, like he thought he'd have to get Con drunk to stand a chance with him. That would never do.

The flats, Tristan realised after a moment or two staring up at the featureless windows above the post office and its neighbours, were accessed via a squarish, drive-through archway. As he penetrated its poorly lit depths, Tristan hoped he wasn't about to step in anything unpleasant. Most people in the village appeared to be remarkably conscientious about picking up after their dogs, but one did see the occasional relic of overenthusiastic consumption of lager and curry. And this close to the river, rats were always a possibility . . . He shivered, and hastened to the door. 6a, 6a . . . Yes, that was it. Tristan pressed the buzzer and waited.

"Yeah?" crackled through the tiny speaker.

Tristan placed his mouth close to it. "It's me. Tristan. Could we have a word?"

Silence. Perhaps Tristan should have bought a bottle of something after all. He could have drowned his sorrows with it if Con refused to speak to him—

The door buzzed, and Tristan hastily pushed it open. The stairway thus revealed was ugly, but at least it was more or less clean, with a slight smell of bleach rather than the more distressing odours one often encountered in cheap accommodation. He'd stayed in worse places, both as a student and as a professional actor. "Con-wards and upwards," Tristan muttered to himself, mounting the stairs.

Con's door was open, the light spilling out from the flat effectively eclipsed by the man himself. He stood there, arms folded and feet shoulder-width apart, the impression of tightly coiled belligerence not the least bit marred by the hole in one sock.

"What do you want?" Con growled in a low voice that rumbled deliciously through Tristan's chest. Among other parts.

Tristan put on his most charming smile, the one with a hint of self-deprecation. "Can I come in?"

"Why?"

Tristan dialled up the self-deprecation a notch. "I wanted to apologise."

Con unfolded his arms. His stance was still tense, but now with much less of a sense of imminent violence. "Yeah, well. Forget about it."

"Please," Tristan said winningly. "I've been feeling terrible about what I said to you."

A hand crept up to rub the back of Con's neck. "'S okay."

"Then I can come in?" Tristan persisted, stepping forward. As he'd hoped, Con stepped back instinctively, and Tristan was in.

Well.

Given that Con was one of the largest people Tristan knew, the flat really was remarkably small. The front door opened directly onto a bed/sitting room, into which were crowded a double bed, sofa, television, and a dining table that would just about seat one, or two if their plates were very small and they were up for a game of footsie. Two doors led off the room, presumably to some kind of washing and cooking facilities respectively.

"Well," Tristan said, his hands on his hips. "Isn't this cosy? May I?" He indicated the sofa and sat on it without waiting for a reply.

Con was still standing there, apparently nonplussed. He had damp hair, Tristan could see now, and had changed into a worn T-shirt and jogging bottoms. His face flushed ever so slightly under Tristan's gaze. "Look, you don't have to—"

"But I insist," Tristan said firmly, leaning back in the sofa so as to be able to look Con in the eye without cricking his neck. "I don't suppose I could trouble you for a glass of water? I came straight down as soon as the Iron Lady released us, and I'm feeling somewhat parched."

"Er, yeah. Right." Con got as far as the left-hand door, then turned, his manner uncertain. "Um. You want a cup of tea or something?"

"Tea would be splendid," Tristan assured him. Excellent.

He spent the time while Con was in, presumably, the kitchen, having a further look around. There was a shelf unit to one side that housed DVDs, CDs, audiobooks, and a photo of Con with an elderly lady, both of them smiling. Grandmother? Tristan couldn't trace any family resemblance—for a start, the old lady was a good foot and a half shorter than her putative grandson—but that didn't necessarily mean a thing.

"You want milk?"

Tristan startled and put the photo down hastily before returning to his seat. "Black, please. Lemon, if you have it. No? Never mind."

The tea, when it came, was in a mug celebrating the last royal jubilee, depicting Her Majesty in a particularly unsuitable shade of lipstick. Tristan's was, at any rate. Con was drinking out of one emblazoned with *Keep Calm and Drink Tea*. After handing Tristan his drink, he hovered awkwardly by the television.

That wouldn't do. "Do sit down," Tristan invited, patting the sofa cushion next to him. Apart from the bed and the dining chairs, it was the only other seat in the room. "Unless neck strain is to be my penance for offending you?"

"Sorry," Con muttered as he sat down, elbows tucked in, presumably to avoid taking up more than his fair share of space. It was rather adorable, really—and where the hell did *that* thought come from? *Focus, Tristan, focus.* Trouble was, with the sheer bulk of Con close enough that Tristan could feel his body heat, focussing on anything but his libido was becoming increasingly difficult.

"No, no, you mustn't apologise," Tristan protested. "That's my job. Which I do. Apologise, I mean." Damn it, had he exceeded his eloquence quota for the day?

Con stared into the depths of his mug. "'S'nuffin'. I shouldn't've got the hump. Just, it's been a long day and all." He shrugged. "Which, yeah, obviously you realised."

"Nevertheless, I shouldn't have allowed my tongue to run away with itself like that." Tristan kept his voice low and leaned a little closer to Con. *That* was better. That was far more like the Tristan Goldsmith A game. "I'm afraid sometimes I can be a little tactless when my nerves get the better of me." Should he have added a self-conscious laugh? Tristan held his breath.

Con looked up at him sharply. "What, you? Nervous?"

"Of course," Tristan prevaricated. "There I was, in an unknown place, with an unknown group of people, all of whom knew each other well, my skills as an actor on trial. Who wouldn't be nervous?"

"Yeah, but . . . you're a professional. I mean, you're *good*."

The praise was so obviously sincere—and so unexpected—that Tristan felt a strong urge to brush it off, deny his own talents. Which was absurd, of course, because if there was one thing Tristan *didn't* suffer from, it was a lack of confidence in his abilities. Well, on the stage, at any rate. If (God forbid) he were forced to be honest, he *was* having the occasional sleepless night over the looming New York job. Father had such high expectations . . . But that was the last thing he wanted to think about right now. "I . . . Thank you," he managed, and took a gulp of tea.

Con smiled in the direction of the carpet. It was a cheap-looking low-pile one with a pattern of flowers in queasy 1970s shades of orange and brown; Tristan couldn't really see what there was to smile at.

"Before you came on board, yeah," Con continued, "Hev was trying to get me to take the part. Bet she's bloody glad now I said no."

Tristan blinked, then rallied. He could hardly let an opening like *that* go by. "Oh, I'm quite convinced you'd make an excellent Bottom," he purred, slipping a hand onto Con's knee and giving a little squeeze.

As a seduction technique, it didn't quite have the desired effect. Con choked on his mouthful of tea and, his cheeks bellowed, went red in the face with the effort of not spraying it over the carpet.

Tristan drew back a few inches and prudently refrained from making any gags on the virtues of swallowing. "I, ah, wasn't aware you acted," he said, once the coughing fit seemed to have died down.

Con took a careful sip from his mug, then cleared his throat. His colour was slowly returning to normal. "Sorry about that. I don't. Act, I mean. I just do the scenery. Shows you how desperate she was getting, though. It's her first time directing, and what with Alan dropping out, she was having kittens over it all."

"What an arresting image," Tristan said politely.

Con laughed. "Yeah. Not so much when you're in the firing line, though."

"There is a certain steeliness to her direction, I'll admit. Have you known her long?"

"Only since I moved into the village." He grinned directly at Tristan. The force of it was a little unnerving. "She saw my card in Tesco and all. 'Cept when *she* rang, it was cos she wanted me to do stuff for free. You know, for the amateur dramatics."

"Oh? And do you provide *other* services for her gratis?" Tristan arched an eyebrow.

Con frowned, then, adorably, blushed. "Oh. No, she's got a bloke. Chris, who plays Flute, yeah? And, well, I'm not really into girls." Once more the carpet received a thorough examination.

Even as he mentally punched the air in celebration, Tristan had to admire Con's constitution. If *he* lived here, he'd make it a point to look at the hideous flooring as little as possible. "And tell me," he purred, sliding so close one couldn't have fit a cat's whisker between them on the sofa and putting his hand on Con's knee once more. "Are there any young men you're particularly, ahem, *into* at the moment?"

Annoyingly, Con stiffened, and not in a good way. Tristan got the distinct impression that if he weren't already pressed up against the arm of the sofa, he'd be edging away. "I . . . Uh. No. Um. You? Um. If you're into blokes, obviously."

"Mmm, I can think of *one* . . ." Tristan ran his hand up Con's thigh.

And had to duck out of the way as Con stood up abruptly. "Um, it's not that I don't . . . But you're going off to New York in a couple of months. It's not gonna work, is it?"

Tristan lolled back in the cushions with a pout, manfully restraining himself from rolling his eyes. "I was after a bit of fun, not your work-roughened hand in marriage."

"That's the point, innit? Look, I don't do casual. It's just not me." Con wrapped his big arms around himself.

Tristan felt a surge of jealousy. "Why on earth not?"

"I just don't, okay? I mean, I like you and all, but I just don't wanna . . ."

Tristan frowned. "It's the height, isn't it? Just because I'm not constructed on Herculean lines—"

"It's got nothing to do with how big you are." Con flushed. "I mean, tall."

"It'd better not be because I'm Jewish."

"You're not bloody listening. We just want different stuff, all right?"

"Sex is a biological imperative. Men are *programmed* to want it. Why would you even try to deny that?"

"I'm not denying nothing, okay? I just don't wanna sleep with you. End of."

One day, Tristan thought dully, he'd be called upon to give a performance as Caesar being shivved by his senators. All he'd have to do would be to remember the precise degree of stabbing pain he could feel now in the chest area, and the Olivier Award would be in the bag.

"Well, you've made yourself perfectly clear," he heard himself saying. He stood up. "And now I come to think of it, good thing too. It was a ridiculous idea, anyway. After all, what on earth could *you* and *I* have in common?"

Con blinked slowly a few times. Then his face hardened. "Right. So I guess you'll be going now, then."

"Well, I wouldn't want to take up any more of your no doubt valuable time."

Tristan was halfway down the stairs before he heard the gentle click of the door shutting behind him. He felt sick. This was . . . This was all wrong.

This *never* happened. Not to Tristan.

CHAPTER SIX
THE RAVELED SLEAVE

Con lay on his bed in the dark, staring at the ceiling. The light coming in from the street lamp outside his window spread in little wavy patterns drawn by the tops of the curtains. Every now and then, a car would go past, and there'd be a flash of light as it went over the speed bump outside, the headlights pointing up for a second or so.

Tristan had left half an hour ago. Con had been so bloody tired, everything ached. He'd brushed his teeth, pulled off his clothes, and fallen into bed, but sleep hadn't come. Right now he felt like he'd never been more awake in his life.

What the hell was Tristan playing at? Was it all some . . . some acting thing? Like he wanted to try slumming it with Con for a bit, so he could *expand his range*, like Heather would put it? Or was he just bored? Yeah, that was it. He was bored, cos let's face it, he'd be used to a lot livelier nightlife than you got around Shamwell.

He was probably used to going clubbing every night . . . Although, hang on, he'd have been at the theatre every night, wouldn't he, what with him being a professional actor? Maybe he went clubbing after the performance. After all, how long would it take Tristan bloody God's gift Goldsmith to land a bloke for the night? Half an hour, tops. Even if the clubs all shut at one like they did round here, he'd have plenty of time.

If Con was honest, he hadn't been surprised Tristan had tried it on. What with all the flirting, and the looks he'd been getting. And some of those posh gits liked a bit of rough, didn't they? Yeah, he'd known Tristan fancied him.

He just hadn't expected Tristan to make it quite so bloody clear a quick shag was all Con was worth to him, that was all.

A tight, painful feeling in his chest, Con rolled over and punched his pillow.

CHAPTER SEVEN
LOVE'S LABOUR'S LOST

"**H**e turned me down, Amanda. Me. *He* turned *me* down."

Amanda's face, which was looking a little on the puffy side as—*finally*—displayed on Tristan's computer screen, showed none of the sympathy Tristan had been expecting. "Have you got *any idea* what time it is here?"

Tristan frowned in concentration. "GMT plus eight, but we're on British Summer Time, so that's only plus seven . . ." He beamed. "Six o'clock in the morning."

Then he realised what he'd just said.

"Oh. Sorry." He made a face at her, the one that was supposed to convey *Aren't I a scatterbrain, but I'm so adorable you forgive me.* It didn't appear to have the desired effect.

God, Tristan was losing his touch with *everyone.*

"So you bloody well should be. I get *one* lie-in here, Tristan, *one*, and it's on a Sunday morning. I do *not* appreciate being woken up from it."

"Then you should have shut your laptop down properly when you went to sleep. Watching naughty pictures before beddy-byes again, were we? Darling, don't you ever worry someone will hack your computer and use the webcam to watch you sleeping?"

"Not everyone has a nasty little imagination like you, *darling.*"

"Or at the very least, you should have turned off that wake-up-when-called function. I don't even know why you have that. I didn't think you were *that* attached to your old friends that you couldn't bear to miss a call from them. Well, present company excepted, of course."

"I do have a family too, you know."

"Sweetie, you hate your family."

"Not as much as I hate *you* right now. The Skype thing's for emergencies."

"This *is* an emergency, darling. I told you. He turned me *down*, Amanda."

"Who did? Oh God—not your mentally negligible village stallion?"

Too downcast to protest the insult to Con's intelligence, Tristan nodded sadly, wondering if it would be overdoing it to let a single tear drop from his eye.

"Maybe he's straight."

"*Please*. You know perfectly well half the men I've slept with have been straight. Which he isn't, by the way. He told me."

"Maybe your particular blend of waspish camp and intellectual snobbery just doesn't do it for him. Perhaps *he'd* rather be off shagging straight men."

Tristan pouted. "Are you implying I'm not manly enough for him?"

"If the diamanté cap fits, darling."

"Ouch. You're going to be back in Britain for Christmas, aren't you? I'll make an appointment with the vet. It's been far too long since we last had your claws clipped."

"Oh, I expect I'll be back, but I don't suppose I'll see you. You'll be in New York, and you know they don't take much time off for holidays there. You won't even have time to get on a plane."

Something seized up uncomfortably in Tristan at that thought. God, that was going to be his life in a few short months. Long days of drudgery in a tedious job, with colleagues who thought days off were for wimps. Still, at least Father would be pleased. And he'd be achieving something. Making a success of himself. Wasn't that what life was all about?

"I *could* come and visit you, I suppose," Amanda said, with the air of one grudgingly condescending to toss a lifebelt to a drowning man. "Christmas in New York would be all right, I expect. You could take me to Macy's, and ice skating in the park."

"Better bring some bolt cutters to unchain me from my desk, then," Tristan muttered, nonetheless cheered by the prospect.

"Poor love. It's just not fair, is it? That you should have to work for a living like, oh, every single other person in the world. In the *real* world, that is."

Tristan frowned. "When we were with the Players, we were working for a living."

"I think the word you were looking for is *pittance*. Remember all those ghastly times we were forced to eat supermarket own brands and get tanked up on cheap wine before we went out, because we couldn't afford to buy rounds?"

Well, yes, but Tristan had actually found it quite fun at the time. Like one of those survival adventures, where they sent you off to the outback with nothing but a penknife and a piece of string and made you forage for your own food. Tristan had become remarkably adept at foraging in the bargain bin at Lidl.

Amanda, he recalled, had never quite entered into the spirit of it. "The point still stands. And anyway, I didn't call you to talk about work."

"Oh yes, the stallion. Are you sure he actually realised you were asking him out? I wouldn't normally accuse you of being too subtle, but you did say he's not the sharpest dagger in the prop drawer."

This was too much. Tristan bristled on Con's behalf. "Just because he's not particularly academic doesn't mean he's *retarded*. Yes, he realised."

"So what did he actually say?"

"I'd rather not repeat it," Tristan said stiffly. "But it was very final." To his horror, the tear he had contemplated shedding earlier in a bid for sympathy was now making its way, entirely unbidden, down his face.

Amanda rolled her eyes. "God, Tristan, for a supposedly nice Jewish boy you have a hell of a lot of ham in you sometimes. Save the tears for your next starring role."

Tristan scrubbed his face vigorously with his hand, and tried to look suitably caught out in counterfeit emotion. "Mmm, not a lot of call for tears in *Dream*—not from Nick Bottom, at any rate."

"What?"

"Oh, didn't I tell you? No, that's right, they only asked me this morning."

"Who?"

"The local amateur dramatics society. Affectionately known as the Sham-Drams. They've asked me to be in their production of *Midsummer Night's Dream*, and I must say they seem rather impressed with my portrayal so far."

There was a pause before Amanda spoke again. "Why would you even want to be in an amateur production? Or should I say, a *shamateur* one?"

Tristan frowned. "Why on earth not? It's *acting*, Amanda. It's a stage. Don't you miss it?" Aware he was likely prodding a raw nerve, Tristan braced himself for an outburst.

It didn't come. Amanda's tone, far from wounded, simply dripped with disdain. "Of course I *miss* it. But a village society? It's hardly the same thing. If you told me I could never eat salmon again, I expect I'd miss that. But it doesn't mean I'd take every opportunity to gorge myself on fish fingers. I suppose it must be a sop to your ego, being the only actual actor in the production, but don't you think it's just a little pathetic?"

"Not in the least," Tristan said icily. "But I'll let you go now, sweetie. I wouldn't want to keep you when you're so clearly behind on your beauty sleep."

She smiled sweetly. "You always were bitchy when thwarted. Some people might say it was time you grew out of it. Do try not to let one humiliating rejection ruin your whole summer, won't you?"

They hung up, and Tristan flung himself down on the sofa, one arm over his eyes. God, when would he learn that calling Amanda for sympathy was like asking a shark to kiss a boo-boo better?

She was wrong about the Sham-Drams. There was nothing pathetic about it at all. Was there? No, no, there wasn't. And yes, all right, perhaps there *was* a touch of the old ego-boost involved in showing a bunch of amateurs how it was done, but mostly, it was just *fun*.

Well, it *had* been fun. Now, he supposed, it was going to be a bloody nightmare, having to face Con all the time.

CHAPTER EIGHT
CONSTANT IN ALL THINGS

"Tristan's trying to get into Con's knickers," Heather announced as Sean put the tray of drinks down on the pub table.

So much for mates keeping your secrets.

Sean grinned. "Yeah? How'd that go, then?"

"It didn't, all right?" Con took a swallow of his beer. They were up at the Sticky Wicket for an early Sunday lunch with Sean's and Heather's boyfriends, so he was already feeling a bit of a sore thumb for not being all coupled up.

"Playing hard to get, are you?" Heather grinned too. "Never saw the point of that, personally."

Chris put his arm around her and squeezed her so tight she squealed. "Yeah, gotta love a girl who's easy."

"Oi! I'm not easy, all right?" She smirked. "Made you buy me dinner first, din't I?"

"Bag of chips, wasn't it?"

"*And* a bottle of Beck's. Don't you go making everyone think I'm cheap."

Sean's bloke, Rob, was looking at them sideways, like he couldn't decide if they were really sweet or just the sort of lager louts with no morals people like him wrote letters to the *Times* about. Sean and him were in their cricket whites, ready for the match at two o'clock, and they'd driven up in Rob's posh car, all white leather seats and looking like it ought to have Audrey Hepburn sitting in the back powdering her nose.

"Speaking of which," Heather went on, "are you going to go and order my lunch or what? Some of us are starving to death here."

"Fine, I'm going. Veggie curry, yeah?" Chris grumbled, standing up with a smile. "Bloody hell, Sean, was she this high maintenance when you were going out with her?"

"Worse," Sean said easily, laughing when Heather gave him the finger with both hands. "And cheers, mate. Me and Rob'll have the ham salad. Don't wanna weigh ourselves down before the match." He handed Chris a twenty-pound note.

Con dug hastily in his back pocket and handed over a tenner. "Lasagne, cheers." His mind wasn't really on his stomach. Was he the only one who found it a bit weird, hearing everyone talk about Sean and Heather being exes in front of the people they were with now?

No—Rob was staring into his lime and soda, looking a bit pink. Sean must have noticed too, as he grabbed Rob's hand and gave it a quick squeeze. "So have you met this Tristan bloke yet?" he asked.

Rob looked up. "No, I was about to ask who he was, actually."

Heather rolled her eyes. "Oh, you'd probably like him. He's dead posh and all. He's our new Bottom."

Rob blinked several times. "Do I actually want to know?"

Heather and Sean laughed. "In Hev's theatre group, yeah? They're doing *Midsummer Night's Dream*. Thought you and me could go and see it."

"*Oh*. Yes, that sounds lovely." Rob frowned at Heather. "And you'll be playing . . . Helena or Hermia? I always manage to forget which is which."

"Hermia. She's the one everyone starts out in love with. And I'm directing it," Heather added proudly.

"Excellent! Well, we shall certainly come along and support your endeavours."

"Long as nothing *else* goes wrong." Heather nudged Con, who'd been keeping quiet through all this. "Oi, you and him getting involved better not cause any problems."

"We're not involved! Told you, nothing happened. Nothing's gonna happen."

"Sure?" Sean put in. "I'd have thought he was just your sort."

Con wished he'd never bloody shown Sean that picture of Mo. Or, all right, spent a good few nights at the pub going on about the bloke. "Look, can we leave it? It's not . . . I don't do casual stuff, okay?"

"Maybe he wants more than that," Rob suggested, which was a bloody nerve seeing as he hardly knew Con and hadn't even met Tristan yet.

"He doesn't."

"Sure?" Heather teased.

"Yeah, I'm sure, because he sodding well said so, all right?" Con stood up. "I'll go help Chris with that order." He stomped off, wishing he'd just stayed in bed instead of coming up here to be got at by his so-called mates.

Course, when he got to the bar, he found Chris had already got to the front and ordered, so he ended up sitting back down with them about two minutes later. Chris gave them all suspicious looks along with their change. "Oi, what's with the awkward silence? You lot been talking about me, or what?"

"Don't flatter yourself, mate," Sean said with a smile. "So when are we gonna get you playing cricket?"

"Cricket? Call that a sport? You spend three hours standing around a field and maybe have a ball come your way once. Telling you, mate, football's where it's at."

"Yeah? And when's the last time you kicked a ball in anger?"

"Kick yours for you if you like, mate . . ."

The conversation stayed light and easy after that, and Con felt a lot more relaxed now it wasn't him in the spotlight.

After they'd eaten, Con wandered over the road to the village cricket ground with the rest of them. Not that he was really into cricket, but, well, it was a nice day and it was right there. Might as well sit out in the sun for a bit longer and cheer on Sean and Rob before heading off home to catch up on the laundry. He supposed it was the same for Chris and Heather—or did she feel she had to watch Sean doing his cricket stuff seeing as he came to her plays?

One day, maybe, he was going to ask one of them how all that worked. But it bloody well wasn't going to be today, with Rob and Chris there with them.

"Right—wish us luck," Sean said, looking over at the pavilion where the visiting team was limbering up. "It's Bishops Langley first team today. League leaders, and they gave us a right thrashing last time."

"Knock 'em dead," Chris told him.

"Yeah, break a leg stump," Heather said. "What? I know my cricketing terms."

"You keep telling yourself that, Hevs."

Rob gave a wave that was sort of half a salute, and Sean and him sauntered over to join their team. They looked good together—both tall and lean, with an easy stride. Con would've looked like a bloody gorilla lumbering along beside them.

Heather tugged on his arm. "Come on, sit down. It'll make it less obvious when you ogle the players."

"I wasn't . . ."

"Nothing wrong with a good ogle, I always say."

"Yeah?" Chris put in. "Cos there's a bird over there with a fantastic pair of—"

He broke off, laughing, as she slapped him.

Con reckoned he was going to be making his excuses sooner rather than later, if they were going to be all over each other all the time. He let his gaze wander around the field. There weren't a lot of spectators—there never were—but he could see a fair few families with picnics scattered around. Mums bringing the kiddies up to support dad and get a bit of fresh air at the same time, he supposed.

The other side of the pitch there was a bloke sitting on his own. Con squinted, trying to make him out. Was that . . . ?

"That's Tristan," Heather said in surprise. She stood up and waved energetically. "Hey, Tristan! Come and join us!"

Oh, bloody hell. "What did you do that for?" Con demanded. The figure over the other side had stilled. He'd definitely seen them.

"What? We can't leave the poor bloke all on his own. Only just moved here, hasn't he? Probably hasn't got any mates apart from us. What's your problem?"

"You know what the problem is!"

She carried on waving. "He asked if you fancied a shag, and you turned him down, that's what you said. Although God knows why. I mean, he's a bit up himself, but he's all right really. But, anyway, so what? *And* we want to keep him sweet. So if he's okay with coming over here, I don't see why you shouldn't be."

Con's stomach flipped over as Tristan got to his feet.

CHAPTER NINE
THE GAME'S AFOOT

"Tristan's Sunday morning did not have an auspicious start. Partly because he'd spent a wretched night in fitful sleep filled with unhappy dreams of large, well-muscled handymen, but mostly because when he finally set one weary foot out of bed, it landed squarely on half a mouse.

Said rodent revenant was soft and damp, and collapsed under his bare toes with a sickening sort of soggy crunch. Tristan yelped, fell back on top of the duvet, and stared in horror at his foot, now liberally smeared with thick, dark blood. He swallowed bile and dared a glance at the floor. Oh God. The sad little remains still clearly showed that the creature had been neatly bisected down the middle, leaving Tristan with its rear end.

Which rather begged two questions. Firstly, was this some sick hazing prank by his fellow Sham-Drams, punning on the name of his character? And secondly, and rather more pressingly, where the bloody hell was the other half?

Thirdly—and Tristan felt very strongly that, in the circumstances, he could be forgiven for not having had the presence of mind to think of this one *first*—just who or what had been in his bedroom while he was sleeping to leave the wretched thing there? Whilst Tristan had always liked to think of his bedroom as having something of an open-door policy, anyone who made a habit of leaving fractional corpses behind them was very much off the guest list.

Had he offended any small-time mobsters, perhaps? Not able to stretch to a racehorse's head, they'd left him instead a mouse's arse?

No, no, that was getting ridiculous. And, oh God, he needed to get his foot clean *right now*. Scanning the floor feverishly for any further rodent casualties, Tristan set his unscathed foot out of bed and began to hop towards the stairs. Nanna Geary's house had been built in the halcyon days of outside privies and tin tubs by the fire, and there was a long, long trail a-winding down the stairs and through the kitchen to the bathroom which had been tacked on as an afterthought several decades later.

Tristan was amazed he managed to reach the ground floor without breaking his neck. He had a narrow squeak (hah!) in the kitchen, when a sudden noise startled him mid-hop. Turning just in time to see the cat flap closing behind a dark shadow he was almost certain was a black furry tail, Tristan cursed as his foot slipped on a patch of grease. His stomach lurching, he made a grab for the nearest means of support. This, unfortunately, was Nanna Geary's Royal Wedding tea towel, hanging on a hook on the wall.

There was a loud ripping sound—and then the hook decided to curtail the lèse-majesté by detaching itself from the wall, taking with it a fair chunk of plaster. Dust rained down on Tristan as he landed on his arse on the tiled kitchen floor a lot harder than was comfortable.

"Bloody, buggering *hell*." He was too dispirited to even come up with a decent bit of profanity. It didn't help that seeing the cat flap reminded him of Con, who would not, now, be coming round to nail it shut or to do anything else, for that matter.

Maybe Tristan should just cut his losses and spend the summer in New York, frying eggs on the sidewalk or getting mugged in Central Park or whatever one did for amusement over there. Village life *clearly* wasn't working out for him.

He took a deep breath. "No. No, this will not do. You are a Goldsmith; comport yourself accordingly. You will rise above minor setbacks, and emerge victorious at last."

Hmm. Not bad, as pep talks went, but the delivery could have been better. Tristan repeated his words several times, with varying emphasis and inflection, and then tacked on a bit of *Henry V* just for the hell of it. "Once more unto the breach, dear friends, *once more*; or close the wall up with our Shamwell dead," he roared into the kitchen, flinging the arm still holding the tea towel out dramatically.

That was more like it. He stood to take a bow—and almost fell over again on meeting the wide-eyed stare of a total stranger, goggling at him through the glass in the kitchen door.

It was at this point that Tristan started to seriously wonder if he should reconsider his habit of sleeping nude. His inner self wanted to curl up into a tiny ball and rock itself gently. Luckily his outer self was made of sterner stuff, and merely fixed the man with a steely gaze. "Can I help you?" he demanded icily.

"Er . . . I can come back," the man said, his voice depressingly audible through the door. "Looks like you're busy."

"No, no, whatever it is, let's get this over with," Tristan said, hopping to the door and holding the shreds of his dignity together with the shreds of the tea towel.

The man backed off. He was middle-aged, casually dressed, and looked vaguely familiar, now Tristan thought about it. Although possibly his expression had been a shade less alarmed last time Tristan had seen him.

"No, it's all right. Some other time."

He turned and ran for the hills. Or, to be strictly accurate, vaulted over the low wall to the house next door, which was, Tristan now recalled, where he lived. It was the neighbour Con had indicated as having taken in bloody mouse-murdering Meggie the Second. Tristan sighed and sank down to the floor again, wincing as his bruised behind hit the tiles.

And then jumped back up so quickly he nearly strained something, when that *bloody* frog hopped out from under the fridge and gave a loud croak from not six inches away.

Things didn't much improve after that. After the wretched, messy business of cleaning dead mouse from between his toes, Tristan had to go back upstairs and start the wretched, messy business of cleaning considerably *more* dead mouse from Nanna Geary's bedroom carpet.

After several gallons of water enriched with an expensive amount of Tristan's shampoo—because surely carpet shampoo couldn't be *that* different from hair shampoo?—only a sad little sandalwood-scented stain remained to reproach Tristan for his abysmal caretaking skills. Damn it. Less than a week in residence, and he'd already allowed infestation and caused wholesale destruction. There'd be nothing of the place left by October. If Nanna Geary were ever to receive the national recognition she so richly deserved, they'd have to mount the blue plaque on a bloody crater.

God, he needed to get out of the house. If only to preserve it awhile longer.

Nanna Geary had mentioned something about village cricket on Sunday afternoons, Tristan was sure. And he'd driven past the grounds, unmistakable with the low pavilion and the big, white sight screen that remained bafflingly free of graffiti, despite the lack of antivandal fencing around the place. It was in a pleasant-looking spot up the hill at the village end of the common, and would be idyllic in today's warm sunshine. Yes, a spot of cricket, that would be the ticket.

Wondering whimsically whether he could manage to spend an entire day thinking in rhyming couplets like a character in a play by a modern-day Molière, Tristan went to get dressed. Hmm. What *did* one wear to a village cricket match? Linen trousers, he decided—dark, so as not to show grass stains—and a casual shirt. Upon reflection, he rolled up the sleeves to display his forearms, which were well on the way to being respectably tanned. There, that would do. Nicely informal, but with a nod to the seriousness of the occasion.

Cricketers, Tristan had learned at both school and college, were wont to take their sport very seriously indeed. Anyone caught reciting the old poem about "flannelled fools at the wicket" was liable to receive very short shrift.

Tristan had never had much interest in or, if he was honest, aptitude for participating in team sports, but he could appreciate it in others. He therefore parked the BMW up at the cricket ground with the anticipation of a pleasant, relaxing afternoon watching vaguely attractive men do vaguely athletic things. Fortunately there was a good-sized car park with plenty of room—the BMW was an unwieldy beast, and would certainly not have been his first choice of conveyance or even second or third, but Father had refused point-blank to lend him the Lamborghini for the summer. And even Tristan would be forced to admit it wouldn't have been particularly practical for clearing Nanna Geary's house. But, damn it, it would have been a lot more fun to drive.

It wasn't until he'd settled himself in a nice, shady spot on the leg side of the pitch that things started to go wrong.

Bowing with bad grace to the inevitable, Tristan walked slowly around the cricket pitch to where Heather appeared to be doing a one-woman impersonation of an American cheerleading squad. Next to, he couldn't help but notice, a very disgruntled-looking Con. And Flute, of course—what was his real name? Chris, that was it.

He felt exceedingly hard done by. Of all the people he'd have expected to bump into at a village cricket match, Con was way down on the list, rubbing spectral shoulders with Nanna Geary's ghost. If anyone seemed likely to be more a fan of the muddied oafs at the goal than of their flannelled counterparts at the wicket, it was Con. He'd noticed him arrive, of course. The day he didn't notice Con within five hundred yards of him would be the day he signed up for a pair of dark glasses and a long white stick. Con towered over the diminutive Heather like an oil tanker over the *Cutty Sark*, with Chris some kind of merchant vessel laden with containers chugging along to starboard. Tristan had hoped they either wouldn't notice his sad, lonely presence, or would at least politely ignore him.

Being alone and friendless in an unkind world, he could handle. Being seen and pitied, however, was more than he could bear.

All he could do was keep the broiling mass of shock and humiliation from showing on his face. He beamed at them all. "I see you share my taste for a spot of organised loafing. Lovely day for it, isn't it?"

"Yeah, gorgeous, innit," Heather said. "Sit down, Rob's about to go in to bowl."

Tristan sat, carefully choosing the patch of grass next to Con to show beyond a shadow of doubt that he was *not* upset by what had passed between them the previous evening. "Rob?" he asked politely, peering at the pitch. A tall, slender, attractive man in gleaming whites was striding out towards the wicket, polishing the ball on his trouser leg.

Tristan had always wondered why they did that. Perhaps they just liked the way it left reddish streaks in the vicinity of their crotch.

"He's Sean's bloke," Heather told him before giving a piercing whistle. The bowler took off his cap and swept it with a flourish in her direction.

There were good-natured cries of "Stop eyeing up the ladies" and "Get on with it!"

"Sean?"

"He's the ginge," she supplied helpfully, jerking her head towards a fielder in mid off. Chris nudged her in the ribs and she yelped. "Oi!"

"In't that ginge-ist or something?" Chris teased.

"So how would you describe him? The bloke in cricket gear standing on the field with all the other blokes in cricket gear? Very bloody helpful I *don't* think." Heather rolled her eyes, then broke into giggling as Chris tickled her.

Tristan wasn't sorry to have his attention distracted from their somewhat embarrassing interplay when, for the first time, Con spoke. "He's the pest-control bloke, remember?" He stared resolutely at the cricket pitch, upon which absolutely nothing had yet happened.

Tristan blinked. "Ah, yes. The one who doesn't do frogs. I now have mice as well. Does he deal with them?"

Con turned to look at Tristan, which was a definite improvement. "Mice?"

"Yes. Small, furry, traditional liking for cheese?"

"I know what a bloody mouse is, all right? I'm not that bloody thick." Con coloured.

Tristan was hurt. He hadn't *meant* anything by his comment. He was cheered to see Heather turn a startled look on Con, before looking back to the match with great deliberation. "Yes, well, I found one in my house this morning. Well, rounding up, I did. It would be more exact to say I found half a mouse in my house this morning. The rear half."

Con gave him a long look. "Not sure Sean can help you there," he said at last. "I mean, I'm not an expert, but I reckon he'd have trouble getting it to take the bait."

Tristan's heart, inexplicably, lightened. "You think so?" He allowed the merest suspicion of a pout to shape his lips.

"Yeah, 'fraid so. Course, if it'd been the front half . . ." Con wasn't exactly *smiling* now, but there was definitely less disgruntlement in his expression. Perhaps even a modicum of gruntlement.

Tristan felt a wholly unwonted urge to punch the air. "I'm still looking forward to finding the front half," he said, his tone drier than Nanna Geary's sherry. "Actually," he added, the weather seeming clement for a spot of hay-making, "I could do with your professional services. There was, ah, some damage caused."

Con's eyes widened. "Just how big was this mouse? Sorry. Half a mouse."

"It was me. The damage, I mean. I, ah, managed to make a hole in the kitchen wall." In for a penny, in for a pound. "Just before I flashed the next-door neighbour with the Goldsmith family jewels and caused him to run away in fright. It hasn't been a very good morning."

"Lot of people run screaming when they see the Goldsmith family jewels, do they?"

"Well, I don't like to brag . . ." Tristan grinned and was unnerved by the thrill that shot through him at Con's answering shy smile. He swallowed. "So is there anyone else I should know on the field today?"

"Well, there's Patrick. Over there, see?" Con pointed towards a sandy-haired figure in leg gully, near where the woodland started at the far edge of the field. "He's playing Puck in *Dream*. He was s'posed to be Bottom, actually, but when Alan dropped out, Patrick said he'd rather play Puck anyway."

"I suppose one can't argue with that," Tristan said, although he was a little miffed that, as their one professional actor and, as it were, the saviour of the Sham-Drams, he hadn't been offered the choice of playing Puck himself.

"You'd make a good Puck," Con said, then looked away as if he regretted his words.

"I would, wouldn't I?" Tristan said, pleased. "'I am that merry wanderer of the night—' God, what a shot! Catch it, man!" He jumped to his feet, quickly followed by Heather, Con, and Chris.

The batsman had hit a cracking, if unwise, shot that soared high into the air and headed straight for leg gully. The putative Patrick was running backwards, his eye firmly on the ball. As it reached him, he leapt—and a cheer rose from the home side at the thwack of leather hitting flesh. The fielder clutched the ball to his chest as he hit the ground with a yell and rolled.

Even as his teammates ran to congratulate him, Tristan could tell something was wrong. The man wasn't getting up, and his shout had sounded more pained than proud.

"Something's up," Con said in a low tone.

"Oh my God," Heather muttered, her hands to her mouth.

Patrick was still on the ground, surrounded by a crowd of cricketers who obscured him from view—but the hushed muttering from spectators nearer to the action told its own story. A man—Sean, from his bright-orange hair—broke off from the group to jog back to the pavilion. The batsman who'd been caught out ran to speak to him, and seemed to get a polite but firm brush-off.

"I'm going over," Heather said grimly.

They all trooped around the outside of the pitch together. Ironically, Tristan thought, if it hadn't been for Heather hailing him earlier, he'd have been right here with a ringside seat for the action.

There was enough of a crowd still around the, presumably, injured man that there wasn't a hope of getting to him, so Heather contented herself with grabbing the arm of the bowler. Rob, that was his name. "What happened?"

Rob looked pained. "Caught his foot in a rabbit hole when he came down. I'm afraid it looks a bit nasty."

The man's accent, Tristan noticed, was several cuts above his interrogator's. He gave Rob another glance. No, no one he'd been at school or college with, or at least, not that he could recall. He wished the man could have been a little more precise. *Nasty* could mean anything from a mild sprain to fatal injury.

"What do you mean, 'nasty'?" Heather demanded. "Is he gonna be all right?"

"Oh yes, absolutely." Rob gave a worried laugh that was probably meant to be reassuring. "It's not like they lop your leg off for a compound fracture these days."

That, Tristan felt rather strongly, was *not* reassuring. From the look on Heather's face, she appeared to agree. "Oh my God," she said again.

The crowds parted, and Tristan was able to see that reassurance, indeed, would have been sadly misplaced. Patrick was now vertical, and supported by his one good leg and two of his fellow cricketers. Tristan hoped they were ready to take his full weight. Unsurprisingly, in view of the grisly red stain spreading down one leg of his whites, he was grey-faced and looked as though passing out was more a matter of *when* than *if*.

A shocked silence fell as Patrick was half carried towards the pavilion.

"You know," Tristan said into the stillness, "I fail to see why everyone's always so desperate to get a man back on his feet after he's fallen. I remember once taking a nasty tumble off my bike as I was coming through King's, and I'd barely got my breath before people were dragging me upright again. I was in no hurry, believe me. People just don't seem to realise how bloody *safe* staying on the ground feels after you've come a cropper once already."

As if to prove his point, the five-legged race halted halfway across the pitch, and Patrick was awkwardly laid down upon the grass once more.

"Shit," Con said, and ran over to them, presumably to be ready should extreme brawn be required. Of course, Patrick wasn't a particularly solid-looking man. Carrying him single-handed shouldn't be a problem for Con. Even as far as the hospital, should the ambulance, which must by now have been summoned, fail to arrive.

"Oh my God."

Tristan turned to Heather, a little perturbed by her imitation of a stuck gramophone record (Nanna Geary hadn't approved of such fads as cassettes and CDs). She still had her hands pressed to her mouth, and her face had taken on a dull, greyish tint against which her freckles stood out starkly.

Chris, too, seemed concerned. "He'll be all right."

"Not to play Puck in two months' time, he won't!" Her face twisted. "And just shut up, yeah?"

No one had spoken.

"I know I'm being a really crap person even *thinking* about that, all right? But it's just—God!" She turned away, her shoulders heaving in the sort of alarming manner that made Tristan want to do a quick impersonation of his next-door neighbour and run far, far away.

Chris cast him a helpless look, and put his arms around her.

Tristan regarded their backs for a long moment, then decided this was his cue to politely withdraw.

Fast.

CHAPTER TEN
OUTRAGEOUS FORTUNE

Bloody hell, that had to hurt. Patrick was breathing hard and fast, and looked like he was about to chuck. Looking at his poor bloody leg, *Con* felt like he was about to chuck.

He knelt down beside Patrick and grabbed his shoulder. "All right, mate. Ambulance'll be here soon."

Patrick's hand came up, groping a bit blindly, and clamped on Con's biceps so tight it hurt. "Gonna be sexy nurses?" he bit out.

"Promise." Con forced a smile. "Tight uniforms and everything. Then when you're better, you'll have all the girls wanting to whip your trousers off so they can see your scar."

"Only the girls? I'm disappointed, mate." He closed his eyes briefly, but didn't let go of Con's arm. "Thought gay blokes were supposed to have more taste."

"Nah," Con said, trying to keep it light. "Taste's nothin' to do with whether you're gay or not. It's what you eat. You know, pineapple's s'posed to be good; Brussels sprouts and broccoli, bad."

Patrick laughed and winced all at the same time. "Gonna write us a cookbook, Delia? *Seriously Delish Spunk*? Bloody hell, where the fuck are those nurses?"

"On their way, mate. Hold on." If he held on any tighter, mind, Con'd be joining him in the fracture clinic. "Hey, here we go."

He could hear the sirens now, getting louder, first gradually and then all at once as they broke through the trees and onto the long, straight road that led through the common to the cricket ground.

It felt weird, letting Patrick go off in the ambulance on his own. Con smiled and shook his head. Yeah, like they'd been having a bloody moment there.

He'd always wondered a bit about Patrick—whether it was just girls he was into. No real reason. It wasn't like he'd ever shown any interest in Con, not that Con would've expected him to. Patrick was, well, a bit too metrosexual to go out with someone like Con. His hair was always perfect like he'd just got out of the hairdressers, and everything he wore looked like it had a designer label even if it didn't. And he'd been single, Con was fairly sure, ever since Con had known him, so even if he went for blokes, which Con had no reason to think he did, he was obviously pretty choosy who he went out with.

But Con had, well, wondered.

Course, the poor bloke wasn't going to be running after anyone for a bit now. Sighing, Con looked around for his mates. He saw Heather and Chris soon enough, standing over by the trees with their arms around each other. Tristan wasn't anywhere in sight, and Con wondered if he should just leave them to it, but then Chris looked up and waved him over.

Heather broke out of his arms and scrubbed at her eyes. "Is he all right?" she asked when Con got near.

"Uh . . ." Con didn't want to give her false hope, but he didn't fancy being shot as the messenger either. "They'll look after him," he said in the end. "He was already looking forward to looking down the nurses' collars."

Chris laughed. Heather sniffed.

"What happened to Tristan?"

"Tristan? He buggered off. Din't even say good-bye." Heather sniffed again.

Con frowned. He'd thought better of Tristan.

"Come on," Chris said firmly. "Let's get back to the pub and buy this girl a drink. Sean and Rob are gonna get changed and meet us there."

"Aren't they carrying on with the match?" Con hadn't thought cricket matches were ever halted for anything but rain. Hadn't there been that bloke in Pakistan who got hit by a ball, and they just marked him on the scoreboard as "retired, dead" and carried on?

"Nah, those Bishops Langley wusses said the pitch wasn't safe to play so they've all packed up and gone home. Bunch of bloody wimps. Sean reckons it's only cos their star batsman got caught out for a duck." Chris looked like he wanted to spit.

Sean was probably right, Con reckoned. "Yeah, it wasn't even like it was their bloke who got injured."

They crossed over the road and headed straight for the bar. "I'll get 'em," Con said quickly. It wasn't his round, but Heather looked like she was about to cry and Con did *not* want to be on his own with her if that happened.

"Cheers, mate," Chris said, already steering Heather over to a table.

"Innit terrible about that bloke at the cricket?" the barmaid said as she pulled Con's pint. "Course, you know why it happened."

"Er, yeah, rabbit hole," he muttered. He should have expected the news to have travelled—it wasn't like it'd had far to come.

"I blame them animal-rights people. They should never have let 'em ban hunting."

Con gave her a look. He'd thought that was foxes. Then again, what did he know?

"All them town folk," she went on. "Coming into rural areas and telling us how to do stuff. It's not right. Bottle of Beck's, was it?"

"Yeah. Ta." Being a town bloke himself, Con wasn't sorry to change the subject.

He took the drinks over to where Heather and Chris were sitting in the corner. Heather grabbed her beer like it was a lifeline. "I don't know what I'm gonna do," she sniffed.

Con frowned as he pulled out a barstool and sat down. "There must be someone who can take over playing Puck. What about Alan? I mean, I know he dropped out, but couldn't he drop back in?"

Chris and Heather sent each other looks. Con couldn't work them out, but they weren't happy ones. "What?" he asked.

Heather took a deep breath. "I might have gone off on him a bit. For leaving me in the lurch like that. I don't think he's gonna want to do me any favours."

Con took a thoughtful mouthful of beer. "There's other blokes in SADS, though. What about Keith? I mean, I know he's a bit old, but—"

"Yeah, and a bit rubbish. He'd ruin it."

"Roger?"

"Like *he'd* ever let me direct him."

"Why wouldn't he?"

Heather rolled her eyes and ticked off on her fingers. "Well, let's see? First, he was against *Dream* from the start. Second, I'm too young. Third, and more importantly, I'm too female. Fourth, and for all I know, this is the sodding deal-breaker all by itself, I'm too black."

Chris frowned. "Come on, you don't know that. I've never heard him say anything racist."

"No? So where were you when he was asking me where 'my people' came from?"

"He probably just meant your family. You know, like my folks come from Hampshire."

"Yeah, right." Heather's expression was getting stormier by the minute. "Cos of course you'd know far more about racism than someone who's actually experienced it."

Con leaned forward a bit desperately. "What about Trevor?"

Chris and Heather stopped bickering and turned matching pitying looks on him. "You know what he's like. Roger says 'heel' and he scampers over with his tail wagging. He wouldn't dare have anything to do with a production once Roger's come out against it."

"Can you double up any more of the roles?"

"Only if you want it to end up looking like Gollum talking to himself in *Lord of the Rings*. Everyone's already playing at least two roles—all except Puck and Bottom, and they can't cos they're on so much. We went through all this when Alan dropped out, remember? There's no way round it, except by finding another bloke to do it."

"You know," Chris started, looking like he knew he was going to get shot down. "You could let a girl play Puck. Loads of productions—"

Heather turned on him. "You *know* how I feel about that! The whole play is supposed to be a war-of-the-sexes thing. And to make the point about men treating women like shit. How's it gonna bloody well do that if Oberon's ally is a girl, hey? You wanna explain that one to me?"

Chris didn't flinch. Which made him a braver man than Con. "Well, it's gotta be better than cancelling the show."

"Oi, who's cancelling the show?" It was Sean's voice, and Con spun on his seat to see him and Rob, now out of their cricket whites and into what they normally wore at weekends, which for Sean was jeans and a T-shirt and for Rob involved a bow tie and braces. At least he didn't have his tweed jacket on today, which always made Con feel itchy and uncomfortable just looking at it.

"No one's cancelling anything," Heather said firmly. Then she collapsed onto the table, her head down on her folded arms, and wailed, "I don't know what I'm gonna do . . ." It came out a bit muffled and with a sniff on the end.

Rob looked alarmed. "Ah, drinks, anyone?"

He wasn't the only one feeling uncomfortable. Con stood up. "I'll give you a hand."

By the time they got back with the round of drinks—all two of them, but Rob was a good bloke and he hadn't called Con out on the fact his help hadn't been needed—Heather had disappeared.

"Ladies'," Chris explained, catching Con's look at her empty seat. "Gone to fix her face. 'Cept she'll probably ruin it all again soon as she gets out. I'm telling you, this play is death to my sex life. She's always either knackered or terminally depressed." He gave Sean and Rob a sad puppy-dog look. "Don't s'pose either of you two lads wanna give acting a go?"

Rob made a face. "I'm afraid September really isn't a good month for me to make such a commitment for, what with parents' evenings and open days. In any case, I'm fairly certain my performance would be as wooden as the scenery."

"Yeah, and don't look at me," Sean said firmly. "Not my thing. I'll come and support you anytime, but you're not getting me up on stage. Not if you paid me." He paused, then turned to Con. "Still think you should give it a go, mate."

Con choked on his pint. "No. No way," he said, trying to shake his head and wipe his mouth on his sleeve at the same time.

"No, but listen, I've been thinking about it, yeah? Hear me out." Sean leaned forward on the table. "You're always telling us bits from your audiobooks, right? And it's dead funny. You know how to tell it, how to, I dunno, make it dramatic. So how different can that be from acting?"

"It's nothing like acting! I just tell it how the voice in the book told it." Con drew back.

"So? So all you have to do is find an audio recording of the play and learn how the actor in that did all the lines. Easy."

"You just wanna see me make a giant tit of myself on stage," Con muttered into his glass.

"Who's gonna be a tit on stage?" Heather demanded, sitting back down. She'd done something with her face but her eyes were still red.

"Con is," Chris said proudly, like it'd all been his idea and more to the point, like Con had actually agreed to do it.

"You're gonna do it?" she squealed. "Oh my God, you're wonderful!"

"No! I never said that." Con glared at Chris, who avoided his gaze.

Heather slumped down in her seat. "Look, just think about it, yeah? Please? For me?"

Con felt like a total bastard, seeing her expression turn from joy to despair. He could kill Chris for dropping him in it like that. "I'll think about it, all right? But I just don't see how it can work."

CHAPTER ELEVEN
BUT BEG ONE FAVOUR

Tristan went to open his door on Sunday evening in a state of high anticipation, leavened with a spoonful or two of trepidation. The chances were good it would be Con—who else in the village knew where he lived? There was, however, a not insignificant possibility that his next-door neighbour still wanted to talk to him, hopefully about permanently adopting Meggie the Second, and had decided to go for a formal approach this time. Possibly bringing reinforcements to protect him against rampaging naked queers.

He wasn't at all prepared to see Heather standing there.

"That's odd," he said, nonetheless with a welcoming smile. "My thumbs weren't pricking in the slightest. Greetings to you, oh benevolent dictator. Step into my humble abode; thou shalt have five thousand welcomes."

"One'll do, ta. Got your address from Con, by the way, in case you were wondering," she threw over her shoulder as she stepped past Tristan and into Nanna Geary's living room. Her beady eyes scanned the room, taking in the no-nonsense, old-fashioned furniture in sombre shades of tweed. "Nice place you got here. Used to be your gran's, right?"

"Actually she was my old nanny. And my mother's before me. Rather a family treasure, you might say."

Heather's eyes widened at that. "You mean she was just an employee, and she left you her house? Bloody hell, your lot have got all that feudal stuff down pat, haven't you?"

Tristan stiffened. "I resent your implications. Nanna Geary was a much-loved family member, even if not by blood."

"Sorry! Not trying to imply anything. What was it, one of those old-fashioned arrangements like *Downton Abbey* or something where the kids spend more time with the nanny than with their own mother?"

"Mother died when I was twelve, so it was somewhat unavoidable after that," Tristan said curtly. She'd been ill for a long time too. Tristan hated that he'd never realised just how ill she was. She'd always seemed so lively when he was taken to see her, lying propped up on a mound of fluffy pillows and always ready to laugh and joke with him. He'd never known just how much of her strength it had cost her to pretend for his sake that things were going to be all right.

"Shit. Sorry. I'm putting my foot right in it today, aren't I? I didn't actually come here to be a bitch." Heather wrapped her arms around herself. "Been a bit of a long day."

Tristan had to give her that. "How is Patrick, by the way? Have you any news?"

"Oh, he's . . . Well, he's still in hospital getting his leg fixed. Which is kind of why I'm here."

Tristan frowned. "You're surely not thinking of cancelling the play?" If he'd been unprepared for Heather's arrival, he was even less prepared for the thrill of horror that shot through him at the thought. He *couldn't* lose this last chance to do what he loved.

"Don't wanna. But we've got to find someone to do Puck. You up for it?"

Tristan eyed her askance. "Far be it from me to criticise your direction, but I feel having one actor play two characters who are on stage at the same time might be a tad confusing to the audience. Or do you have another Bottom in mind?"

Heather nodded. "Look, you like Con, don't you?" she said.

"Con?"

"Big bloke, not bad looking, muscles on his muscles, plays for your team?"

"I know who he *is*. I'm just not sure quite how he's relevant to the present discussion."

"But you like him, yeah?"

"He's not without his charms," Tristan agreed cautiously.

"Wouldn't mind spending a bit more time with him, am I right?"

"I imagine I could endure it, yes. But are you seriously suggesting he's agreed to play—"

"Nope. That's your job."

"*What*?"

"You've got to get him to say yes."

"*Moi*? *Pourquoi*? I mean, why *me*, of all people?" Tristan elaborated hastily.

"Cos you're gonna have to help him out. No way he's gonna be able to learn his lines from the book." She stopped. "You know he's dyslexic, right? And he never got a lot of help, cos his gran who brought him up . . . Well, he's never *said*, but I reckon she wasn't any better at reading than he is. Worse, probably. I mean, don't get me wrong, Con can read, it just takes him a while, yeah? Makes it hard for him to learn stuff. So someone'll have to help him."

"And again I feel compelled to ask, why me?"

"Well, it's not like you're doing anything else, is it? The rest of us have all got jobs to go to."

"I do *have* a life, you know."

"Do you?" she challenged, quick as lightning and twice as painful. "Cos it looks to me like you've got everything on hold. One last summer of lazing around before you go over to America to run a bank or something. I'm right, aren't I? So why not use the time to do something useful."

"But . . ." Tristan could feel his resolve crumbling under the unexpected force of her gaze. "Does he even act? *Can* he even act?"

Heather scrubbed at her face with both hands—fortunately she'd had the foresight to wear very little makeup; Tristan had seen Amanda do that once or twice, and she'd emerged looking like a clown caught in a deluge—then slumped down on Nanna Geary's sofa. "That's gonna be part of the job—convincing Con. See, me and Sean, we've thought for ages he'd be great on stage, but he's got this idea he'd be rubbish. You know, cos of the reading thing. But I thought, if you give him enough help, maybe, I dunno, record the speeches so he can listen to them? I reckon he'd do really well."

Tristan frowned. "I see your point, but should he really be your first choice for an important role like Bottom?"

"Yeah, well, prob'ly not, but we're shit out of second choices. So, you gonna do it?"

"You do realise we're not on the best of terms right now?"

"What, cos he didn't wanna shag?"

Tristan winced. He'd hoped that *hadn't* become public knowledge. "Is it too much to ask that a gentleman should not kiss *and* not tell?"

"Oh, for God's sake. So you got turned down. Get over it. You telling me that's never happened to you before?"

"Yes! I mean no. I mean . . ." Tristan pressed his thumb and forefinger against his forehead. "I fail to see why that's any of your business. And I resent your implication that rejection must be a daily occurrence for me."

Heather leaned forward and smiled. It didn't bode well, that smile. Meggie the Second, Tristan considered, had probably worn such a smile an instant before this morning's mouse became a stranger to his own hind quarters. "Poor you. Must've been a bit of a shock, Con saying he didn't want you. Bet you'd like to see him eat his words, wouldn't you?"

"Possibly," Tristan conceded reluctantly.

"And let's face it, the only reason he'd turn you down is cos he doesn't know you well enough, yeah?"

Tristan nodded. She undoubtedly had a point.

"So he needs to get to know you better. See the real you. Trouble is, he's a bit shy, Con is. He's probably feeling awkward around you right now."

Tristan didn't mention it was mutual. She didn't need to know that.

"So," Heather went on, "all you need is a way to spend time together focussing on other stuff, yeah? So you can both forget to feel embarrassed"—damn, she'd noticed—"and just get on with getting on."

Tristan had been nodding so much he was starting to feel a little dizzy. "That does sound quite logical."

Heather clapped her hands together and stood. "Brill! So you're gonna do it, yeah? Right, next rehearsal's tomorrow night, but I reckoned I'd give you till the end of the week to talk him round. So you just need to come up to the hall ready to play Puck. Might wanna practice your lines a bit first, yeah?"

And she was gone. Tristan replayed the conversation in his head.

He was still totally unable to identify any point at which he'd actually *agreed* to do what she asked.

By the time he was able to talk to Amanda, Tristan was feeling much more sanguine about the whole thing. Technically, of course, he *could* have Skyped Amanda the minute Heather had skipped gaily out of Nanna Geary's house, mission accomplished, but luckily Tristan had the foresight to calculate that it was then around three in the morning in Hong Kong, and the wisdom to realise that if waking her at six on a Sunday morning was bad, then doing so at three on a Monday morning would most likely be apocalyptic.

Amanda, when he called, was already online and eating her breakfast.

It appeared to be the remains of last night's dinner. "Is that really healthy?" he asked, frowning at the takeaway carton of gelatinous gloop displayed fuzzily on his screen. He couldn't quite work out what it was supposed to be.

"Fat shaming? You've got a nerve."

"Fat shaming? Who said anything about fat? I'm simply concerned about your well-being. Although now you come to mention it, you *are* looking a trifle puffy around the jowls—"

She hung up.

Tristan gave it a good five minutes, then called her again. "Are we caffeinated now?"

"Are we going to refrain from personal comments now?"

"Possibly. Do you have a mo?"

"Of course, darling. All the time in the world. It's only Monday morning in the world of the gainfully employed; what possible other demands could I have on my time?"

Tristan pouted. "So you're saying I should call you back tonight?"

"Don't be ridiculous. So come on, what's the news? *Please* let it be something dire enough that I won't have to go in to work. Have you caught something incurable?"

She didn't have to sound so excited at the prospect. "I've had a breakthrough."

"Not a breakdown? Because I would have thought that seemed more likely."

"Oh, ye of little faith. I've—"

"Does your family know you go around quoting the New Testament? I can't see *that* going down too well at synagogue."

"Wouldn't know. Never been. And don't interrupt. There's no trust, no faith, no honesty in you—that better?"

"Much. Do continue."

"There's been a sea change in the production. Instead of playing Bottom, I'm now to be Puck—a role I feel far more suited to my sprightly nature. All jokes about fairies to be taken as read, please. And you'll never *guess* who's now to be my Bottom."

"With a lead-in like that, it can only be your grunting handyman. Has he even heard of Shakespeare?"

"I do wish you'd stop talking about him like he's a complete idiot. He's dyslexic, not mentally subnormal. And yes, he's a member of the company, so he's quite familiar with the Bard. I'm to be his acting coach." Tristan beamed. "I'm telling you, Amanda—if ever proof were needed that the gods are on my side, this is it. Think about it. The man's never acted before, and he's barely literate. Through no fault of his own, I might add. I've a good mind to write to the *Times* about the shocking failings of the state school system. But in any case, I'll have to spend half my waking hours with him." Soon to be followed, he hoped, by the majority of his nonwaking hours.

"So you're taking on an unpaid post as a remedial English teacher. This is good, *why*?"

"Amanda, dearest darling, haven't you been listening to anything I've told you about him? The man is a marvel of genetics. Well, in the physical department at least. Why he isn't in pornography, I'll never know."

"And the fact that he's become your own personal Everest has nothing to do with it?"

"Meaning?"

"You're determined to mount him or die trying. You just want to conquer him and plant your little flag—"

"Less of the *little*, please, darling."

"I wouldn't know, would I? As it's only straight *men* you bestow your favours upon."

"Jealous?"

"In your dreams. So. The educationally challenged odd job man you're about to go all Professor Higgins on and turn into the star of the show, he's agreed to all this, has he?"

"Well, not as such. Not yet. I, well, I haven't actually asked him yet."

"So what if he says no?"

"Of course he won't say no. Pass up the chance of expert tuition like that? Trust me. He'll say yes."

CHAPTER TWELVE
THOU DOST INFECT MY EYES

"**N**o," Con said flatly, putting down his mug on the flowery coaster on Mrs. Geary's dining table. Tristan's. Whatever. "No way. Come on, there's gotta be loads of other people you could ask." And why was it Tristan doing the asking, anyhow? Had he taken over the whole of SADS? He'd only been in the village five minutes.

Tristan, who was standing next to Con's chair, clapped a hand on his shoulder and smiled down at him. God, the bastard had done this on purpose, hadn't he? Sat Con down with a cup of coffee just so he could get the height advantage for once. "But you'd be perfect," Tristan purred in his nice voice, the one that wasn't all sarcastic. "Nick Bottom is a craftsman; so are you."

"I'm a *handyman*. He's a weaver."

"Pish tosh."

Con stared. Jesus, who even *said* that? "That's why you called me over this morning, remember? To be a handyman. Urgent repairs to your back door to stop people coming in and murdering you in your sleep, *you* said."

"False alarm. Just needed a good kick. I've seen your sketches for the forest scenery," Tristan just went on smoothly, as if being caught out in a lie didn't bother him at all. "Heather showed me. It's inspired. You have true artistic talent, dear boy. And a feeling for the text."

"I haven't even *read* the text."

Tristan leaned in close with a smug smile on his face. It suited him, the bastard. "I bet you've listened to it, though. Or seen a film adaptation."

Con didn't say anything. He'd actually done both, but that wasn't the point, was it?

"And in any case," Tristan was saying, "you'll have *moi* to help you."

He made it sound like that was the clincher, like anything Con said now couldn't *possibly* stand up against it. "Hev put you up to this, didn't she?" Con's face burned. He was going to *kill* her next time he saw her.

"That's a very cynical way to look at a heartfelt appeal from one of your closest friends. Heather needs you. She was here—yes, I don't deny it—weeping anguished tears over the cruel fate—"

Con frowned. "No, she bloody wasn't." Heather, coming over to cry on Tristan's shoulder? It sounded about as likely as Con winning an Oscar.

Or the Nobel bloody prize for literature, come to that.

"—that's left her bereft of the means to fulfil her bright potential as a director. Not to mention potentially robbed her of her first starring role—"

"She's starred in lots of stuff. She's one of the best actors we've got."

"—and a chance to prove herself against the naysayers who dismiss her simply because she's a young mixed-race woman." He stopped and looked expectantly at Con, as if he was politely waiting for another interruption.

Con gave an embarrassed little shrug. "That one's a fair point."

Tristan beamed, like he thought that one concession meant he'd won the whole bloody argument. "Then how can you deny her this?" His face fell way too quick to be natural, and he gazed at Con like a puppy whose tail Con had just stepped on. "I really hadn't thought you'd be selfish."

"What?" That was so unfair Con didn't even know where to *start*.

Tristan took Con's mug from his numb fingers, moved it way over to one side, and hopped up to sit on the table facing him. "Think about it, dear boy. When will you ever get the chance of personal tuition from a classically trained actor?"

"Who says I *want* personal tuition from a classically trained actor?"

"All of your friends, for a start. I'm told you're quite the raconteur when amongst convivial company." Hands gripping the table edge, and a mischievous smile on his face, Tristan leaned forward so far Con could feel the warmth of his breath. He smelt fresh and sort of spicy, like he'd had something with cinnamon in for breakfast. "Nobody joins a dramatics society if they don't have a secret yen to perform. Why not grasp this opportunity? Carpe, as they say, diem."

"I'm not..." Con sighed. It was almost tempting... And he really didn't want to let Heather down ... But he'd just make a total cock of himself in front of everyone he knew. *That* was what'd happen if he gave in and grasped anything or bloody well carpe-d it either. "I just do the scenery, all right?"

"But you could do so much more! And ... God, you don't know what you're missing." Tristan's smile turned dreamy, and he hopped back off the table to pace around the carpet. "It's a buzz, a natural high ... The audience hanging on your words, taking their meaning from the life *you* give to them. And the words themselves, God, the rhythm of them, the back-and-forth ... *Dream* isn't *Much Ado*, I'll grant you that, but then that's in your favour, as a novice. And just seeing it all come together, seeing those dry lines in the book every schoolboy hates to study transformed into a living, breathing, ephemeral work of art ..." He spun on the spot and fixed Con with a childlike stare, his hands flung wide in a gesture that somehow seemed totally natural. "How can you *not* want to act?"

Oh God.

Something was squeezing Con's heart in his chest. Either that or it'd grown too large for his rib cage. He wasn't sure which.

He'd always thought Tristan was all, well, *acting*, all smoke and mirrors, nothing real and honest about him, but right now ... Right now Con felt like he'd seen Tristan's soul. And it'd nearly fucking blinded him.

He couldn't tear his gaze away from Tristan's face. Even as it changed, lost some of the enthusiasm and the wonder, and turned uncertain.

Oh shit. Just what was Tristan seeing right now?

The spell broken, Con looked away. "Look, I'll think about it, all right?"

Con jumped as Tristan clapped him on both shoulders. "Excellent! I *knew* I could count on you. Let me call and give Heather the good news." He spun away again and picked up the receiver of Mrs. Geary's phone.

Con stood up hastily. "No! I said I'd think about it, yeah? Don't go telling her stuff that's not true."

Tristan gave him the puppy-dog look again.

Bloody hell, Con was in so much trouble right now. "I'll give it a go, all right?" he said, because, fuck, how could he look at that face and *not*? "Just . . . just don't tell anyone. Not until we've tried it a bit first." He was betting Tristan wouldn't be so keen after Con had tried and made a complete tit of himself.

Fuck. He was going to have to make a complete tit of himself in front of Tristan. How the hell did he manage to get into this?

No. No, it was good. Tristan would see how crap Con was, and then he'd stop all the flirting and the offering him stuff he wasn't going to get to keep. Because Tristan was only here until the end of September, wasn't he?

Con's guts felt like someone had shoved a knife in and twisted. Hard.

"Not a problem," Tristan was saying. "My lips are sealed." He put a finger across them to illustrate.

That just made Con look at them, which really wasn't helping right now.

"So shall we?" Tristan went on, looking like he hadn't noticed all the turmoil going on inside Con, thank God. "You're not busy right now, are you? No, of course not, silly me. You've just had a job cancelled. Well, then. Are you sitting comfortably?" He gestured at Con's chair and waited pointedly until Con sat down again. "Then I'll begin. The time has come, the walrus said, to speak of many things, but we shall eschew the usual alliterative efforts and get straight down to business." He leaned in close with a—yeah, all right, Con was going to think of it this way—Puckish smile, his eyes dancing with mischief. "Bottom," he breathed.

Con swallowed. "Yeah," he said, and stopped.

"Well, tell me about him. About how you see him."

"He's . . ." Con screwed up his eyes. "He's a bit, I dunno. Up himself. Thinks he can play all the roles in the rude mechanicals' play all by himself. Wants to take charge of everything. And when the queen of the fairies falls in love with him, he doesn't think that's anything weird, cos he thinks he's God's gift to women and fairies." Yeah, and somebody remind him again why Tristan wasn't still playing the role? Con felt a rush of relief at the thought. At least he wasn't so far gone on the bloke he couldn't see him like he really was.

Then again, there was a difference between Tristan and Nick Bottom, wasn't there? They both thought they were hot stuff, but Tristan had the looks and the talent to back it up . . .

Shit. Time to shut off that line of thought. "And he gets loads of stuff wrong," Con went on quick. "Like calling a lion a wildfowl, and he doesn't even notice his head's been changed into an ass's head. He just thinks he needs a shave."

"Excellent! You see? You know the part already."

"Yeah, but that doesn't mean I can play it. And that's even if I manage to get the lines into my head in the first place." Con bit his lip. "You know I'm dyslexic, right?"

"It has been mentioned, yes." Tristan gave an airy wave. "But this isn't the Dark Ages. You must have had extra help at school."

"You reckon? Don't think we went to the same sort of school."

"Surely your parents—"

"Yeah, well, they weren't around. Well, my m-mum—" Con thumped the table, not sure if he was angry at himself for the stutter, or for calling her that. "Caroline. She was around sometimes, but those weren't exactly the good times. And I've never met my dad." He stared fiercely at Tristan, daring him to make some flippant comment.

Tristan just gave an odd little grimace. "Well, fathers can be overrated. I've never really got on all that well with mine. Particularly since Mother died. The constant paternal disappointment does get a little wearing, after a while."

That was . . . That was so not what Con would've expected to hear. "What? What's your dad got to be disappointed about?" He stared at Tristan, trying to work out if he was on the level.

"Where to start, dear boy, where to start? Shall we just put it down to my essential frivolity, and move on?"

"Frivolity. That a posh way of saying you're gay?"

"No, although I'm oddly taken with the idea of it being the new euphemism. The twenty-first-century equivalent of *earnest*. And I'll admit my disdain for the distaff side hasn't helped. Moving on now . . ."

Con was frowning so hard he was getting a headache. "But you've got a degree from Cambridge, some other thing in classical acting . . . What's so bloody frivolous about all that?"

Tristan shrugged. "Or, as my father would put it, and frequently does: I've read a few dusty old books and farted around on stage for a bit."

"You mean he's not proud of you? That's just . . ." Con couldn't even finish that sentence. "Your gran was proud of you," he said instead.

"My . . . Oh, you mean Nanna Geary. Well, yes, I'm afraid she always had a bit of a blind spot where I was concerned."

Blind spot? For being proud of someone who got into the top university in the country? Who got into some posh drama school afterwards even though his first degree had been in English, not drama? Con would've thought Tristan was having him on, but he seemed, well, not so much serious as *resigned*.

Bloody hell, some families needed to get their priorities straightened out.

"She wasn't my grandmother, by the way," Tristan went on. "Nanna, in her case, was an honorific."

"What, she was like a godmother or something?"

"Yeeesss . . . Something like that. In any case, we are straying ever further from the point. Am I to take it all written material is to be avoided?"

Con nodded, his jaw clenched. Put like that, it sounded like he was a total thicko.

Tristan didn't seem like he was having a dig, though. And his tone was still businesslike as he went on. "Not to worry, not to worry. Easy enough to work around. I'll make recordings for you, and you can listen to them while you drive. Or work, even. Now, let's take a look at how we first meet Nick Bottom. Act one, scene two . . . Book, book, my kingdom for a— Aha!" He grabbed a slim, new-looking paperback from behind the carriage clock on the mantelpiece. "Here we are. So, we start with the rude mechanicals—"

"Why are they called that?" Con interrupted, thinking if anyone knew, it'd be a bloke with an English degree from Cambridge.

Tristan blinked. "Oh, *mechanical* simply meant manual labourer, in the Bard's time. And *rude*, well. Ignorant. Uneducated."

Right. There was a tight, unpleasant feeling in Con's chest, like pins and needles or something. "So, basically, me," he said, his voice sounding funny. "No bloody wonder Hev was so keen for me to take the part."

"What? No, I think you underestimate the difficulty of playing a comic figure in one of Shakespeare's plays. After all, consider in whose footsteps you follow. Samuel Phelps, Herbert Beerbohm Tree . . ." Tristan paused, maybe because he'd seen Con's blank look. "He was Oliver Reed's grandfather," he added, sounding like Con's gran when she'd told him off for not putting his plates in the dishwasher again. "How about these, then? Ralph Richardson, James Cagney, Kevin Kline?"

Con nodded. He'd heard of them. Even seen some films they'd been in. Gran had liked her old black-and-white movies.

"Good. So you see, Bottom isn't a role one gives to the man off the Clapham omnibus." Tristan flashed that Puckish smile again. "I, for one, am most particular whom I allow to be my Bottom."

Hopefully the faint tingling in Con's face and neck wasn't an actual blush at the innuendo. "So you're not pissed off about me doing it, instead of you?" he asked, a bit surprised at himself.

Okay, so now Tristan's smile was more like a Cheshire cat's, or at least, how Con had imagined it when he'd listened to the old story cassette he'd had as a kid. Gran had got it for Caroline when she'd been little, but that didn't mean Con couldn't enjoy it. "By no means. Turnabout is fair play, I always say."

Okay, this time he'd *definitely* blushed. Con swallowed. "So. Act one, scene two, yeah?"

CHAPTER THIRTEEN
WHAT PLIGHTED CUNNING HIDES

Tristan sprawled on Nanna Geary's sofa, his hands behind his head and a contented smile on his face. He'd still got it. Con had been putty in his hands. Figuratively speaking, of course. He still hadn't managed to get his *literal* hands on the man, but that would surely follow. And when it did, any comparisons with soft, malleable building materials would hopefully be *entirely* inappropriate. This summer was going to be a glorious swansong, before the death of the soul that would follow in the fall . . .

No. He wasn't going to think about the job in New York. Plenty of time to dwell on that when he was actually there, slogging away at a desk on matters fiscal for, oh, the next forty years . . . Oh God.

Tristan flung himself off the sofa, his good mood melted into thin air, leaving not a rack behind. Were his revels truly ended? Was it really too late to get out of this? He tried to imagine telling Father he wouldn't be working for Goldsmith & Klein, but was assailed by nausea at the very thought.

Tristan paced into the kitchen in his socks, too dispirited to even watch where he trod for small animals, living or dead. With any luck he'd step on one, skid, and take another chunk out of Nanna Geary's kitchen wall, this time with his skull. Rounding his little life with a sleep was sounding rather attractive right now.

Hmm. To sleep . . . Perchance to dream about Con once more? That *would* be a consummation devoutly to be wished . . . Damn it. Sometimes, Tristan deeply regretted the fact that his brain had not come equipped with an off switch.

Reaching the fridge freezer without, alas, having managed to shuffle off this mortal coil, he cursed his luck and got out the pizza he'd planned to have for dinner. It was in fact barely lunchtime now, but damn it, he needed some comfort food.

One thing he hadn't been able to persuade Con to do was stay to lunch. He'd run off shortly before midday like an inverted Cinderella, pleading a backlog of jobs that needed doing. While Tristan was all in favour of a sound work ethic in the labouring classes in principle, in practice it'd proved annoyingly inconvenient. Hmm. Tristan really needed to keep in mind all the work he could legitimately pay Con to do around Nanna Geary's house. Unfortunately, every time the man appeared, all practical considerations seemed to fly straight out of the window and flit off to play with the fairies.

Tristan closed the oven on the pizza, and sat down at the dining table to make a list.

He'd got as far as *fix cat flap in kitchen dor* (the spelling of which he hastily corrected, somewhat appalled at his sudden attack of sentimentality) when the phone rang. Tristan hesitated, then popped into the kitchen to pick it up. Nanna Geary didn't have caller ID. Caller ID had probably not been invented yet when Nanna Geary's telephone, which was so incredibly ancient it actually had a curly cord attaching it to the wall, had been constructed. "Hello?"

"Tristan, darling, I've been trying to get in touch for *days*. What on earth have you done with your phone? I had to call your father to get this number, and he didn't seem very pleased to give it to me."

Tristan beamed as Suki's familiar throaty tones filled his ear. "Suki, my cherub, how delightful! Well, not that you've had trouble getting in touch. Mea, as they say in Rome, culpa. I keep forgetting to charge the thing." Actually, he'd been rather enjoying using Nanna Geary's landline instead; it even had an honest-to-goodness *dial*, for heaven's sake. He'd taken to keeping a pen nearby, not so much to take notes as to use it to dial the numbers, like an elegantly coiffed, scarlet-lipped secretary in an old-fashioned film. "How are you, darling? And how's my replacement settling in?"

Suki gave a bitter laugh. "Not well. Not at *all* well. He's an opinionated, self-aggrandising little sod. And not in a *good* way, like you." There was a pause, and Tristan could almost see her dragging on her cigarette. "I don't suppose I can convince you to come back to us?"

"How about we make a deal, darling? You persuade Father it's a sensible career move, and I'll come back to the Players."

"Worried he'll cut you off without a penny like some disgraced Victorian debutante who's let the footman get her in the family way? Well, if *money's* all that's important to you—"

"The money has nothing to do with it."

"Please. Is your nose itching? Or did you already scratch it?"

"Neither," Tristan lied once more, scratching his nose again and wishing neither of them had ever attended that body language workshop. "All right. It's not *just* the money. It's time I got out in the real world. Recognised my responsibilities." Did something worthwhile in the eyes of the world, or at least that portion of it represented by his family.

"I've heard all those lines before, darling, and your delivery remains less than convincing. In any case, the theatrical world seems perfectly real to me. Particularly while I'm restraining myself from strangling your successor. And what responsibilities? Unless you've suddenly acquired a wife and an unspecified number of children to support, I can't recall a single one. You haven't even got a pet."

"Actually, that last may no longer be entirely true . . ." Scanning the kitchen, Tristan saw no signs of Meggie the Second or even Froggy the First, and forced himself to focus. "But anyway, as Father has graciously pointed out, I've had an extremely expensive education and upbringing and he's yet to see any return on his investment."

"So children are an investment, now? I suppose investing in property *is* rather last-century. Tell me, how much of a return does he expect on his money? Ten percent? Twenty? More? What happens if you fail to realise that? Will he strip your assets and leave you to the bankruptcy courts?"

"Ouch. Suki, *darling*. You don't know what it's like. Goldsmith & Klein is Father's *life*. He needs to know it'll be in safe hands when he retires."

"Which rather begs the question, why put it in yours? No, listen," she went on immediately over Tristan's outraged spluttering. "Why not get in someone to head up the company who actually has a flair for that sort of thing? Someone who'll enjoy it? Because I know you, darling. You'll hate every single tedious minute of it." There was the rasping click of a cigarette lighter as Suki lit up again. Tristan was hit with a vivid sense memory as smoky aromas flooded his nostrils—no, wait, that was the pizza. Stretching the cord to its utmost, Tristan managed to turn off the oven. Oops.

God, he missed Suki. He even missed the smell of her vile French cigarettes, and all the companionable times they'd huddled by the stage door as he kept her company while she smoked to stave off hunger pangs. Staying thin was apparently *much* harder once one passed thirty, darling, and Suki took her art *seriously*.

Amanda had never joined them—in fact, she'd generally told Tristan he was ruining his voice for nothing and then complained vociferously if the merest whiff of cigarette smoke clung to either of them when they returned. Tristan had strongly suspected, however, that it was less to do with preserving her vocal cords—admittedly a valid concern—and more to do with the intense mutual loathing that had, regrettably, sprung up between her and Suki almost the moment they'd met.

"You know the young me," Tristan protested. "The *now* me. After a couple of years, I'll . . . I'll settle into it. There's no reason I shouldn't develop a flair for business. Get to like it, even." Perhaps he should adopt this as a mantra, and start repeating it twenty times before breakfast every morning.

He'd have to start believing it then, wouldn't he?

"Seems like a poor trade for a career you have a real passion for. And since when are you in such a rush to get old?"

"Not to get old. To . . . to mature. I can't just carry on having fun all my life." Oh God. Tristan died a little even as he said the words.

"Can't you? I think I've discerned who's writing your scripts, darling. It's your little drama college chum again, isn't it? Dear, sulky, little Hamanda. How is she these days? Still bragging about the salary she's earning in Hong Kong?"

"*A*manda," Tristan corrected, "is perfectly well. Shall I remember you to her next time we Skype?"

"Oh, lord. The evils of technology. Heaven forbid, darling. She might hire some Chinese hag to put a curse on me from afar. But why you should continue to be affected by the jealous ramblings of someone who simply couldn't hack it in the profession—"

"Amanda's a dear friend," Tristan said stiffly. "I don't know how I'd have got through my MA if she hadn't befriended me."

"So you said when you charmed me into hiring her, but the evidence has so far failed to convince. I cracked open a bottle of bubbly when she announced she was leaving—then had to drown my sorrows with it when you told me she'd somehow persuaded you to follow her."

"It wasn't *all* down to Amanda. Father had been on at me for ages to get a proper job."

"*And* you'd ignored him, as well you should. Do you really think he'll start respecting you now that you've done what he told you to?"

Tristan winced. Suki's aim was as good as ever, and her arrows as barbed.

"In any case," she went on, "I see absolutely no reason why one shouldn't keep having fun all one's life. I certainly intend to. Tomorrow we may all be dead, darling, so let us gather us rosebuds while we may."

"Rosebuds wither," Tristan reminded her, a sharp edge to his voice.

"So will you, darling, trapped in a desk job. So will you."

Three hours later, his stomach still weighed down with somewhat singed pizza, Tristan found himself unable to settle. He'd packed up three more boxes of Nanna Geary's worldly goods—small ones, admittedly, but still, *three*—and taken half a dozen to the local charity shop. Well, one of them. Bishops Langley seemed to be one of those places with a somewhat split personality: the high street was composed almost entirely of high-end women's clothiers dotted in between charity emporia staffed by grey-haired old ladies. Tristan wondered if any of the middle-class ladies who shopped at JoJo Maman-Bebe and Country Casuals ever stepped into one of those cheerful little shops with their eclectic stock and jumble-sale smell by mistake and fainted on the doorstep, perhaps having to be revived with a cup of Earl Grey.

And there was *no* parking. After circling for the third time in vain, Tristan pulled Father's BMW in to the kerb directly beside a *No loading* sign. After all, he'd only be five minutes. What were the chances of a traffic warden happening along at this precise moment?

He'd reckoned without the chattiness of old ladies. After listening politely to over-effusive thanks—really, he'd only brought them a load of old clothes, and whilst they'd originally been of the first quality, some of them were no doubt on their umpteenth generation of moth holes—and consenting to filling in a Gift Aid form, Tristan finally escaped only to see the waspish colours of a parking ticket being tucked under his windscreen wiper.

He sighed. "Might one ask precisely what you have against—" Tristan glanced back at the shop to remind himself which charity he'd been supporting "—cancer sufferers?"

The traffic warden, who happened to be tall, well-built, and vaguely menacing even in the bright-blue uniform favoured by his ilk in this area, turned slowly. His face did a passable impersonation of world-weary obsidian, or possibly black jasper, like a jaded Othello in the face of yet another best friend's betrayal. "Me? I got nothing against cancer sufferers. What I *do* have a problem with, mate, is blokes like you who think just cos they've got a posh car they can park it anywhere they bloody well like. You wanna help cancer sufferers? Sell that bloody gas-guzzler, give 'em the money, and stop driving around like you bloody own the bloody place."

Tristan blinked, a little taken aback at the man's hostility, not to mention his somewhat restricted vocabulary. "I can't. It's not mine." Then he realised how that might sound. "I mean, I haven't *stolen* it. It's borrowed. And there was *literally* nowhere to park," he added with a touch of righteous indignation.

"Yeah? There is *literally* a bloody big car park just round the other side of the shops. Next time, try parking there and bloody well *walking*. That's what us poor people do. Blokes like you don't have a bloody clue what it's like for the rest of us. Bloody privileged bloody *establishment*." He turned and walked away, disdain in every heavy step.

Tristan sagged. Then he rallied. "I *am* Jewish, you know," he yelled after the man's retreating back. "And I'm gay!"

A passing gaggle of teenagers burst into helpless giggles. Well, the female ones did. The male ones gave him narrowed-eyed looks like they'd be watching him. One of them even did the pointy-fingers gesture. Defeated, Tristan got back into the BMW and drove off, the parking ticket flapping gaily in the breeze.

That had been hours ago, and he was still rattled. Not by the parking ticket—after all, what was forty pounds to the salary he'd be earning in mere months?—but by the traffic warden's tirade. Which had been total and utter codswallop, of course. Tristan wasn't *privileged*. Well, yes, he supposed he was, actually—but honestly, just having been born to a particular background wasn't a sin. There wasn't a lot he could have done about the circumstances of his birth or his upbringing either, for that matter.

But . . . did he really take things for granted? Think a life of ease was somehow *owed* to him?

Tristan's conscience pricked uncomfortably when he thought of Meggie the Supplanter. There might just possibly be a grain of truth in the man's accusations after all. Having taken over Nanna Geary's house, Tristan supposed he might very reasonably have been expected to take over responsibility for all remaining inhabitants, yet he'd blithely accepted the neighbour's care of her cat. All Tristan had done in return was provide a free viewing of his firm, supple body, and he strongly suspected the man hadn't really appreciated it.

Damn it. Clearly he owed his neighbour an apology. And probably some form of remuneration. Tristan hadn't the least idea of how much cat food cost, but like most things, it was probably ridiculously overpriced. And while he had no direct evidence that the neighbours had been feeding her, he presumed that if they hadn't, she'd have eaten the whole of her mouse instead of deciding in a fit of misguided generosity to share it with Tristan.

Of course, come to that, he had no direct evidence Meggie Mark 2 even existed, seeing as he'd yet to set eyes on the wretched animal. Shadows disappearing through cat flaps didn't count. That tail, if indeed it had been a tail he'd seen, could have belonged to anyone—a young and inquisitive fox, an opportunistic squirrel, perhaps even a rodent of the wrigglier variety such as a stoat or weasel. Tristan shuddered. On the whole he'd prefer to give Meggie the

Second the benefit of the doubt, as opposed to attributing the frog and mouse incursions to some other agency.

So. Tristan hesitated. Should he offer the man money? Or would a gift of some kind be more neighbourly? Perhaps he should do both.

Having reached a decision, Tristan hunted quickly through Nanna Geary's kitchen cupboards for something both new and vaguely bottle-shaped. Hm. The gravy browning probably wouldn't be appropriate, which was a shame as Tristan had never made gravy in his life and had no intentions of starting anytime soon.

Perhaps in the living room? There, he met with more success. In the bottom of the cabinet that held Nanna Geary's sherry glasses, he found a bottle of champagne. He wondered what Nanna Geary had planned to celebrate, and felt a renewed pang of grief that she hadn't lived to pop the cork. There was an unopened bottle of sherry in there as well, which Tristan decided would do. Thus armed, Tristan checked himself to ensure he was decently clad, then hopped over the garden wall to rap on his neighbour's back door.

Tit, as they say, for tat. And in any case, Tristan was a life-long fan of rear entrances.

He waited, and after a minute his neighbour appeared, a wary look on his face. Tristan beamed at him through the glass, and held up the bottle.

The door opened. "Yes?"

"I wanted to apologise," Tristan said smoothly. "I'm afraid you were subjected to something of an exhibition the other day. I'm Tristan Goldsmith, by the way."

The man's ruddy cheeks took on an even less attractive hue. He coughed. "Kenneth Onslow. Quite all right. You were in your own home. No reason to think anybody would, ahem, *see*." Based on current evidence, it was hard to believe that the man in front of him had *seen*. His gaze, Tristan couldn't help but notice, darted towards all points of the compass in turn except, it seemed, the true north that was Tristan.

Tristan began to feel a little irritated. Here he was apologising when, as Onslow had just admitted, he hadn't been in the wrong, and the man wouldn't even look at him.

"Although," Onslow continued, "I'm not sure Shamwell is really the place for that sort of, well, *lifestyle* is I believe the modern term. We're quite an old-fashioned sort of place. Now, I don't mean to say there weren't, ah, your sort of people back then, of course there were."

"Actors, you mean?" Tristan queried with wide, innocent eyes.

"Ah . . . possibly."

"Or did you mean, *earnest* young fellows? In the Wildean sense."

"I . . . Ah." Onslow rallied. "I think you know what I mean. And in my day, people had the good sense and common decency to keep such things firmly out of sight. I say this purely as a friendly word to the wise, you understand."

Tristan nodded solemnly. "Pure, disinterested advice is so rare these days. I also wanted to thank you," he added with treacled spite.

"Yes?"

"For taking such good care of my pussy." Tristan was proud of himself for keeping a straight—hah!—face as his neighbour choked. "I'm really *very* grateful," he purred, when the coughing fit died down. "Is there anything I can do for you in return? Perhaps something for that nasty cough of yours? You know, I'm sure I have something I could rub on your chest." It was perfectly true; Nanna Geary had been a firm believer in herbal vapour rubs.

Onslow's colour had reached potentially dangerous levels, and he appeared lost for words.

Tristan frowned. "Are you quite well? I think perhaps you need to lie down for a bit. Why don't I help you?" he added, stepping forward.

Jolting visibly out of his stupor, Onslow took a large step back and closed the door without so much as a *thank you* for Tristan's offers.

Tristan looked at the bottle in his hand, smiled, and hopped back over the wall with it.

Nanna Geary's sherry would have been wasted on the man, anyway.

CHAPTER FOURTEEN
ALL THE WORLD'S A STAGE

Con had left Tristan's place with his head in a whirl. He was going to be an actor. Going to be up there on stage with Heather, Chris, and all the rest he'd only ever watched before.

Not to mention Tristan, who was an amazing actor and had actually made a living at it, instead of just playing at it like the Sham-Drams. Bloody hell, had Con completely lost his mind? What the hell was he even *thinking* of, trying to keep up with that? Trouble was, it'd all seemed so easy when he'd been with Tristan. Like the fact he was barely sodding literate wasn't gonna be a problem learning lines and stuff.

And there was another thing. Con had expected all kinds of digs about his lack of education, but Tristan hadn't been like that at all. Not this time. More than that, he'd even tried to make Con feel better about it.

Maybe it hadn't actually been Tristan. Maybe he'd been a changeling, and the real Tristan had been stolen away by the fairies ... Con grinned as he drove the van down the high street, and a lady in a bright-red Golf smiled back at him as they passed one another. He felt all light-headed, like he'd drunk too much coffee or shared some wacky baccy with that bloke over in Bishops Langley with the greenhouse that kept needing fixing. Good job he was only going down the road to hang a couple of doors for Chris's mum's next-door neighbour.

He was trying really hard not to think about the *other* thing. The way his insides had all sort of melted when Tristan had come alive talking about acting. That was ... That was just a ... a thing. Which he was going to get over really soon, because nothing was ever gonna come of it. Ever. All Con would ever be to Tristan was another notch on his bedpost, and face it, there were probably so many on there already it was a miracle the whole bed hadn't collapsed.

Although, come to think of it, chances were he was sleeping in Mrs. Geary's bed right now, and Con didn't reckon there would have been all that many notches on *that*, and anyway, if the bed was in that sort of state, Tristan would probably have asked Con to fix it, seeing as he was so keen on any opportunity to get flirty, and . . .

. . . And seriously, Con was thinking *way* too much about this.

He pulled up outside Chris's mum's neighbour's house and yanked the handbrake on sharply. Time to get back to the real world.

It was getting on for teatime by the time Con had finished with the doors. The job had been a bit of a bastard—it was an old house, and the doorways weren't straight—but Mrs. Rogers had been really friendly, even making him a sandwich for lunch. She'd kept saying how nice it was to have a man about the house again, asked him to call her Steph, and offered to cook him dinner if he didn't mind hanging on a bit, but Con hadn't wanted to outstay his welcome, and anyway, he'd thought he might drop in on Mr. Smith again. Alf, he reminded himself. Though it felt weird, calling his grandad's mate by his first name. Gran had been a bit old-fashioned about that sort of thing—all her friends had been either Mrs. So-and-so or Auntie Whatsit to him.

Con had felt a bit bad about freeloading the other day, so he took round a pie he'd made last night, using the bag full of cherries one of his customers had given him from her tree. Con wasn't much for cooking—not fancy stuff, anyhow, or anything that needed a recipe—but pastry was easy. You just rubbed a lump of fat into a bowl full of flour until it looked right, and added a bit more of one or the other if it seemed to need it. And the filling was dead simple too—just fruit cooked up with sugar and a bit of cinnamon. Gran had showed him how to do it when he was little.

Alf looked bowled over to see Con standing on his back doorstep. He blinked at him, a slow smile blooming on his face. "I'd have thought you'd have had enough of an old man rambling on."

Con grinned. "What? Never. Nah, I thought you might like this for your pudding. Made it myself." He held out the pie. "It's cherry. You can eat it cold, but it's better if you bung it in the oven for a bit to warm it up. Nice with custard too."

"I'm sure it is. Well, don't stand on the doorstep all night. Come in, come in. I was just about to put some sausages under the grill." He turned to shuffle back into the kitchen without waiting for a reply, his worn slippers making a *shushing* sound as he walked.

"Um, I didn't come round to invite myself to tea again . . ." Con said, feeling a bit awkward.

"Nonsense. They put far too many sausages in these packets anyway. Can't eat them all myself. Don't have the appetite I used to these days. A strapping young man like you can always use a little extra food." One hand on the counter to support himself, Alf bent down to bung a string of sausages in the grill pan, turned on the gas, and heaved himself up again. "And the potatoes will only go off if I leave them any longer. Can't stand waste. They're in a plastic box in the fridge, if you wanted to give me a hand."

"Yeah, course." Con put the pie on the table quick and crouched down by the small fridge. Sure enough, there was a Tupperware container with a generous number of boiled potatoes nestled inside, probably left over from the last time Alf had failed to cook for one. "Want me to slice 'em for you? You're frying 'em, right? Want the lard?"

"My daughter always says I should use olive oil. Says animal fats are unhealthy." Alf chuckled. "I keep telling her, if the food's going to kill me, it'll have to get a move on or old age is going to get there first."

"Nah, you've got years left in you," Con said encouragingly as he pulled out a half-used packet of lard, the paper wrapper carefully tucked around the opened end. "My Gran always reckoned lard was best for frying potatoes. Well, if you haven't got any beef dripping, that is. Which she never did, cos if she ever had any she used to eat it on her toast for breakfast."

Alf was chuckling again. "Toast and dripping? That takes me back. I haven't eaten that in years. Did you ever try it?"

"Er, yeah. Once." Con tried not to shudder. He couldn't even *describe* what it had tasted like. Pureed slugs that went off last week, or something. You probably had to have been alive while rationing was still on after World War Two to actually like that sort of stuff.

"My daughter would be horrified, but what's life without a few simple pleasures? Yes, that's right," Alf went on, looking at Con's efforts with the potatoes. "Not too thin, mind. If I want to eat crisps, I'll go down to the shops and buy a packet."

"You're the boss," Con told him cheerfully, cutting the slices a bit thicker from then on. "We having any veg? Just to keep your daughter happy."

"There's a packet of frozen peas in the freezer." Con got them out as Alf put a small saucepan on the stove.

Quarter of an hour later, they were sitting down at the kitchen table to eat, Con's plate piled high with sausages at Alf's insistence. Good thing his job was so physical.

"You know," Alf said, as he speared a slice of potato on his fork and inspected it carefully, probably to make sure it was regulation thickness. "There's someone else in the village who could tell you about Bill Izzard. Mary Wellbeck. She's the vicar's daughter. The vicar as was, I should say. Pretty little thing, she was—the brightest blond curls you ever saw, and always with a ribbon in them. She used to pester Bill and me to play with her, when I came round to the vicarage to see him. Of course, we weren't very nice to her, not then. Used to tell her we'd play hide and seek, and when she'd hidden, we'd run for the hills." Alf sighed. "Served me right, later on, when she wouldn't give me the time of day."

Despite his keen spark of interest at Alf's words, Con grinned. "Old flame?"

"Never burned very brightly on her end, I'm afraid. Or at all, come to that. No, she didn't think much of me, when I was of an age to be interested in girls. Or perhaps it was young men in general she didn't think much of. She never did marry."

"But she's still in the village, right? Do you still see her at all?"

"Every now and then, in passing. I've never been sure if she knows it's me, these days—would you believe I had as fine a head of hair as you, once? She lives in one of the new sheltered flats, down by the river. Six Elms, you know it?"

"Yeah—not done any work there, but I've been past." Con chewed on a bit of sausage, frowning. "Think she'd talk to me if I went round? She might think I was trying to scam her or something."

"Well, I suppose I could go with you, if you'd like? Not that my company would be much of a recommendation, of course..."

Con jumped on that as quick as he could swallow his mouthful of peas. "Yeah? Seriously, that'd be great. If you don't mind doing it, I mean. Any idea when'd be a good time?"

"Anytime, I should think. We old people don't tend to have a lot of standing engagements. Mid-morning would probably be best—I tend to doze off after lunch, and if she has the same problem, she won't appreciate us waking her from her nap."

Con left Alf's place with a pleasantly full stomach and an arrangement to go round to see Mary Wellbeck in a couple of days. Alf had been all keen to go sooner—since he "wasn't getting any younger"—but Con had a job on tomorrow morning, regular gardening work he did for a lady in a wheelchair over Bishops Langley way, and the next day he was supposed to be clearing some guttering.

It'd give him time to think what he wanted to ask her, anyhow. *If* she agreed to talk to him, and *if* she still actually remembered a kid who got billeted with her way back in the 1940s. God, it seemed weird there were still people alive who remembered that far back. Even Gran hadn't been born back then—she'd been a fair bit younger than Grandad. She'd always known he'd go before her, but she hadn't expected him to die just a few years after they'd married. Only forty-one, he'd been. Had a weak heart, they'd told her, brought on by rheumatic fever when he'd been young.

Bloody hell, Con was glad he'd been born after they'd discovered antibiotics and the National Health Service.

He'd been in the village a year and never met anyone who remembered his grandad before—never expected to, to be honest, seeing as he'd spent such a brief time here—and now he'd found two of 'em. Well, *if* Mary Wellbeck still had all her marbles, he reminded himself. Couldn't expect too much at her age.

Tea had been a bit earlier than Con usually ate, and what seemed like a long evening stretched ahead. Sprawling on the sofa, he flicked through a few channels on the telly, then turned it off. He had half a mind to head up to the pub and see who was there, but then again, he had stuff to do, now, didn't he? Acting stuff.

God, he felt like a total poser. "I am an ac*tor*," he said out loud in his poshest voice, the one that sounded a bit like Tristan, then nearly killed himself laughing. Thank God he'd had the living room window shut so no one could have heard him. Shaking his head, Con got out his phone, where Tristan had recorded Bottom's first speech for him to learn.

The most important thing, Tristan had said, was for Con to *feel* like the character. To wear Nick Bottom like a second skin. "The costume," he'd said, "does not make the character. The character *is* the costume." Which, yeah, Con had the thicko rude mechanical part down all right, but Bottom was all stuffed up with his own sense of importance, and that bit was harder to get.

Con had a pretty fair idea of his own importance, and it wasn't anything to get stuffed up about. He tried to imagine feeling like he was the centre of the world, like he could get any bloke or girl he wanted, like he could play all the parts in a play as easy as breathing . . . Like, say, Tristan? Con grinned, and tried to imagine it. Him as Tristan.

He stood up straight as he could and puffed out his chest a bit. Yeah, that was it. Tristan was always trying to make himself look taller, where Con tended to have the opposite problem. Funny how much difference it made, just changing how you stood.

Course, he'd have to remember to dodge the light fitting when he moved around. Right. He was a weaver, so he was a bit of a cut—heh—above a bellows-mender, or a tinker, for that matter. If Gran hadn't thought much of someone or something, she'd say they *weren't worth a tinker's*, although she'd never actually told him a tinker's *what*. So yeah, Bottom thought he was better than them.

What about Starveling, the tailor? Well, you couldn't be a tailor without someone to weave the cloth, could you? And he ended up with a crap part in the play-within-a-play, just being Moonshine. So yeah, actually, Bottom *was* the most important of the rude mechanicals. Satisfied, Con smiled at himself in the mirror on the wall by the wardrobe. Yeah, that looked nice and smug.

He played the first part of the speech, just to listen to it. Tristan's voice rang out through his living room, tinnier and more crackly than the original, but just as pompous and, yeah, energetic. Larger than life, which he'd said you had to be, on stage, cos people were seeing you from a distance.

Funny how voices stayed, well, voices. Tristan's accent wasn't anywhere near as posh as it usually was, and he was obviously playing a part, but Con would still have known it was him anywhere. There was that warmth, that sense of fun in the way he spoke, the way his words just rolled over you, like ripples on a pond or someone stroking your skin . . .

Right. Time to give the acting a try, Con told himself firmly, taking a deep breath. "'That will ask some tears in the true performing of it: if I do it, let the audience look to their eyes; I will move storms, I will condole in some measure. To the rest—'" Con broke off like the recording did, and did his best to turn into pouty Tristan instead. "'Yet my chief humour is for a tyrant: I could play Ercles rarely, or a part to tear a cat in, to make all split.'"

He'd had a bit of trouble getting his head round the "tear a cat" line until Tristan had told him to think of Bottom as Hercules, wrestling with Snug the lion.

Course, then Tristan had gone off about it possibly being a pun on *catin* which apparently was an insult for a woman, and about characters in other plays called Tear-Cat, and Con had got hopelessly lost again, but at least Tristan had stopped when he'd seen Con's blank looks. Not that it hadn't been *interesting*, but there was only so much Con could keep in his head at once, 'specially when he was trying to learn something.

Catching sight of himself in the mirror again, Con realised his smile wasn't looking so smug now. He winced. It'd looked *soppy*. Fond.

Sod it. "'Man is but an ass,'" he quoted to himself, and set to learning his lines again.

CHAPTER FIFTEEN
THAT GLIB AND OILY ART

Con's first official masterclass in Bottoming wasn't until the Wednesday evening. They'd all agreed it would be best to rehearse Con privately for the first couple of weeks, until he was a little more confident in the role.

Tristan had been a very paragon of restraint while he waited for it. He'd fairly soon prepared a CD for Con with all of Bottom's cues and speeches recorded on it, helpfully arranged in separate tracks for each scene, but he'd contented himself with dropping it through Con's letterbox while the man himself was out.

All right, Tristan had knocked first, ever hopeful. He was, after all, only human. But he *hadn't* sat on Con's doorstep awaiting his return like a lovesick stalker.

Now, though, he was fairly fizzing with excitement. He'd made as much space in the living room as possible by taking another trip to the charity shop—this time, parking in the car park and lugging the boxes over one by one. Well, until the last couple, when he tried to save a little time and tedium by stacking one upon the other.

Fortunately, the good weather meant the ground was perfectly dry, and several people had been kind enough to help him pick everything up and repack the boxes when the inevitable happened. One young man had even taken one of the boxes off his hands and accompanied him to the charity shop. He'd been rather good-looking, actually, as well as more than helpful, and under other circumstances Tristan might have been tempted to ask for his number. But, well, Tristan had his hands full with Con. Or at least, *hoped* to. And the man on the street didn't really compare, upon reflection. He'd been disappointingly short—barely half a head taller than Tristan—and decidedly lacking in the biceps department. The seams of his T-shirt sleeves hadn't strained at *all* as he lugged Nanna Geary's sensible shoes and cast-iron handbags to the charity shop.

Anyway, the point was, the house was now clear of clutter; not just the lower levels, but an optimistic trail leading from the living room up the stairs to Tristan's bedroom. Not that Tristan actually thought it would be used—softly, softly, catchee monkey and all that—but it didn't do to be unprepared. So the stage, as it were, was set.

Trouble was, it was set well in advance of the actual curtain time. Tristan had occupied himself by studying his new part, and by Skyping Amanda, having first made sure he shouldn't be waking her from slumber.

She greeted him with a less-than-friendly "You again? I told you you'd get bored out in the sticks."

"Amanda, darling. Perhaps I just wanted to see your ravishing face?"

She sniffed. "Well, I'm glad you called, anyway. I wanted to remind you about posting dates."

"A little over-anxious, aren't we? And in any case, I thought you were planning to visit me for Christmas." In New York. Oh God. "That's ages off," he said firmly, more to himself than to her.

"My *birthday*, however, is in two weeks. Which is roughly how long it takes for airmail to reach us here, although God knows why, seeing as the flight itself is only twelve hours." She pouted. "You hadn't forgotten, had you?"

"Of course not," Tristan lied hastily. "Your present is winging its way to you even as we speak." Oh, bloody hell, postmarks. Well, she probably wouldn't remember exactly what day they'd had this conversation. He hoped. "Amanda, my sweet, I wanted to ask you something."

"What?"

"Well . . . Do you really think I'm doing the right thing? The job in New York, I mean. Rather than trying to make a go of it as an actor." The back of Tristan's neck prickled, as though his father stood behind him, the dagger of parental disapproval poised. Tristan defiantly did *not* turn to check this was no mere fancy.

Amanda tutted. "Don't be silly. Of course it's the right thing to do. We were never going to get anywhere with the Players."

"But we never really explored any other options. To stay in the profession, I mean."

"One garret is much like another when you're starving in it. Don't tell me you're getting cold feet. We agreed we were better off out of it."

Tristan was honestly struggling to remember why. "Not *all* actors starve. In fact I believe some in a place called, now, what was it? That's it, Hollywood. Apparently some of *them* manage to earn quite a modest competence."

"As if we were ever going to end up in Hollywood, working with the Players."

"One doesn't have to leave the country to—"

"And of course it was fine for you," she interrupted, her voice heated. "You were always Suki's *darling*. Always got the best roles despite your *obvious* disadvantages, whereas I was lucky to get the character parts."

"Character parts are fun," Tristan protested. "And what do you mean, my obvious disadvantages?"

"Character parts are for ugly, fat people nobody would believe in a leading role, and *Pukey* made it *quite* clear that was what she thought of me."

"And apparently I am to infer that that is what *you* thought of *me*?"

"Oh, for God's sake, Tristan. Stop being so bloody precious and look at yourself in the mirror. Without, for once, striking a pose. You're never going to be anyone's leading man. At any rate not on stage, which you appear to regard as your métier, God knows why. Nobody ever made a fortune on *stage*. And why not go for film, where they can stand you on a box like Tom Cruise?"

Tristan flinched.

Perhaps realising how deeply her words had cut him, Amanda softened her tone. "Look, do you want a decent standard of living, or don't you?"

"Well . . ."

"There, you see. Anyway, I've got to go and get ready for dinner. I'll speak to you again soon."

She hung up.

Tristan stared at his dim reflection in the dark laptop screen. Was she right? Would defying his father and trying to make a go of it as an actor be a waste of both time and parental goodwill? Had his little sojourn with the Players been nothing more than Father thought it to be—a pleasant interlude? An extended gap year?

All in all, it was something of a relief when Con's self-effacing knock finally sounded at the front door. Tristan squared his shoulders and strode over to fling the door wide, a confident smile on his face. Maybe he wasn't destined to play the Dane opposite any modern-day Ellen Terry, but he could damn well make it as Con's leading man.

"Come in, come in." Tristan ushered Con inside with appropriate gestures. "Sit down, Con, and welcome."

"Uh, thanks." Con's answering smile was a balm to Tristan's hurt mind. "How are you getting on with Puck?" he asked, settling his impressively large self on the sofa and improving its appearance by several hundred percent. "I mean, you're getting time to work on your own part, right?"

It was rather touching, how worried he seemed. Tristan grinned.

"'Thou speak'st aright; I am that merry wanderer of the night.

"'I jest to Oberon and make him smile

"'When I a fat and bean-fed horse beguile,

"'Neighing in likeness of a filly foal.'"

He let his eyes turn sultry at the last two lines and was rewarded with a bashful smile.

"You're brilliant at that," Con said in gratifyingly awestruck tones. "I dunno how you do it—you say the lines, and it's like they *are* you."

Tristan gave a stage shrug. "Well, to be fair, playing a cheeky little fairy isn't all that much of a stretch for me."

Con laughed. "Nah, s'pose not. Guess we're both typecast, then. Um."

He hesitated.

Tristan waited.

"I was just wondering," Con went on finally, "what other sort of plays you'd been in and, you know, what characters you played."

"Oh? Doubting my qualifications? Surely it's a tad late to be asking to see my curriculum vitae?" Tristan enquired, his eyebrow arched and his tone sardonic.

Con's eyes widened, and his face fell. "No—I didn't mean—" He broke off. "You're just winding me up, aren't you?"

"Would I?" Tristan grinned. "Well, let me see. I've been Dick Dudgeon in *The Devil's Disciple*—you know it? No? George Bernard Shaw. Set in the colonies during the eighteenth century. Dudgeon is something of a virtuous rebel, a heroic antihero, who sacrifices himself for another but gets reprieved at the last minute." And nobody could dispute he was the lead role in the play. Take that, Amanda.

"Yeah? Sounds good." Con nodded. "He was from round here, you know, Shaw. You can go and visit his house."

"It's a date," Tristan purred distractedly. Now, what had been his other triumphs? That might actually mean something to Con? Hmm. "And I was Caliban in *The Tempest*."

"That's Shakespeare, right? Is he the main character?"

"Well, arguably he's *a* main character." Tristan gave a self-deprecating grimace. "Caliban is a monstrously ugly, evil would-be rapist. So no quips about typecasting, please. But he does have quite a pivotal role. And he has his poignant moments." Tristan's body fell almost without conscious instruction into the twisted, hunchbacked shape he'd assumed to play the role, and he looked around the room in unseeing wonder.

"'Sometimes a thousand twangling instruments

"'Will hum about mine ears, and sometime voices

"'That, if I then had waked after long sleep,

"'Will make me sleep again: and then, in dreaming,

"'The clouds methought would open and show riches

"'Ready to drop upon me that, when I waked,

"'I cried to dream again.'

"Of course, it's a lot more effective in costume and makeup, when you get the contrast between the lowly monster and his eloquent words," Tristan added, straightening his back and loosening up his jaw.

Con was staring at him. "How do you keep all that stuff in your head?"

"Well, to be fair, that's his most famous speech. And God alone knows how many times I delivered it on stage. I seriously doubt I could give you much of the rest of his part without studying it again first, though. And, in any case, it's my *job*." Was. Damn it. Tristan carried on. "I'm sure there's any amount of knowledge in that well-shaped head of yours about the kind of jobs you do. And take Sean," he added, seizing the opportunity to turn the conversation in this direction. "I've no doubt he has a vast quantity of professional know-how concerning pests and how to deal with them."

"Yeah, I guess," Con said, sounding like he didn't really think it was the same thing.

Not that Tristan actually gave a tinker's cuss about the argument itself. "I suppose you met Sean through Heather," he went on, dropping gracefully to the sofa and flicking through his copy of *Dream*. He was especially pleased with the artless nonchalance he'd managed to imbue his tone with. No casual listener, he felt, would have the slightest inkling he was fishing for information on whether Con and Sean had ever slept together.

He only hoped Con was in a similar state of ignorance.

"Well, sort of. That's how I got to know him. But we'd met before, actually."

Oh God. They'd had a one-night stand. Tristan was certain of it, and equally certain he did *not* want to hear the details. Probably. "Oh?" he said with polite disinterest.

"Yeah, bit of a funny story. See, he was with a couple of other blokes—"

If this was going to turn into the tale of an orgy, Tristan was going to put his fingers in his ears.

Well, maybe *one* ear.

"—up on the top floor of this old barn."

Tristan glanced up from his book, startled out of character. "I always thought *rolling in the hay* was a euphemism. Nowadays, at any rate. Wasn't it a trifle itchy?"

Con frowned. "What? They were clearing pigeons' nests. It was a job."

"*Ohhh.*"

"What, did you think I was about to tell you about some foursome I had with him and two other blokes the first time we'd met?" The furrow between Con's brows deepened. "That the sort of thing you get up to, is it?"

"Good God, no. I prefer the *pas de deux* to the ensemble. Or, to put it in terms with which you may be more familiar, I find that turning the horizontal mambo into a conga line is seldom as enticing as it sounds," he added drily in the face of Con's suspicious glare.

"Right," Con said, still looking a touch doubtful. "Well, anyway, like I said, they were clearing a load of pigeons' nests out of the place. Bagging them up and chucking them out through the door. You know, that high one they have on barns where if you walked out of it you'd splat yourself on the ground? Dunno what it's for."

"Some . . . grain thing. Probably," Tristan contributed vaguely. "But did it really need three of them to clear a few birds' nests?"

"You ever seen the mess pigeons make? They've got pigeons nesting under the eaves of the church—you walk past, you see 'em roosting in the stained glass windows. I helped the churchwarden clear out the mess they made one time. We had three bin bags full of pigeon shit at the end of it, and they clean that up regular. So yeah, a barn that's been left for years with generations of pigeons nesting there? Too bloody right they needed three of them."

Tristan inclined his head graciously. "I bow to your superior knowledge in the area of pigeon shit. So where did you come into this barn story? Did they feel compelled to send out for reinforcements?"

"Not exactly. Nah, I was just walking past—been doing a job for one of the neighbours. And I heard someone calling for help. Took me a while to realise it was coming from twenty feet up in the air." Con smiled. "One of 'em had been a bit energetic chucking a bag out, and he'd knocked their ladder down and trapped 'em up there. So I put it back up for 'em, and Sean offered to buy me a pint to say thanks for the rescue." He laughed. "Thought it might be to bribe me to keep quiet about it, but Sean's all right about stuff like that. He doesn't mind having a laugh at himself."

Tristan felt a surge of irrational jealousy. It must be nice to be so secure in oneself. "And did he also bestow upon you the traditional reward for a rescue?"

"Do what?"

"A kiss. Or, of course, any other sexual favours?"

"What? No. Me and Sean have never been like that." Con paused. "Not really my type, to be honest."

"Oh? What were your objections? He seems personable enough." If one liked that kind of thing, although personally Tristan found the kind of thing he was looking at right now to be far more attractive. But he was curious as a cat to see what Con might say.

Con shrugged. "Too . . . blokey, I s'pose." He grinned suddenly, but went a tad pink with it. "And too, well, ginger. Not that there's anything wrong with that, obviously."

Tristan raised an eyebrow. "Let me guess: some of your best friends are ginger?"

"Well, yeah. That's what we've just been talking about. I just mean, I like blokes who are a bit . . . I dunno. It's just a look you go for, innit?"

"You prefer the traditional tall, dark, and handsome?" Well, Tristan certainly did, so he could hardly fault Con for that.

Con went even redder. "Well, dark, anyhow. And yeah, handsome, obviously."

Oh, that was *very* interesting. Tristan was about to make some remark congratulating Con on his lack of a height requirement when the man himself changed the subject somewhat abruptly.

"What did you think of Robert?"

Tristan blinked, then shrugged. "Well, from what little I saw of him, he seems to be a competent bowler."

Con was frowning again. "I meant . . . what do you reckon about him and Sean being together?"

Tristan had thought they were rather sweet together, but decided, on reflection, that he didn't want to sound like a thirteen-year-old girl by saying so. "They seem oddly compatible," he said in the end.

"Yeah," Con said, his gaze appearing to focus somewhere just short of the wall. Then he closed his eyes and took a deep breath. "We probably ought to get on with the play."

CHAPTER SIXTEEN
QUICK BRIGHT THINGS

Con's emotions were in a bit of a tangle when he left Tristan's house Wednesday night. It'd been a bloody good evening—they'd really got on with learning his part for the play, with Tristan showing him how to move and stuff. And it'd just seemed so easy to talk to him about other things too.

There had been a bit of flirting, yeah, but Tristan hadn't pushed it. Hadn't done anything that made Con feel on the spot or uncomfortable. None of the touching or the outright propositions.

If Con was really, *really* honest with himself, he'd sort of missed it. But this was better, really, wasn't it?

Yeah, course it was. Definitely.

Con wished he knew if Tristan had been serious about them going to visit George Bernard Shaw's house together. He'd said it was a date—but Con had had the feeling he wasn't really thinking about it at the time. But, well, it'd be good to do something like that with him. Con hadn't honestly ever thought about going before—it was way too literary for someone like him—but with Tristan, it'd be fun. Con could see him now, flouncing around the house and grounds quoting stuff from the plays. And, well, Con knew some bits of *Pygmalion*, cos the Sham-Drams had done it last year, so he'd even be able to join in.

It'd be . . . fun. Even with them just going as mates. Which was all they were ever gonna be, obviously.

Yeah. Mates.

Mates was good. And, well, a mate would still miss Tristan when he left the country. So, yeah, it wasn't surprising Con didn't want to think about him going away.

At all.

Thursday morning, Con was due to meet Alf to go and call on Miss Wellbeck. He was on his way, and for the first time since last evening, *not* thinking about Tristan, when Con came out of the archway that led from his flat and bumped into the bloke. Almost literally.

"Well met by—" Tristan glanced up at the sky. "Hmm. Rather indifferent sunlight, actually. I *would* say, fancy meeting you here, but seeing as we're only three feet away from your bedroom as the sat-nav flies, it's hardly the greatest surprise of the century. In fact," he went on without even pausing for breath, "for all I know, you were gazing idly out of your window like Juliet upon her balcony, saw me coming, and ran down to intercept me."

"No," Con said a bit shortly, thrown off track by meeting Tristan unexpectedly like that and worried it was going to make him late to meet Alf. Then he felt bad about it, probably cos Tristan's smile had done an instant disappearing act. "You, um, going to the post office?" he asked, trying to sound apologetic.

Tristan gave an exaggerated nod and held up a small parcel he'd had under his arm, somehow managing to make Con feel like the bloke had just laid on the sarcasm with a trowel and asked him how on earth he'd managed to work that one out, all without saying a word.

Shit. They'd got on so well last night. Con opened his mouth to say he'd better be going before he could fuck things up even more, but Tristan beat him to it.

"I'm sending a care parcel to Hong Kong," he explained. "Well, an early birthday present. Well, I say early, but apparently these things travel by carrier snail, so it'll probably be late by the time it gets there." Now *he* sounded like he was apologising.

All this was starting to do Con's head in. *And* it must be getting on for time he met Alf. Con looked at his watch.

"In a hurry, are we?" Tristan asked sharply. "Or simply tired of the present company?"

"Nah, it's just I'm s'posed to be meeting up with this bloke, and I don't wanna be late."

"Anyone I know?" Tristan asked. His voice sounded a bit funny, but when Con glanced at him, Tristan just looked normal. He must have imagined it.

"Nah, shouldn't think so. Name's Alf. Alf Smith. He lives up on The Hill."

"Alf? How delightfully old-fashioned. And how did you meet this *Alf*?"

Con shrugged. "Same way I met you. Did some work for him. Digging out a tree stump. He's a good bloke—gave me dinner after. But I gotta go now. I'll see you Saturday, yeah?" He jogged off, not quite hearing what Tristan said as he left. Probably something literary anyhow.

Alf had insisted on meeting Con in the high street—said he didn't want to make Con go at his old pace, walking down from The Hill. He was sitting in the bus shelter when Con jogged down there, hands folded on top of his walking stick like he'd copied the pose from some old geezer in a cartoon. He'd dressed up posh, Con realised—Alf was wearing cream-coloured trousers with sharp creases down the front, a crisply ironed short-sleeved shirt with an open collar, and even a straw trilby. He looked pretty cool for an old guy.

Con was glad he'd put a clean pair of jeans on, and a T-shirt without any holes. He still felt a bit underdressed, but at least he wasn't a total scruff.

"'Lo Alf—you're looking good," he said with a grin. Actually, now he was closer, the old guy seemed a bit nervous, so Con was glad he hadn't gone as far as teasing him for putting on his pulling clothes.

"Ah, excellent. Right on time." Alf heaved himself to his feet and picked up a bunch of flowers wrapped around with newspaper Con hadn't noticed lying next to him on the bench. "Come along, then. We mustn't keep a lady waiting."

Con frowned. "Does she even know we're coming?"

"Ah. Well, no, I suppose she doesn't, but we wouldn't want to stray too close to lunchtime, would we? Wouldn't want to inconvenience her."

It was half past ten. Still, Con wasn't going to argue. Now they were almost there, he was pretty keen himself to hear what

Miss Wellbeck might have to say about his grandad. "Course not," he said, and reminded himself not to offer the old boy his arm as he shuffled slowly down the high street.

Maybe that worry about getting too close to lunchtime wasn't so far off the mark, at that. The Six Elms flats were only about three hundred yards from the bus stop, but it seemed to take forever to get there at Alf's pace.

It was a pretty new development, with the buildings designed so they looked like something you might actually want to live in, not like the boxy 1960s block in Bedford where Gran had lived ever since Con could remember. There were communal gardens in front of the flats, with benches where the old folk could sit and look at the flowers—from what Con had heard, the actual gardening was done by a service that was part of the rent. Seemed a shame for any of the residents who actually liked gardening, but then, if they were that active and independent, they probably wouldn't choose to live in sheltered flats in the first place.

Mary Wellbeck's flat was a first-floor one, so Con reckoned she must be reasonably mobile, at least. Well, probably. There was a lift, though, so maybe not. Gran had had to walk up four flights of stairs to get to her flat, and when she got ill, that just meant she didn't go out much.

They didn't have to ring the bell because an old lady who was on nodding terms with Alf was just going out and let them in, so they walked up the stairs, which were so clean you could have eaten your dinner off them, to Miss Wellbeck's front door.

Well, Con walked. Alf sort of creaked. "Ready?" Con asked at last, fist raised to rap on the door.

Alf held up a hand and took a few deep breaths. "Ready," he wheezed, then thumped his chest and cleared his throat. "Ready," he said again, sounding a lot more like it this time.

Con knocked.

There was a silence. "Maybe she's out?" Con asked—but then the door opened and a face appeared, a bit lower down than Con was expecting.

"Yes?" Miss Wellbeck asked with a friendly smile. She was a skinny old girl, straight backed and neatly dressed. Con could see Alf's "pretty little thing" in her high cheekbones and big blue eyes, only slightly faded with age.

Alf's eyes misted as he smiled back at her. "Mary? Remember me? Alf Smith. Alfie. And this—you won't believe it, but this young man is Con Izzard. Bill Izzard's grandson, do you remember old Bill?"

Miss Wellbeck's smile wobbled, then disappeared altogether. Her face paled, and Con realised with alarm she was swaying a little.

"Are you all right, Miss Wellbeck?" he asked, stepping forward in case he needed to catch her. "Want me to get anyone?" They had staff at these sort of places, didn't they? Wardens or something? They'd know what to do—might even be used to her having a funny turn.

She gripped the doorframe with one tiny hand, the skin paper-thin over the finely shaped bones. "No—no, I'm quite all right. Just something of a . . . I'm so sorry. I'm afraid I can't . . . I'm very sorry, but I can't ask you in. So kind of you to come, but I'm afraid . . . So sorry."

She closed the door. Con stared at the blank, white-painted wood with its little spyhole for a moment, gobsmacked, then he turned to Alf.

Alf didn't just look gobsmacked. He looked like he'd brought Miss Wellbeck a kitten and she'd drowned it in front of him, the poor old bloke. He gazed down sadly at the flowers in his hand. "Seems a bit pointless taking them home, now. Would you put them down by the door for me?"

"Yeah, course," Con said quickly, taking the bunch and laying it just to one side of the door. They were sweet peas, and their cheerful, honey fragrance reminded him of stuff he used to buy Gran for Christmas—talcum powder and soap, all done up in straw-filled baskets so they'd look like a proper present. "She'll probably like them when she's feeling a bit better. Must have been a bit of a shock, us turning up like that. Tell you what, why don't we go and get a cuppa in the café on the way back? My treat, yeah? Seeing as I've had all those meals on you."

CHAPTER SEVENTEEN
FOND FOOLS

"'**P**arting is such *sweet* sorrow,'" Tristan had muttered sourly to Con's departing back. And just who on God's green earth was *Alf*? There had been no mention of any Alf at their previous meetings. Tristan was *quite* certain he should have remembered. Was this someone new? The name told him annoyingly little. Alf Smith might *sound* aggressively working class, the sort of man who wore paint-splattered overalls and drank real ale, but he could just as easily turn out to be, say, Alfie Fortescue-Smythe, dropping the hyphenated name in a form of inverted snobbery.

Then again, with all due respect to Con, the overalls and ale salt-of-the-earth type did seem more likely. After all, they'd have much more in common.

Much more than, say, Con and *Tristan*. Damn it.

Tristan realised he was crushing the parcel in his hands and smoothed out the brown paper hastily. It still looked rather ill-used, but luckily he'd had the foresight to buy Amanda one of those scarves that came pre-crumpled, in his lightning-fast visit to the department store in Bishops Langley this morning. And undoubtedly she would blame the Royal Mail rather than him in any case. Speaking of which . . . He glanced at the post office outside which he was currently standing. If he were to go inside, he'd be able to post his parcel and he'd be in an excellent position to see anyone Con brought back to his flat.

But then again, if that had been the ultimate destination, why not meet there? No, they must be going to one of the village pubs . . . or perhaps a café? It *was* only ten thirty in the morning. Not really drinking time. Barely even breakfast time, in Tristan's days with the

Players, but he'd been trying to accustom himself to the hours at which people with mundane jobs operated.

And he was losing time and with it, any chance to set eyes upon the mysterious *Alf.* Tristan came to a decision.

The view up the high street was most inconveniently blocked by a large, old mill building that now housed various bijou establishments, several of which had the word *artisan* in the name, presumably to justify their outrageous prices. Lodging Amanda's present firmly under his arm, Tristan crept up the path between the former mill and its adjacent mill stream that split off at right angles from the main river to rush merrily along, unhindered these days by any water wheel.

Damn it. An enormous double buggy hove into view and halted on the footbridge over the river. It was turned side-on to allow its kicking occupants, their juvenile fists clasped around mangled slices of stale white cut-loaf, to view the water—or rather, its inhabitants. A vast number of freeloading ducks tended to congregate here during the day, clearly knowing which side their bread was, metaphorically speaking, buttered. On its own, the buggy would merely have meant a tight squeeze for Tristan to get past. Together with the large, leggings-clad rear end of the proud mother-of-two bent over her children's heads to point out the "quack-quacks," however, it proved an impassable obstacle.

Tristan tried to seethe silently. "Excuse me," he said with unctuous politeness. "Might I possibly get past?"

"Oh, sorry, love. They won't be a mo, though, will you, darlings?"

Darling #1 responded with a frown and a shout of "Wack-wack!"

Darling #2 made no reply, but managed to imbue the way it slowly tore off a corner of stale bread with subtle menace.

"I *am* in something of a hurry," Tristan said with an ingratiating smile.

"Well, I *suppose* I could move the buggy." She started halfheartedly to manoeuvre the unwieldy object. Twin wails of dismay arose from childish throats, their owners convinced their quack-quack time was about to be cut unreasonably short. "Hush, you two. I'm just letting the man get past."

The latter remark was said with wilful disregard for its inherent lack of truth. "Perhaps if you left them, and merely removed *yourself*?" Tristan suggested desperately.

Mother stood up straight, her hands on her ample hips. "Just what are you saying?"

That you have a rear end the size of Covent Garden? Tristan had a sudden vision of himself flying over the railings of the bridge to be pecked to death by a feeding frenzy of quack-quacks. "Ah . . . simply that it would be a terrible shame to upset the young ones?"

"Oh." Grumbling, she nevertheless *finally* got out of the way.

"Thank you *so* much," Tristan said, his smile starting to make his cheeks ache as he squeezed betwixt wall and buggy, grazing his elbow on the former in his attempt to avoid any risk of contact with the latter. Mother would probably take it as some kind of slight to or even attack upon her little darlings if he so much as nudged the buggy. Justice would no doubt be both swift and draconian.

Safely through, he emerged at last onto the upper section of the high street—only to find that Con, by now, had gone, presumably taking the mysterious Alf with him. Still, there remained the village cafés, of which there were two, both of them on his way back home. Tristan could saunter past and cast a casual eye through the window of each. Yes, that would do. Not everyone, he flattered himself, could pull off an air of nonchalance like he could. He adjusted the parcel under his arm—

Ah. The parcel. Having said he'd made the trip to post it, Tristan might look a trifle odd walking home with it still in his possession. Con, were he to see Tristan, might conceivably wonder about that. And Amanda would *definitely* wonder why her birthday present was so bloody late if he didn't get the wretched thing posted, well, post haste. Damn it. Tristan turned to retrace his steps.

Only to find that Mother and Darlings #1 and #2 were still in determined occupation of the bridge. Noticing Tristan's approach, Mother glared.

Tristan crumbled. "I'll, ah, I'll just go around the long way, then."

The queue at the village post office having grown exponentially during Tristan's failed attempt at stalking his lover-elect, it was almost half an hour later when he finally walked his weary way back up the high street, heading towards Valley Crescent and a soothing cup of tea. God, he could almost taste the tannin already.

Maybe it was the association of ideas, but Tristan found himself idly glancing at the lower of the two cafés as he passed—only to see Con sitting at a table with a smartly dressed elderly man.

Was that *Alf*? Laughter bubbled up inside Tristan. He'd been jealous of a geriatric. And true, the old man *was* dressed up as if for a date, but somehow Tristan couldn't quite stretch his credulity far enough to believe Con had suddenly acquired a superannuated sugar daddy. He wondered what the true story between them was.

And then he thought, damn wondering, and opened the café door.

Con looked up and smiled at him. "All right, Tristan?" Then he frowned. "Has it seriously taken you all this time to get that parcel sorted?"

"I stopped on the bridge," Tristan said smoothly, pulling out a chair to join them at their table. "To admire the qua—the ducks." He coughed. "I take it this nattily dressed gentleman would be Alf?"

"Oh—yeah, sorry. Alf, this is Tristan. He's Mrs. Geary's grandson—well, sort of. Lives in her house now. Um. Did you know old Mrs. Geary?"

"Only to say good morning to." Alf gave Tristan a long and searching look. "You're, ah, friends with Con here, are you?"

Tristan strongly suspected Alf already knew the answer to that question. "Absolutely," he said with his smile set to medium charm. "Con's told me a *little* about you, but . . ."

"Alf Smith. I live up on The Hill. I was at school with Con's grandad during the War," he added, the sharp look in his eyes disappearing as his thoughts lost themselves in memory. Then his gaze snapped back into focus. "But I'll leave you two young people to it now. Time I was heading back home." Leaning on the table, he heaved himself to his feet.

Tristan rose hastily. "Please, not on my account," he said, feeling genuinely bad he'd allowed his curiosity to interrupt Con and Alf's tête-à-tête. "It was terribly rude of me to invite myself to join you. Perhaps I could get you another cup of tea? Some . . ." he darted a glance at the counter, "rock cakes, or scones, or whatever those rather lumpen things are supposed to be?"

Alf's gaze, when he bestowed it upon Tristan once more, was definitely kindlier than it had been. "No, no. I've done what I came down to the village to do, even if it didn't . . . Well, never mind. They do say you can't go back, after all." Clearly these cryptic murmurings meant something to him, as his eyes turned misty. "Why don't you get Con a bite to eat, hmm? That young man needs feeding up."

He shuffled off, impervious to Con's pleas to be allowed to walk the old man home or give him a ride in his van. Con sat down again, a little awkwardness in his mien.

It was nothing to how Tristan felt. "If I say I'm sorry, can we assume I just mean for interrupting you and leave it at that?"

Con frowned. "What else have you gotta be sorry for?"

"I think your antediluvian friend Alf may be under the impression our *friendship* is more than just platonic." Fiddling with a packet of sugar, Tristan did his utmost not to make it apparent just how closely he was studying Con's reaction to what he'd just said.

To Tristan's surprise, Con reddened. "Nah. 'S my fault. He was just asking me if I had a girlfriend. I mean, I didn't exactly tell him I was gay. Just, you know, that I wasn't into girls."

Tristan sighed. "And that's what passes for subtlety on planet Constantine? You might as have waved a little rainbow flag and jumped up on a Pride float in a sparkly thong. Why the interest in your love life, in any case? Was the old man after some vicarious thrills?"

"Nah, it just sort of came up."

Tristan smirked.

Con gave him a hard stare belied by just the hint of a twinkle, and continued. "Well, we just went to see an old girlfriend of his. Didn't go too well." Con stared down at the dregs of his tea—Tristan might have assumed he was searching for some meaning in the leaves, had it not been made with a bag that had been thoughtfully left in the mug.

"Let me get you another of those," Tristan said, having been reminded of his own thirst. He waved a hand in the direction of the counter, adding a winning smile. "Waitress? We want the finest teas available to humanity." He prudently decided not to add *we want them here, and we want them now.*

The middle-aged, middle-sized woman behind the counter gazed at him stolidly. Perhaps she wasn't a fan of 1960s-set cult classic films, or people who quoted them. "We got Yorkshire Gold or English Breakfast."

"Yorkshire Gold's fine again, thanks," Con said, sounding a little harassed for some reason.

"Oh, and some of your . . . cakes, are they? Apparently, my *friend* requires feeding up." Tristan turned back to Con. "Although, honestly, if we feed you up any farther, you'll be a danger to low-flying aircraft."

"You're supposed to order at the counter, you know," Con muttered.

"Why? She heard me perfectly well from here. And I was planning to leave a tip."

Con shook his head. "My gran always used to say good manners don't cost nothing."

Tristan ignored both Con and the pricking of his conscience as it reminded him Nanna Geary had used to say that exact same thing. Although with rather better grammar. "So go on, tell me about Alf's date and why you went along. You know, when you put on your card 'all jobs considered,' you really did mean all jobs, didn't you? Although I can't imagine you get too many calls to be a chaperone to the aged. Is that why it didn't go well? Alf seems remarkably sprightly for someone of school age during 'the War'—I assume he meant the Second World War, not the First—but at risk of making you conceited, the comparison between the two of you isn't all that favourable to him."

Con smiled. "Glad to hear you think so. No, he, well, he said she—the lady we went to see—used to know my grandad. Used to live with him, actually, her being the vicar's daughter. So I was hoping she might be able to tell me stuff about him. But she didn't wanna know. It was a bit weird, really."

Tristan sniffed the air. "Hm, I scent a scandal. They lived together, you say?"

"Yeah, but my grandad was thirteen at most, and she was even younger."

"It's not *totally* beyond the bounds of possibility . . ."

"Yeah, but if my grandad was getting up to stuff with a ten-year-old, I don't wanna know."

"What *I'd* like to know is what your grandad was doing in the village in the first place. I thought you said you didn't come from around here?"

"Oh—yeah, I used to live in Bedford. But my grandad was evacuated out here in the war."

Tristan leaned forward to carry on the interrogation, then moved back hastily as the waitress appeared with a tray. She dumped it on the table between them with a surly clatter of crockery.

"So kind," Tristan murmured, beaming at her.

"That'll be eight pounds twenty," was her only reply.

Tristan took out a ten pound note. "Keep the change," he said to see if that would move her granite features to a smile.

It didn't. She merely snatched it and left.

"Some people are *such* hard work," he murmured once she was safely behind the counter once more.

He didn't quite catch what Con said, as it was all but drowned out by the ear-splitting scrape of a chair leg as their charming hostess tidied up, but it sounded an awful lot like "You're telling me."

Tristan took a sip of his tea. It was hot and strong, and he'd definitely had worse. Even the rock cakes, on closer inspection, didn't appear so bad. He broke off a corner of one of them. "So, your infant grandfather, evacuated to Shamwell. Any particular reason, or was it simply the nearest available country village?"

"Well, actually, he was born here. See, the vicar of St. Saviour's found him in the churchyard—when he was a baby, I mean, he'd been abandoned—"

"Sounds fishy to me."

"—and named him after a gravestone. Then he got sent to a kids' home over in Bedford. And when the bombing started, the vicar offered to have him back here to stay. I s'pose he felt like Grandad was his responsibility, or maybe just cos his parents must have been from the parish."

"Or possibly he just felt guilty for landing him with such a morbid choice of name."

Con grinned. "Yeah, s'pose it was a bit. It's still there—the gravestone, I mean. Wanna see it?"

Tristan was surprised to find he very much did want to. "After we've finished our tea and cakes, yes. These are actually rather good."

"Yeah? Go for it, then." Con pushed the plate over to Tristan's side of the table. "If I have anything now, I won't eat my lunch."

"Your loss," Tristan said, digging in greedily. "You can tell me how you ended up back here," he added with his mouth full, just about managing not to spray Con with crumbs.

Nanna Geary would *not* have approved, he reflected guiltily, and took a smaller bite next time.

Con shrugged. "I just dropped by one day I was in the area, you know, to see the grave and that, and really liked the village. Then when Gran died and I was thinking of moving out of Bedford, I just thought 'Why not?'"

"Well, I can think of a few reasons why not," Tristan pointed out, gesturing with his rock cake. "You had to leave the area you'd grown up in, all your friends, your clients if you were in the same line of work, and it must be a lot more expensive to live here." Hm, when he put it like that, Tristan started to wonder if he could scent a scandal here too.

Con looked down at his tea. "Yeah, well . . . There was this bloke. Mo. Sort of wanted to go somewhere I didn't have to see him all the time."

Tristan put down his rock cake, not entirely certain he was hungry any longer. "What did he do?"

"Nothing!" Con's eyes were wide. Perhaps Tristan's tone *had* been a little sharp. "It's just, we were together and we broke up, that was all."

"Oh. Well, he sounds like a complete idiot in any case."

"I haven't told you anything about him except his name." Con's gaze had significantly narrowed. "Oi, has Hev been saying stuff to you?"

"Nooo . . . Is there," Tristan asked delicately, "*stuff* to say?"

"No." Con's cheeks were red again, and Tristan decided to leave well alone.

Well, for now, at any rate. He stood. "Time for us to talk of graves, of worms, and epitaphs? If you're ready, that is."

"Yeah, I'm good," Con said, scrambling to his feet and almost knocking his chair over in the process.

The distance to the churchyard was only a few feet as the crow flies, since the café backed onto its boundary. Not being crows, Con and Tristan had to walk a rather longer route around the buildings of the high street to reach the northernmost gate. Technically the lych gate was nearer, but that seemed available for the use of the living only when accompanied by a corpse.

Tristan felt his usual sense of vague unease as they stepped inside the pale—not that he expected the vicar to come rampaging out and persecute him personally for daring to set foot inside; in fact, when he'd been to friends' weddings and christenings (their children's, not their own) he'd at times been given an exaggerated welcome by the incumbent once his Jewish identity became known. But still, the Church of England was more than this quaint little stone building surrounded by graves (and, one had to assume corpses) in varying states of decay. It was an institution; it was the Establishment, to which Tristan's kind traditionally did not belong. And it was a symbol, in a way, of centuries of persecution and pogrom.

"You all right?" Con asked, peering down at him with an expression of concern.

Tristan forced a laugh. "Just being morbid."

"Yeah? You've come to the right place, then."

This time the laugh came naturally. "Quite right." Tristan shook his head free of such gloomy thoughts. "So where are we headed?"

"Round the back of the church. See that house through the trees? That's the vicarage. The vicar was on his way into the church to get ready for morning service when he found my grandad."

They ambled over to a weathered stone that still stood straight and proud, unlike many of its fellows which lay like broken teeth around it. "You know, looking at all those fallen stones, it strikes me a grave isn't the safest of places to leave a baby. What if the stone had happened to topple while the poor thing lay there?"

"Well, you wouldn't be here with me now, for a start. Anyway, this is it. William Izzard, born 1789, died 1838." Con grinned. "Think he's up there somewhere, thinking, *Oi, who's this bastard who's gone and stolen my name?*"

"Hm, not sure, but you might want to stand away from the headstone to be on the safe side."

They parted after that, Con pleading work which, it being a weekday, Tristan supposed wasn't *totally* unreasonable. He wished, though, as he made his way back to Nanna Geary's house, that he'd had more time to pry out the story of Con's foundling forebear. And just why would Alf's inamorata refuse to talk about old Bill?

Hm. She was the vicar's daughter during the war, he mused, arriving at his front door. Once inside, Tristan opened up his laptop. St. Saviour's Church, Shamwell, proved to have a very informative, if rather badly laid-out, website which readily yielded the name of the wartime vicar, a Reverend Thomas Wellbeck, along with far greater detail about the church bells than anyone could conceivably want to know. No details of his children were forthcoming, alas.

However . . . she still lived in the village—in the centre, no less, as she'd been within doddering distance from the café for old Alf—and was probably old-fashioned enough to have her telephone number listed in the phone book. Tristan quickly searched the "people" pages for Wellbeck, crossing his fingers the lady was still a spinster of this parish.

Success! M. Wellbeck, flat number twelve, Six Elms. Well, if it wasn't her, it must be a brother and hence, a route to the woman herself. Tristan sat back in his chair and drummed his fingers on the table in satisfaction.

He hadn't got a clue what he was actually going to *do* with this information, but nevertheless, he was rather pleased he'd got it.

CHAPTER EIGHTEEN
THE QUALITY OF MERCY

Con wasn't sure how he felt about going round to Tristan's for rehearsal on Saturday afternoon. He'd . . . well, to be honest, he'd missed Tristan. Hadn't seen him for a couple of days, not since that thing with Alf and Miss Wellbeck went a bit pear-shaped. It'd been . . . All right, it'd been a bit weird, to start with, that day, but it'd got a lot better. Showing Tristan Grandad's grave—well, not his *actual* grave, the one he'd been found on—had been . . . Sod it. The only word he could think of was *nice*.

He'd never really told anyone about all that stuff before. Gran had been a bit funny about people knowing her husband had been born out of wedlock, even though Con's birth certificate had *Father: Unknown* written on it and no one had seemed to care much about that. Half the kids in his class at school, if they even had dads, they weren't the ones they'd started out with. Then again, back in the 1930s, or even in the 1950s, that sort of thing had mattered, hadn't it?

Con would bet his van Tristan knew *his* family tree right back to the Norman Conquest. Which they were probably on the winning side of. Con could just see Tristan as some French nob, looking down his nose at Con's peasant ancestors.

Except . . . Tristan's family were Jewish, weren't they? Con's knowledge of history wasn't great, but he had a pretty good idea the Nazis weren't the first lot to treat Jewish people like shit.

Con had pulled out his laptop and typed *Jews in the middle ages* into the search bar (well, close enough—it had known what he'd meant, anyhow), and he'd managed to find a website that wasn't too hard to read when he made the text a bit bigger. Enough to get the gist of it, anyway, which, to be honest, was more than enough. It wasn't exactly cheerful reading. Jewish history seemed to consist mostly of lending money to kings and that sort, then getting chucked out of the country when the king didn't want to pay them back. Apparently Christians weren't supposed to lend money to people. Con hadn't known that, although come to think of it Gran had been fond of saying, "Neither a borrower nor a lender be." He'd thought that was just, well, a saying.

And when they weren't being chucked out of their homes, Jews were getting blamed for everything that went wrong, like plagues and fires and bad weather and stuff, and having to leave the country off their own bat so they didn't just get murdered in their beds.

There were some medieval pictures on the website, showing the Christians as straight-backed, handsome, clean-cut men, while the Jews were all hunched over with cartoon big noses, looking sneaky and sly and like they deserved to have their heads cut off, which was what was generally happening or about to happen in the pictures.

Christ.

Con felt ill at the thought of anyone doing any of that stuff to Tristan. Which, yeah, obviously wasn't going to happen these days—he was much more likely to get beaten up for being posh or gay or just generally annoying than for being Jewish—but still.

Anyway, he didn't want anything like that to happen to Tristan. More than he just generally didn't want that sort of thing to happen to *anyone*. Because it felt like they'd, well, shared stuff. Were getting closer. And that was . . .

Good, his heart said. *Bad*, his head knew. Con shouldn't let it happen. Because Tristan was buggering off in a couple of months, wasn't he? He just . . . He just had to remember that. Tristan couldn't be more than a friend.

He told himself that all over again, just to be on the safe side, as he knocked on Tristan's door.

Tristan opened it with a big smile that didn't help Con's resolve. "Excellent. Come in. I thought we'd skip lightly ahead to Bottom's awakening, once morning has come. It's actually extremely poignant."

Con looked at him, startled, as he toed off his trainers. It was a bit embarrassing how much bigger they were than the pair of posh shoes he left them next to. "Yeah? I thought it was, you know. More stuff for laughs. Like, he talks about hands tasting and ears seeing. Gets it all wrong."

"Oh, he does, he does. And yet . . ." Tristan paused, his hands frozen in mid-gesture. "It's actually a very profound speech about our inability to say what we really mean. To share our thoughts, our feelings, our experiences with another person. Nick Bottom has had the most bizarre, most magical experience of his life—of the life of anyone he knows—and he's doomed to struggle hopelessly with his words whenever he tries to relate it to anyone else. I read a book once—"

"Good for you," Con teased. It was about time he got some of his own back.

"Shut up. I can't remember what it was about, but one of the characters said something to another—to a lover—that really spoke about how we can never truly connect to another person. 'All we have is a touch and a voice,' that was it. No matter how much we want our loved ones to really know us, we're limited to words and gestures." Tristan laughed, but he didn't look all that happy. "The whole of human interaction: just one endless, and rather poorly organised, game of charades."

God, he looked sad, staring into space. It did weird things in Con's chest to look at him, and he almost reached out to touch Tristan, maybe even hug him—

But then Tristan was off again, striding around the room and waving his hands around like knocking stuff off the mantelpiece was something that only happened to other people. "And of course, Bottom is the only human character to actually cross over into the magical world of the fairies. We mustn't forget that. He may be a fool, but he's the only one who sees what's really going on. The fact that he can neither comprehend nor express it is comic, on one level, and tragic, on another." He stopped suddenly, dead in the middle of the living room, and sent Con a bright, brittle smile. "But I think we'll work chiefly on the comic, for the benefit of our audience."

"Yeah. Yeah, that'd be good," Con managed, his throat a bit dry. "Um. Could I get a glass of water first?"

Tristan stared at him. "Didn't I offer you a cup of tea? Flask of wine, loaf of bread, et cetera?"

"Uh, no."

"Good God. Nanna Geary would have *conniptions*. Sit down and I'll put the kettle on."

Con sat on the sofa and wondered what exactly conniptions were while Tristan banged about in the kitchen with cups and stuff. After a moment, Meggie poked her furry head out from behind the armchair and padded over to rub her cheek on Con's jeans. Pleased to see her, Con gave her a stroke.

There was a picture of Mrs. Geary on the mantelpiece that hadn't used to be there—the frame had used to hold a picture of Tristan in his university gown, Con remembered now. It looked like quite an old photo, and Mrs. Geary was dressed up all tweedy, holding a baby. "Hey, is that you?" Con asked, giving Meggie one last pet on the head before getting up to peer at it more closely. The baby was just a pink blob in a white shawl, really.

Tristan came back into the living room holding two mugs and a biscuit tin. "Yes. Of course, I hadn't quite grown into my looks, back then. We've actually got a very similar picture of her holding Mother. We're even wearing the same outfit."

Funny to think of her looking after generations of someone else's children, and never having any of her own. "You know, I always wondered if there was ever a Mr. Geary," Con said, sitting down again.

Tristan smiled. "Oh, there was, there was. It's my belief," he added in ringing actor-y tones, "she done the old man in."

Con blinked. It sounded like Tristan was quoting something, but he was buggered if he knew what it was. Then it came to him—Eliza Doolittle said something like that in *Pygmalion*. That'd been the first Sham-Drams production he'd helped out with, back last autumn. Con smiled, pleased to have got the reference. Tristan had probably expected that one to sail *right* over his head.

Then it hit him what the bloke had actually said. "*What*?"

"Well, not really. Mother used to joke about it, though. He seems to have disappeared in mysterious circumstances. He definitely existed—Mother was sent a piece of the wedding cake. She said it was rather dry. And then there were a few years when Mother didn't really hear from her—just cards at birthdays and so on, and she was never sure she had the right address. But Nanna Geary finally wrote to her when she—Mother, that is—became enceinte—"

"What?"

"Preggers, dear boy. Where was I?"

"In the womb, then, I 'spect."

"Stop being witty. It's unnerving. And, I might add, that gesture you just made is *extremely* vulgar."

Con grinned and put down the finger he'd been holding up.

"So anyway," Tristan went on, "Nanna Geary just reappeared at the house one day shortly before I was born, and didn't have a word to say about *Mister* Geary—not that he was Mr. *Geary*, in actual fact. Some other name. But it was all terribly convenient for us, of course. Anyway, shall we to business, if you're now suitably refreshed?"

"Yeah. Course." Con looked around, but Meggie had disappeared again. "You're getting on better with Meggie now, then?" he asked idly.

Tristan looked at him like he'd suddenly sprouted an ass's head. "What? Oh, the cat? Haven't seen a whisker of her. Or the frog, for that matter, but then again I'm fairly sure they don't actually have whiskers."

"But . . ." Con shook his head, hiding a smile. "Never mind. Bottom's speech, yeah?"

"Absolutely. Now, try to imagine you've woken up in a forest with a hazy memory of having shagged a fairy you'd never met before . . . Feel free to draw on experience here." Tristan gave him a wicked grin.

Con might have known the Saturday afternoon session would end up with him getting talked into going to the evening's rehearsal up at the hall. Even though it was way ahead of schedule for anyone else but Tristan to see him trying to act. He only really agreed to it in the end because, well, if it was a total disaster, it wouldn't look good for Tristan, either, what with him being Con's acting coach. So maybe Tristan was telling the truth when he said Con was ready for it?

He hoped.

Con had a feeling Tristan might've been talking to Heather behind his back, though, seeing as the first scene she wanted to go through that night was the one where Bottom wakes up in the forest.

"Yeah, we did that one this afternoon." Con bit his bottom lip and winced at its soreness. His stomach was tying itself in knots and all. Shit, could he even remember the words? Let alone be all profound, and poignant, and all them other words Tristan had been chucking around earlier?

Heather nodded. "Okay, let's hear it. Don't worry if you're not word perfect," she added, which Con supposed was meant to reassure him but just made him feel even *less* confident. Like she wasn't expecting much from him.

He took a deep breath and lay down on the floor, pillowing his head on his arms. Right. He could do this. What was the first thing? Yeah, that was it. He was Nick Bottom, and the last time he'd been awake, he'd been half donkey. He let out a loud, hee-hawing snore, and startled up and looked around. The others were laughing, which made him feel a bit better. "'When my cue comes, call me, and I will answer . . .'" Then he frowned, and looked all around the room, shading his eyes as if against the sun. He couldn't remember which of the others he was supposed to call for, so just called for all of them in turn. He knew the next bit. "'God's my life, stolen hence, and left me asleep!'"

"Okay, gonna stop you there," Heather interrupted. "When you're calling for the others—nice improv, by the way—I'd like to see you moving around the stage a bit more, yeah? Have a really good look, like you think they're hiding behind a tree or something."

Con nodded. "Want me to do that bit again?"

"No, carry on—but next time, yeah?"

Shit. Straight on with the hard part. Con took a moment to pull the character back around him, like a warm coat on a winter's day. "'I have had,'" he began slowly, "'a most rare vision. I have had a dream'"—he nodded to himself, then looked straight up at the audience—"'past the wit of man to say what dream it was: man is but an ass, if he go about to expound this dream.'"

He frowned and rubbed his face, imagining his skin felt strangely smooth, instead of a bit bristly with five-o'clock shadow. "'Methought I was—'" He shook his head firmly. "'There is no man can tell what. Methought I was,'" he tried again, gesturing, like Tristan had said, to where the ass's ears would have been in his previous scene—"'and methought I had . . .'" This time, the gesture was downwards, by his crotch because, well, if he was going to get an ass's head, he might have got something else at the same time, mightn't he? It'd certainly explain why Titania was so bloody fond of him.

There was a burst of laughter, thank God. Con had thought that bit up himself while he was having his tea, and he hadn't been sure they'd get the joke. "'—but man is but a patched fool, if he will offer to say what methought I had,'" he went on, and managed to get to the end of the speech without forgetting the rest of his lines. The gestures Tristan had showed him really helped—made the words seem more natural, somehow.

When he got to the end and smiled at his audience, still in character, he wasn't prepared for the burst of applause he got. Course, Tristan was clapping the loudest, but Heather wasn't far behind.

"Oh my God, that was brilliant!" she squealed. "I *knew* you could do it. I knew it!"

"Yeah, good stuff, mate," Chris added, and everyone else was nodding and stuff.

Con just stood there, gobsmacked. The most he'd hoped for was that they'd think he was all right. It was like . . . Shit, he couldn't even *think* of anything that was like this. Maybe that one time he'd been playing football at school and managed to score a goal more or less by accident—he'd never really been quick enough on his feet to be good at team sports.

No wonder Tristan loved this.

The warm, fuzzy haze around him was still glowing as Heather got him to go through it again, this time moving around more, and even lasted through the rest of rehearsal while the others were doing their stuff.

CHAPTER NINETEEN
'TIS AN ILL COOK

Tristan felt rather as Professor Higgins must have upon Eliza's glorious debut in society. Or Victor Frankenstein, upon his creature's springing to independent life. He'd had no doubt he'd be able to coach Con into a passably successful mimicry of Tristan's portrayal of Bottom—but Con had actually started to put himself into the role. Was coming up with his own ideas.

Tristan's insides were a turbulent mélange of justifiable pride and inexplicable melancholy as he trooped to the pub with the rest of the cast. He'd congratulated Con on his performance already, of course. Con had looked like he couldn't believe his ears, which had added anger to the mess of emotions seething inside Tristan like an overambitious prop for the witches' scene in the Scottish play. No doubt it had been the teachers at that execrable state school he'd attended who'd made him feel he'd never amount to anything. Boiling in a cauldron, Tristan considered, would be entirely too good for them.

The company being too large for any one person to be expected to buy a general round, once arrived at the Three Lions they separated into smaller groups. Tristan found himself buying drinks for Con, Heather, and Chris, who immediately detached themselves to join Rob and Sean in the corner. They were seated at a large table, no doubt thoughtfully chosen to allow the others to join them.

Con accompanied Tristan to the bar. "That was amazing," he said as they waited for their order to be filled. "I never thought they'd go for it that much. I mean, I know half of it's probably just them being supportive—"

"Bite your tongue." Tristan was determined to nip such unwarranted modesty in the bud. "Supportive has nothing to do with it. Your performance was a tour de force."

"Yeah? Nah." Con shook his head, still smiling in a glorious, joyful way that was entirely too distracting. "I mean, it's good of you to say so—but anyway, if I was any good at all, it's all down to you."

"Poppycock. Whether you like it or not, you're a natural at this."

"It's like . . ." Con's brow furrowed. "You know when you were telling me how much you loved acting? I mean, I *sort* of got it—but now I *really* get it. It's just . . . I dunno how you're giving it up."

Something inside Tristan twisted so hard it hurt. How in God's name *was* he going to give all this up? He was inordinately grateful that the barmaid chose that moment to place the last of the drinks on the bar and name her price, saving him from having to answer.

Taking two of the glasses and leaving the other two to Con, Tristan led the way over to the table and took the seat next to Rob. Sean was eating a packet of pork scratchings and offered them round once the others had sat down. Tristan politely declined the revolting snack—really, how could anyone eat something described as *scratchings*?

Con, who was seated on Tristan's left, frowned, although he'd followed Tristan's example and refused likewise. "I thought you didn't keep kosher?"

Interesting. Tristan was a little surprised to hear the phrase *keep kosher* falling so naturally from Con's lips. Perhaps someone had been doing some research?

Very interesting.

"You're Jewish?" Rob asked before Tristan could say anything.

"Yes, what of it?" It came out perhaps a tad defensive, but then there *had* been something about Rob's tone that implied there was more coming.

"Just . . . I wonder you're so fond of Shakespeare, then. He can be read as anti-Semitic."

Oh, *that* old chestnut. Tristan rolled his eyes. "Opinions vary; Marlowe was worse; Shakespeare probably never met a Jew in his life. Et cetera, et cetera. Do you also ask every female actor how she can bear to take a part written by a man who penned *The Taming of the Shrew*?"

Rob laughed. "A fair point. Heather, do you have anything to say on the matter?"

"Yeah, and what I have to say is, I'm knackered, and I just want a nice quiet drink without a discussion on whether a bloke who died five hundred years ago had modern attitudes or not. Cheers, Tris," Heather added with a smile in his direction, raising her bottle of Beck's.

Tris? "I'm quite certain I never agreed to be truncated like that," Tristan muttered, low enough that she probably wouldn't hear him.

Rob shrugged. "It just seems to be something that happens around here," he whispered back. "Best not to make a fuss, or you'll wake up one morning and find you've been christened something even worse."

Tristan raised an eyebrow. "What? Jew-boy? Kike? Yid? I'm assuming, given present company, any homophobic epithets would be avoided."

Rob stared at him. "I was thinking 'Goldie,' actually, for your surname, but to each his own."

Ah. "Hm. Goldie wouldn't be so bad, actually. I'm a Cambridge man myself, so being named after the university's second boat would be quite respectable—after all, even their reserve rowing eight has to be a damn fine crew." Tristan smiled as a wicked thought hit him. "Plus, Goldie regularly has eight strapping young men at the peak of physical fitness pumping away inside her."

Rob blinked several times, rapidly. Tristan hoped he wasn't experiencing a petit mal. Still, in for a penny . . . "And of course, one mustn't forget the cox."

"Oi, you," Sean put in, edging his stool around the table a tad so he could fling an arm around Rob's waist. "No flirting with my bloke."

Con, Tristan was *very* interested to note, was frowning. "Flirting? *Moi*?" Tristan asked rhetorically, hand on heart. "We were having a serious discussion about sport."

"Oh yeah?"

"Actually, yes," Rob said, smiling rather adorably at Sean. "Well, technically about sport, anyway. But perhaps not entirely *serious*."

"Oi, you lot, budge up." The other rude mechanicals had arrived en masse, each clutching a pint. For a moment, Con seemed frozen in indecision—*Which way to go?* Tristan imagined him thinking.

To the safety of Sean, or the temptation that is Tristan? Then he shifted his chair around so far Tristan-wards that when he stopped, their thighs were pressed up against one another.

The surge of triumph in his breast, Tristan had anticipated. The frisson of yearning desire—or at least, the overwhelming strength of it—he had not. He was utterly, painfully aware of every inch of Con which touched him. All the more so, perhaps, because he was in no position to do anything about it.

Tristan cleared his throat and turned to his unwitting tormentor, feeling a desperate need for distraction. "I've been meaning to ask, have you seen anything more of our retired Romeo?"

Con appeared startled. "What— Oh, you mean Alf? Yeah, I went up to his on Friday, just to check he was okay."

"And was he?"

"Yeah—well, you know. Still a bit down about Miss Wellbeck not wanting to talk to him."

Hah. Spinster of this parish. Tristan had known it. "I've been thinking about this. I wonder if an approach by a disinterested third party might work?"

Con gave him a suspicious look. "You mean you, don't you? Why would she wanna talk to someone she doesn't know from Adam?"

"Because, dear boy, she clearly has some painful associations with your aged acquaintance. Something must have happened between them."

"That's the whole point, though. Alf reckoned *nothing* ever happened between them. He knew her when she was a little girl and my grandad was living with them, but when they grew up she wouldn't even speak to him."

Tristan frowned. "And the reason for this?"

"Alf reckoned it was cos him and Bill used to tease her when she was little."

"And she's borne the grudge for the last seventy years? A little extreme, one would think. What on earth did they do to her?"

Con shrugged. "Nothing *that* bad. But she was definitely upset about something when I saw her."

"Oi, who's upset?" Heather leaned over the table.

"I am," Tristan lied easily. "Devastated. All the time I've spent learning my new lines, and you didn't call upon me tonight for a single word."

"Well, 'scuse me for thinking you might want a bit of time to learn a whole new part."

"*Moi*? In the matter of learning lines I, dear child, am swifter than arrow from the Tartar's bow. I'll put a girdle round about the earth in forty minutes—"

Heather appeared unimpressed. "That's two different speeches, you know. And who are you calling *child*? If you're old enough to be my dad, you're hiding it well. Had some work done, have you?"

Tristan narrowed his eyes. "Con, dear boy, remind me why I'm doing this woman a favour by appearing in her wretched play?"

"Uh..."

Heather interrupted with a grin. "Oh, we *all* know why you're doing it. 'Nother drink?"

She swept off to the bar, leaving Tristan more than a little discomfited. But then Sean chipped in with a snippet of local news, and conversation remained on safer ground until closing time.

Although they all trooped out of the pub together—minus a few of the older Sham-Drams who had already fallen by the wayside—Tristan contrived to be alone with Con as they walked the short way down the high street before their paths would diverge. They'd had a triumphant rehearsal followed by an hour and a half sitting *very* close indeed. It was a Saturday night, and they were pleasantly mellowed by several drinks. The iron, he judged, was as hot as he could make it. Time to strike. "I, ah, wondered," he said, unwonted nerves swirling in his stomach, "if you'd like to come to my place for a coffee?"

Con stilled, and it was a long moment before he answered, one hand rubbing the back of his neck. "Nah, thanks, but I, well, it's been a long day, you know? Think I'd better get to be—to sleep."

"It *is* Sunday tomorrow," Tristan coaxed without much hope. The butterflies in his stomach had apparently been constructed out of modelling clay, judging from the way they were now coalescing into one leaden mass.

"Yeah, but... You know. I'd better go."

No, thought Tristan as he trudged home alone, more than a tad miffed. He didn't know at *all*. He'd thought they'd been getting on well. And what was all that business about pressing so close to Tristan when they were in the pub? If that wasn't a come-on, he didn't know what was. Yes, granted, they'd been tight for space, but *still*.

Con, Tristan reflected, needed to sort out once and for all these mixed signals he was sending.

CHAPTER TWENTY
LIFE'S FITFUL FEVER

It was a good thing Con didn't have anything to get up for on Sunday morning, he thought, staring at his darkened ceiling. He reckoned it was going to take him a bloody long time to get to sleep tonight. He was still buzzed from people actually liking how he'd played Bottom.

And yeah, all right, he was buzzed from being in the pub after too. Sitting so close to Tristan had been torture—Christ, they'd been pressed together like sardines. Con had been fighting a stiffy half the time. Thank God he'd got his round in early and hadn't had to stand up again until the end, when he could hold his jacket in front of him to hide the evidence.

He'd been so close to saying yes when Tristan had asked him round for a coffee. What with the buzz, and the beer, and, well, *Tristan*, Con was pretty sure it wouldn't have been coffee he'd have got if he'd given in and gone. And, God, yeah, he'd wanted it . . . Even now he was half-tempted to sling his clothes back on and jog round to Valley Crescent. It'd only been half an hour. Tristan would almost certainly be up.

Con bloody well was.

And it'd be good, he knew it would be. He knew Tristan well enough now, trusted him enough, that it'd work between them. God, would it really be such a bad idea? They both fancied each other—why not just give in and get it out of their systems?

Except . . . it wouldn't work like that, would it? For Tristan, maybe—probably—but not for Con. Sod it, he was half in love with the bastard already, if he was honest. Sleeping with him would just make it so much worse when Tristan jetted off to his new life in New York. Face it, once he was out there with his new job and his new friends, how likely was he to even think of Con? Even if he went out with the best of intentions, which . . . which wasn't all that likely, was it? *"Not after your work-roughened hand in marriage,"* he'd said.

Shit. It hurt, thinking about that.

Con needed to remember that hurt.

God, though, if they did sleep together, it'd be bloody amazing. Con could just imagine Tristan flashing him that wicked, Puckish smile of his before dropping to his knees . . .

Oh, *bloody* hell. Con was going to have to jerk off again.

Twenty minutes later, with one cause of sleeplessness sorted, Con was still wide-awake and staring at the ceiling. Now he'd got rid of one problem, all the rest were ganging up on his mind.

Like, was Heather right about Con needing to do something proper with his life? Needing to have plans for the future? He'd thought it was all bollocks when she'd said it, but now he was starting to wonder. He'd never really thought there was anything he could do apart from being an odd-job man—but then he'd thought there was no way he could be an actor, and that seemed to be turning out a hell of a lot better than he'd expected, didn't it?

Not that he was daft enough to think he could make a go of it as a career—for a start, he couldn't expect Tristan as an unpaid coach all his life—but it showed it might, just might be worth trying something else. Like getting his reading up to speed, or maybe even trying to get some qualifications? Despite what he'd told Heather, he'd always wished he could do a proper carpentry and joinery course, maybe get a diploma. Something that'd mean he'd be able to take on proper jobs, not just handyman stuff. But he'd checked online, and even practical courses like that had entry requirements. They didn't ask much, but you had to have passed a few GCSEs or the equivalent. And Con . . . hadn't. Maybe it was time he did something about that.

There'd be stuff starting at the local colleges in September. Evening classes, adult education, all that guff. He could ask them in the library if they could help him find something. Everyone kept saying there were resources available if you were dyslexic, and Con reckoned he was well overdue for his share.

And then there was Miss Wellbeck. After talking to Tristan, it did seem a bit weird that she'd still be pissed off with Alf for stuff that happened when they were kids.

Maybe Con should go round there again, on his own this time, and ask her.

In the end, though, it was Alf who Con went to see Sunday evening. He made sure it was after seven, cos he was *not* gonna invite himself to anyone's Sunday dinner. 'Specially as Alf might not be so pleased to see him anyway, this time. What with things going badly with Miss Wellbeck and, well, the whole *gay* thing. Con wasn't ashamed of being gay, but he knew it was harder for old folks to accept, what with them growing up when it was still illegal and all that. Then again, half the "larks" Alf had told him about getting up to during his National Service had been pretty dodgy in the eyes of the law.

But, anyway, Con still had to take a deep breath before knocking on Alf's door.

He needn't have worried. Alf's wrinkled face still broke into a smile when he saw who it was. Then he frowned and wagged a stern finger. "You're late. Here I was with a whole chicken to myself, and where were you? Never mind, never mind. Come on in and I'll cut you some meat off the carcass." He turned and shuffled back into the kitchen.

"Uh . . . I've already eaten. Sorry," Con said, following him.

"Not to worry. I'll wrap it up for you. You can make one of your pies. How about that? My wife always used to make pies from the Sunday roast, but I'm afraid I never learned how."

Con grinned. He could bring it round and share it one night. "That'd be great." He sat at the kitchen table while Alf stripped the bird of way more meat than he'd have thought it possible to get off one small chicken. Con snaffled a couple of bits while he was at it, because, well, it smelt bloody good and it'd been at least an hour since tea. Well, half an hour, definitely.

Neither of them mentioned Tristan—or Miss Wellbeck, for that matter—but Alf *did* tell him about a couple of lads he'd known in the army who'd used to sneak into each other's bunks after lights out and had almost got caught more than once when they'd had surprise inspections.

It was a good evening.

CHAPTER TWENTY-ONE
FORTUNE'S FOOL

By Sunday afternoon, Tristan had come to a momentous decision. It had become clear to him that his homophobic neighbour was *not* a fit person to be looking after Nanna Geary's cat. He would only lead her into bad habits and indeed quite probably already had. Action needed to be taken.

Not least because that *bloody* frog was back.

Tristan had developed a theory, while nervously scanning the kitchen for other unwelcome invaders as he stirred milk into his tea. Meggie, or so his theory went, was only leaving these little living or, as it might be, not-so-living billets-doux because she was unsure of her welcome. She was trying—misguidedly, but then she *was* only a cat, so one could hardly blame her—to ensure that, when she finally judged it safe to introduce herself to Tristan, he would already be predisposed to like her.

He therefore needed to assure her of his lack of enmity. And then, please God, the stream of visitors of the rodent, amphibian, and for all he knew (his knowledge of biology was, it must be admitted, a tad sketchy) every other genus and phylum of the animal kingdom, would cease.

To that end, he had dug deep in Nanna Geary's store cupboard and located a tin of rather horrid-looking, reeking chunks of unidentifiable meat, which he had painstakingly forked out into a bowl marked *Cat*. He then placed the bowl upon the kitchen floor, where he would no doubt tread in it within the hour and spend the rest of the day stinking of offal.

But he was *trying*, damn it.

What else did cats like? Judging by Meggie the Original and Best, they liked sunny spots, warm laps, and sleeping. Preferably all at the same time. Trouble was, he could hardly spend his life sitting in the sun in hopes the cat would magically appear and jump up for a snooze.

Also, Tristan remembered more hopefully, chicken breast and tuna fish. Right. Those went straight on the mental shopping list.

Along with air freshener. Hmm. Perhaps he should prop open the cat flap? That would serve the dual purpose of sending Meggie a welcome message *and* ventilating the kitchen. Initial efforts using pencils tied together with string were not, alas, successful. Of course, Tristan mused, Con could probably knock something up in a jiffy. Perhaps he should call him . . .?

No, no. That way madness lay. Well, extreme frustration at the very least, which no doubt would turn into madness given half a chance. Extended contemplation of Con's many fine physical attributes with no release in sight could *not* be good for a man. And, damn it, now he needed a distraction.

Tristan sat down with his book to read through Puck's speeches once more, but even the words of the Bard could hold him only so long. Huffing with annoyance, he opened up his laptop and called Amanda.

She was already online, which struck Tristan as a trifle sad— surely it was high time she'd got herself an actual life out there? Tristan thought about mentioning it to her, but she wasn't looking in the most receptive of moods, so he decided discretion would be the better part of not getting his head snapped off.

"You'll be happy to hear your birthday present is even now in the ever-capable hands of the Royal Mail," he led with instead.

Amanda did not appear mollified. "You said that last time we spoke. Am I to infer it's actually true this time?"

Oops. "I might simply have forgotten I'd told you, darling."

"Occam's razor dictates otherwise, *darling*. So what have you got me?" For the first time, she showed some animation.

"A surprise, naturally. Get back upon your monument, patience."

Amanda pouted. "You're no fun."

"Au contraire. I am the very definition of fun. You'll find me in the abridged Oxford Dictionary, nestling between *fuck* and *fundament*."

"Oh?" She seemed to perk up a tad. "Is that what your extremely rude mechanical tells you? Come on, darling, if you want me to pay up, you'll have to provide all the juicy details. In fact, I should probably demand pictures as proof you've won the bet."

Tristan deflated. "He's proving surprisingly resistant—"

"Oh, for goodness' sake. How long do you *need* to seduce one village idiot?"

"I don't know," Tristan replied, his temper rising. "How long do you suppose it'll be before you take some notice of what I've been telling you and *stop calling him that*?"

"My, we *are* touchy, aren't we? Don't tell me you've developed tender feelings for the oaf."

Tristan shut up his laptop with a snap. Out of the corner of his eye, he caught a flash of movement—as, say, of a cat that had nervously crept in to say hello and fled, startled, at the noise.

Damn it, damn it, *damn* it. Slings and arrows of outrageous fortune? Tristan was besieged by the entire might of the US bloody army. And as a distraction from thoughts of Con, the call to Amanda had been positively counterproductive.

Had he developed tender feelings for Con?

That would be ridiculous. He'd only known the man a matter of weeks—and would be leaving the country in a matter of months. Sudden fear pierced him. *Was* it still months? Yes, yes, he had over two months to go. Relief trickled over Tristan like a lukewarm shower in indifferent digs. God. Two months was *nothing*.

All the more reason to enjoy what little time he had left.

Con's next rehearsal with him was scheduled for Monday morning, but suddenly that seemed far too long to wait. Tristan glanced at Nanna Geary's clock. Just past seven. Was that too early for a Sunday evening visit? Trouble was, if he left it much longer, it'd be too late. No, now was the time. Tristan checked his appearance. Hmm. Jeans. Too casual?

No, that was ridiculous. Con would prefer casual. And, hopefully, appreciate the way they fit around Tristan's arse. Jeans it was. And the shirt? It was a faded Edinburgh fringe T-shirt from three years ago. Casual, yes, but possibly not the most flattering garment. Tristan raced upstairs to exchange it for a plain black one.

Much better.

Tristan strolled through the village to Con's flat and pressed on the buzzer. And waited.

Nothing.

He pressed again.

After a long moment, a voice came through the intercom. "Are you after number 6a?"

"Yes," Tristan admitted cautiously.

"Think he's out, dear."

And once again, fortune vomited on Tristan's eiderdown. Of course Con was out. Of *course*. Because unlike Tristan, Con actually had a life here, damn it. He was probably out carousing with Heather and Sean and no doubt every single other attractive young person of the village. Probably of the *county*.

Damn it.

Tristan trudged home, his mood as black as his shirt.

Might as well get an early night.

Monday morning, Tristan was feeling a lot more sanguine. For a start, he'd just poked his head out of his bedroom window and seen Con ambling down the street. Beaming, Tristan checked his clothes—present, good—and scurried downstairs to fling wide the door.

"All right?" Con said, his voice equally cheerful.

This boded well. This boded *very* well. And at ten o'clock in the morning, if called upon for some extracurricular activities, Con could hardly plead the lateness of the hour.

"Come in, come in," Tristan urged him genially. "Tea? Coffee? Pound of flesh?"

"Nah, I'm good, thanks. We can just get straight down to it, if you like."

Tristan reminded his libido sternly that *it*, in Con's mind at least, undoubtedly referred to rehearsing. "Oh, no hurry," he purred. "I thought we could have a little chat first."

"About what?"

"About . . . Well." Damn it. Tristan cudgelled his brain, out of which all thought had fled like a classically educated young lady pursued by a centaur. "Did I ever tell you how I got into acting?" he asked with sudden inspiration.

"Uh ... no."

"*Well*. It was quite by chance, as a matter of fact. I was approached—much as has happened here, in fact—to take over a role at the last minute when the actor playing it was sent down."

"Sent down where?"

"God, I don't know. Ah—I see what you're getting at. No, this was in my Cambridge days. Getting *sent down* meant expulsion. He was a chemistry student, and, shall we say, a little too interested in the commercial opportunities presented by his subject. Anyway, he was supposed to be playing Malvolio in *Twelfth Night*, which happened to be a play I'd studied—and, well, to cut a long story short, I was asked to do it instead. I believe alcohol may have been involved."

"Let me guess—instant success?"

"Unmitigated disaster. It was an open-air production, in the Master's Garden at Clare. And nobody had thought anything of the fact that Trinity had their May Ball the same night. Except that the music from the band *entirely* drowned out the dialogue for the whole of the first half." Tristan paused for effect. "And then in the second half, the fireworks started. Oh, the audience applauded politely enough at the end, but it was quite plain none of them had had the first idea what had been going on." He grinned.

Con smiled back.

A curious fluttering sensation arose in Tristan's breast. "Are you familiar with the play?" he asked quickly.

"Nah—but Malvolio's the hero, yeah?"

"God, no. A thousand times no. He's a steward with delusions of grandeur who is duped and humiliated in the course of the play."

Con frowned, but a half smile still played upon his lips. "And ... that's what made you want to be an actor?"

"But of course! He's ..." Tristan stalled, neither words nor gestures sufficient to explain, in a few words, the joy of playing a character who excites both ridicule and sympathy. "We'll find a reputable production, and I'll take you to see it," he decided. "We're only twenty-five miles from London; there *must* be one that's easily accessible this summer."

"Yeah? That'd be ... Yeah. We should do that."

Con's face was aglow as he leaned unconsciously towards Tristan. Now was the time. The iron was hot; the sun, shining. Tristan opened his mouth to say the words that would make Con his.

"So, rehearsal," he was appalled to find himself saying. "I thought we'd go back to the scenes with Titania. How's your singing?"

Con looked supremely uncomfortable. "Dunno. Never really done any."

"Excellent. Just remember, this is *supposed* to sound bad." Tristan took a moment to berate himself for his epic failure of nerve, then another to breathe in the character of Nick Bottom. A puffed-up idiot who utterly failed to live up to his own expectations.

No, that wouldn't be too far a stretch of his abilities right now. Tristan began singing in a nasal monotone, clapping his hands to the beat.

"'The ousel cock so black of hue,

"'With orange-tawny bill,

"'The throstle with his note so true,

"'The wren with little quill.'" He broke off for a moment, a thought striking. "You *could* go for the laughs with *cock* and *little quill*, but remember you'll be in full ass's regalia then, so any subtle expressions are likely to be lost." Tristan frowned. He never *had* had that conversation with Heather over Bottom's costume. "Do we know yet what you're going to have in the way of headgear? We should find out sooner rather than later."

"Yeah. It's just gonna be this sort of hood thing—Hev reckoned it'd be funnier. And, well, cheaper than a full ass's head."

Tristan nodded. "No, that's good—we could work with either, but it does make a difference. How about a tail?"

Con blinked. "Dunno. Is that in the play? I thought it was just his head that got changed."

"Oh, you mustn't underestimate the efficacy of a tail. One can do all *sorts* of things with a tail." Remembering his goal, Tristan smiled flirtatiously and added a little of a leer for good measure.

Con, predictably, flushed.

"Ah, well. Onwards and *tup*wards, as the saying goes." Con was frowning, but Tristan ignored it. "You, dear boy, are about to be seduced by a fairy. Are you ready?"

"Uh..."

"I'll be the fairy. 'Come, sit thee down upon this flowery bed.'" Tristan patted the sofa impatiently until Con perched upon the edge like a very large, very nervous bird preparing to take flight. Beaming, Tristan continued with both words and actions. "'While I thy amiable cheeks do coy, and stick musk-roses in thy sleek smooth head, and kiss thy fair large ears, my gentle joy.'"

Con swallowed audibly. "Uh, that was my real ear you just kissed."

"Well, of course it was. You're not wearing any false ones right now."

"Yeah, but ... shouldn't you, you know, pretend?"

"Do remind me which of us is the professional actor here, won't you? I seem to have forgotten. Actually, I think it would be better if you put your head in my lap instead of just sitting next to me. This isn't the nineteen thirties; neither of us is required to keep one foot on the floor."

Con's head noticeably failed to move lapwards. "Shouldn't we be talking about this with Linda? She's the one who's actually playing Titania. I mean, she might get a bit pissed off with me if we're rehearsing the scene and all of a sudden I've got my face in her crotch."

Not having met Linda yet, Tristan couldn't comment on her in particular, but he could damn well pass judgement on generalities. "You really have no idea of your own allure, do you? Trust me, dear boy, there are very few people around who would object to your face coming into contact with any portion of their anatomy." Tristan cocked his head. "Well, perhaps my neighbour over there. He seems to get a little hot under the collar about anything *gay*."

"Mr. Onslow at number twenty? He's always been all right with me."

"Well, *flamboyant* or, for that matter, *camp* are the last words anyone would use to describe you. Quite possibly he hasn't noticed your rampant homosexuality." Tristan leaned towards Con and lowered his voice in both volume and pitch. "Trust me, though; *I've* noticed. Now. Head; lap."

Con scowled and resolutely failed to move. "'Where's Peaseblossom?'" he ground out with no regard to character while delivering the line.

Tristan ignored it and smiled brightly. "I can be Peaseblossom, if you like. Just put your head down on that cushion. There, that's it." He leaned over, allowing a sultry look to slink into his eyes. "Now, where's that itch that needs scratching?"

Con stood up abruptly, his face red. "Look, you gotta stop this, all right?" His voice was hoarse but nevertheless ominously earnest.

Tristan's stomach took on a sudden whim to visit his socks. "I thought you were enjoying our little acting classes?"

"Not the acting. The . . . the other stuff. All that . . . you know. Suggestive stuff. You gotta stop it. I told you before, I'm not interested."

Tristan forced a laugh. It sounded painfully hollow, as if uttered by a corpse in a cathedral crypt. "Oh, that? Dear boy, you didn't really think I was *serious*, did you?"

Con blinked. "Oh."

"I do apologise if I've offended your rustic sensibilities. I shall try to be a little more innocent in my amusements in future. Don't worry, your rough-hewn virtue is *entirely* safe in my hands." Ashes. That was the taste in Tristan's mouth. He laughed again, more lightly this time. There, that was better. Still haunting a cathedral, but at least above ground. "But do recall the Bard's comedy is *supposed* to be bawdy."

"Oh," Con said again. "Yeah. Right." His stance, which a moment ago had been that of a gazelle about to flee from a lion, now took on the aspect of a gazelle that had just realised said lion was, in fact, merely a trick of the light upon a tuffet of grass.

Tristan smiled—a good smile, a thoroughly convincing one. He'd practised it in the mirror many times so was quite certain of that. "Shall we continue?"

"Um." Con swallowed. "Think . . . think I'd better go. Gotta job," he added unconvincingly, the quick rub to the nose merely the perjured icing on the forsworn cake. "I'll, um. Give you a call."

CHAPTER TWENTY-TWO
STRANGE BEDFELLOWS

Con barely knew which way he was walking as he left Tristan's house. Stupid, fucking *idiot*. Course Tristan wasn't serious. Why the sodding hell would he be? They'd had that conversation already, hadn't they, about Tristan fancying him—but he hadn't, had he? He'd just been horny, that was all. Con had just been, well, *there*. Tristan had even admitted it. He'd *said* Con wasn't in his league—well, he'd said it politer and posher than that, but it meant the same thing.

God, Tristan must think Con was just like Nick Bottom—thinking he was God's gift to men, women, and fucking fairies. Why the sodding hell couldn't Con have kept his stupid, big mouth shut? He could have played along with the flirting, it wouldn't have killed him. Yeah, so it was awkward and uncomfortable, and made him *want* stuff he knew he couldn't have—so what? Con was a big boy. He ought to be able to handle it.

It was just . . . Con couldn't stop thinking about the way Tristan's face lit up when he talked about things he really cared about. The way he waved his hands all over the shop while he talked, and his face was like . . . like one of those flip books Gran had helped Con make when he was a kid, where you drew a little stick figure on the corner of each page and then flipped it quick so it looked like he was running . . .

"Con?"

Startled, Con looked up, blinking back something in his eye. "Oh—Mr. Onslow. You all right?"

"Fine, fine. Glad I caught you, actually." He frowned. "Have you just been at Mrs. Geary's?"

"Uh, yeah."

The frown deepened. "Hmm. There's something very *odd* about that young man. He's not at all what I was expecting. I mean to say, I've personally got nothing against homosexuals—nothing at all. I believe one of my great-uncles was what used to be called a confirmed bachelor, although of course such things were never really talked about—but it does seem a little distasteful the way he seems determined to *flaunt* it."

Con stared. Words weren't exactly the thing he was good at even at the best of times, and right now the only ones he could think of were the sort Gran would have given him a clip round the ear for saying in public. He wanted to punch the bastard on his ugly, prejudiced nose. Course, Gran wouldn't have liked him doing that either.

"Dunno what you mean," was all he ended up saying roughly as he pushed past Mr. Onslow and legged it up the road.

"But I wanted you to . . ." Con didn't hear the rest. He was round the corner and jogging past the village hall before he slowed down again, sweating a bit in the hot sun. God, Tristan had been right about that bastard. Not got a problem with homosexuals? No, not at all, just as long as they didn't dare do anything *gay*. Why the bloody hell *shouldn't* Tristan flaunt who he was?

If he wasn't who he was, he wouldn't be Tristan, would he? Huh. Argue with that, Mr. Nothing-against-gays Onslow.

Con had calmed down a bit by the time he got back to his flat—he'd kept seeing people he knew on the high street, so he'd had to at least give them a smile and a wave. Five minutes in his living room, though, had him pretty much climbing the walls again. He needed something to *do*. Preferably somewhere a bit cooler, but he'd take what he could get. Maybe he should go and see Alf?

Yeah, right, because spending all your time hanging round some old bloke you'd only just met, simply because he'd once been mates with your grandad, was in no way sad. Trouble was, all Con's mates would be working.

He could . . . He could go and see Patrick in hospital, Con realised. They weren't really that close mates or anything, but the poor sod would probably be glad of the company. And at least Con wouldn't get teased about Tristan. Course, Patrick being a Sham-Drammer too,

Con probably wouldn't be able to get away without talking about Tristan at all, but still, it ought to be easy enough to change the subject.

Con hadn't thought they made you stay in hospital so long these days just for a broken leg, but Heather reckoned they were doing all kinds of surgery and stuff to the poor bastard. It sounded horrible. She'd been to visit already, taking a big card she'd got all the Sham-Drams to sign. Well, most of 'em anyway. Con was pretty sure she'd faked Roger's signature so she wouldn't have to go round to his house and deal with the git.

Con ought to take him something too. People liked stuff to read in hospital, didn't they? Con had never stayed in hospital himself, and Gran had never been one for reading even before her eyes got bad, but she'd liked having her old audio books with her, 'specially the last time she'd been in.

That time she hadn't come out again.

But yeah, he could remember other people in the ward having books and magazines and stuff. Trouble was, he didn't have a bloody clue what Patrick might like to read. Better be something general interest, then. And there was a lot less chance of Con making a really stupid choice if he stuck with the magazines, so he'd do that.

Nodding to himself, Con toed on his trainers and grabbed his keys.

God, he hated the disinfectant smell of hospitals. It always reminded him of Gran dying. That, and the weird metallic sounds you got, mixed up with the squeaking noise his trainers made on the floor. And the lighting, too bright like it was all one big kitchen. And the plastic chairs, and the way they always clashed with the green-painted walls with the scuff marks . . . Actually, come to think of it, Con hated pretty much everything about hospitals.

Still, it wasn't like he had to stay here, was it? He'd rung Heather before he set off to find out what ward Patrick was in—and to check he hadn't actually been allowed to go home already. She'd rattled off the ward and the visiting hours and said good-bye—maybe she wasn't supposed to take personal calls at work? Then again, it might just be her being focussed on the job. She was like that.

There were half a dozen beds in Patrick's ward, and the other five were all occupied by elderly people, so it wasn't hard to spot the man himself, even though he had his nose stuck in the *Daily Mail* and was looking a bit different than he usually did.

Con walked over to his bed. "Hey, mate, how you doing?"

Patrick looked up from his newspaper, both eyebrows raised, which made Con feel a bit awkward. Maybe they weren't good enough mates for Con to come and visit after all? Then he smiled, and Con felt a lot better. "Con! Good to see you."

He looked pale and a bit tired—there were dark circles under his eyes—and he hadn't shaved for a few days. And his hair was the worst mess Con had ever seen it. Without any product slicking it back or spiking it up, it looked lighter, sort of straw colour. Right now it looked like someone had dumped a haystack on top of Patrick's head.

"Yeah, personal grooming hasn't been top of the priorities list while I've been in here," Patrick said with a crooked smile, leaving Con feeling like a total bastard for being so bloody obvious about what he'd been thinking.

"Sorry. How's the leg?" Con nodded at the lump under the thin white blanket, mercifully hidden from view, as he sat down on the plastic chair by Patrick's bed.

"Ah, you know. Still there, at any rate. So how's it all going with the play? Hev told me you're in it now, which, seriously, that's great. Can't believe they managed to persuade you."

Con shrugged. "It's going okay. Oh—I brought you this," he said, reaching into the carrier bag he'd dumped on the floor and pulling out a copy of *Men's Health*.

Patrick laughed. "Oi, is that supposed to be a hint to stop lying around on my arse and get back into training? Harsh, mate. Harsh."

Shit. He'd *still* got it wrong, even sticking with the safe option. Con grimaced. "Didn't mean it like that. Sorry."

"Hey, no worries. Just having a laugh. Seriously, thanks, mate. It's a lot better than what my mum brought. Copy of *Alice in Wonderland*, can you believe it?" He laughed again at Con's puzzled frown. "It's a joke—s'posed to be, anyhow. She fell down a rabbit hole, remember?"

Con groaned. "That's terrible. And that's your mum?"

"Yeah, that's her. She's signed up on a couple of dating sites, and I read her profile. *Good sense of humour*, she put. I told her, 'No, Mum. No. You have a *terrible* sense of humour.'" He shook his head, a fond smile on his lips. "But she brought me a couple of thrillers too. Tell you something, I never thought I'd say this, but I'm getting so bloody sick of reading now I've got bugger all else to do all day."

"Oh—sorry." Con winced and held up the magazine he'd brought. "Want me to take it back with me?"

"Oi, no you bloody don't. Don't have to read it, do I? I can just look at the pictures. That one's got David Beckham in—he's well fit, long as he keeps his mouth shut." As Patrick made a grab for the mag, Con's expression must have given away his surprise. "What? Seriously, you thought I was straight?"

"Wasn't sure."

Patrick grinned. "What, cos I never tried it on with you? Hev told me you were getting over a bad breakup. Mind you, that must have been a year ago now, mustn't it? Could be time to get back on the horse, don't you reckon? Or is it true what Hev said about you and that Tristan geezer?"

Oh, *bloody* hell. "There's nothing going on between me and Tristan," Con said a bit sharper than he'd meant to.

Patrick held up both hands. "Oookay. Moving on now. They're gonna let me out of here in a few days—wanna take a gimp out for a drink?"

"Uh . . ." Caught by surprise, Con wasn't sure what to say. *Did* he want to go out for a drink with Patrick? As in, on a date, not just a drink with mates? Patrick was a good bloke, and he was definitely good-looking—'specially when he had his face on—but, well, he wasn't Con's type, was he?

Shit. He wasn't *Tristan*.

"Thanks, but, uh, I think I'm gonna be a bit busy for the next few months," Con said at last, when the silence got too excruciating. "You know, with the play and all. Seeing as you've decided to put your feet up," he added with a weak smile.

Patrick didn't look too upset at being turned down, thank God. "Yeah, yeah, you don't have to rub it in. So how's it going, anyway?

Go on, give us a line or two. You were there for most of my rehearsals, so you must know some of it by now."

"What, here?" Con looked around. They were in an open ward, with other patients and visitors in easy earshot if he stood up and started declaiming stuff.

Huh. Declaiming. That was one of Tristan's words.

"Well, if you do it anywhere else, it's not gonna do a lot for me, is it? Come on, let's hear something."

Shit. Well, if he was going to look stupid anyway . . . Con took a deep breath. "'An I may hide my face, let me play Thisby too.'" He remembered seeing Patrick cover his head with a shawl for this bit in rehearsals. Reckoning it'd be a bit rude to nick the bloke's blanket, he grabbed the copy of *Men's Health* instead, opened it, and held it over his head to make a sort of bonnet shape. "'I'll speak in a monstrous little voice. *Thisne, Thisne,*'" he went on squeakily. "'*Ah, Pyramus, lover dear! thy Thisby dear, and lady dear!*'"

Patrick burst out laughing. "That's brilliant! Shit, I'm gonna have some competition next time I go for a part, aren't I?"

"Nah, this is just a one-off," Con said uncomfortably, determinedly not looking around the ward to see if anyone was staring at him after that.

"No way, mate. You're good. You oughtta keep at it."

Con shook his head. "Couldn't do it without Tristan's help. And he's not gonna be here after September." Like he'd want to carry on spending time with Con after that anyway.

"Oh, that's it, is it? Yeah, don't go there, mate. Long-distance crap's a load of bollocks."

Con was feeling a bit weird when he left the hospital. And a bit annoyed with Heather, seeing as it sounded like she'd gone round telling every bloke in sight he was off the market for the foreseeable. Or maybe Patrick had just meant he hadn't fancied being a rebound thing? At any rate, he definitely seemed interested *now*, which was . . . weird. Good weird? Con wasn't sure.

No, that was bollocks, it was definitely good. Good for the ego, at any rate. Still, weird. Him and Patrick weren't in the same league looks-wise, and he'd never seemed all that into Con before. Maybe he'd just heard about Tristan supposedly fancying Con, and that had made Patrick take a second look himself?

Course, they did have the poor bastard on some pretty strong painkillers. Still, it was nice to know there were . . . options.

Maybe.

Trouble was, anytime he thought about being with anyone, all Con could think of was Tristan.

CHAPTER TWENTY-THREE
WHAT KIN

Oh God. Tristan was an *idiot*. He'd *known* Con was skittish—what on earth had possessed him to come on so bloody strong? And now he'd ruined everything. All he'd achieved with all the embarrassing display of over-the-top desperation had been a categorical statement that Con wasn't interested in him.

Not just that he didn't fancy a fling. This time, it had been a firm rejection of the idea that he could ever fancy *Tristan*. So much for striding forwards. He'd taken a giant bloody leap *backwards*.

God, he was an idiot. And it *hurt*, damn it. And not just his pride.

Oh, damn it all to hell. Amanda had been right, curse her for a clod of wayward marl. He *was* developing tender feelings for Con. No, scratch that. He *had* developed tender feelings for the man. Perhaps even lo—

The phone rang, its jangling tone administering the coup de grâce to his thoughts. Tristan ran to answer it. Suki. It must be Suki again.

It wasn't.

"Tristan?" The tone was peremptory; the voice, familiar.

"Father, how lovely to hear from you," Tristan lied smoothly enough, he hoped, to hide the jolt he'd just received to a stomach already roiling with disappointed hope. He was twenty-three years old; not a fourteen-year-old schoolboy who'd been caught behind the changing rooms after rugger with his hands in his teammate's trousers.

Actually, that had happened at fifteen and sixteen too, come to think of it, and whilst the sharpness of Father's ire had dulled with the repetition, his weariness shone more piercingly than ever. If indeed weariness could be said to shine. Perhaps it merely glowed?

An impatient clearing of the throat alerted Tristan to the fact that he'd missed something. "Sorry, Father, what did you say? Bit of a bad line on this end." He cast an eye around the kitchen for some cellophane to crackle to add a touch of verisimilitude to his claim, but alas, none was forthcoming.

"I need to know when you'll have that business of the house wrapped up."

"Well, certainly by October." Honestly, that was *ages* off.

"Hm. That's not going to be good enough, Tristan. I'm going to need you in New York by the end of August—early September at the very latest."

"*What*?" Tristan cringed as his voice cracked. "No, I'm sorry, Father, that's impossible. I have commitments—"

"You'll have to cancel them. There's a deal we've just confirmed that's going to put Goldsmith & Klein right on the front of the financial pages, and there's no point you turning up after the fact. I want you there."

"But you promised I'd have the summer!" Why did Tristan always devolve into a whining child around his father? *Why?*

Father might have been asking himself the same question. "Enough of that nonsense. I've been far too indulgent of you for far too long. It's time you grew up and started contributing."

Contributing? To what? The coffers of Goldsmith & Klein? Last Tristan had heard, they were bulging quite admirably without his help.

Then again, what had he been living off all his life before joining the Players? Perhaps Father had a point, and it was time to start putting something back.

Oh God.

Father was speaking again. "You've got until the end of August. Anything that's not settled by then can be put into the hands of our solicitors."

Tristan had a brief, unsettling vision of old Mr. Endicott donning horns and buckskin trousers to play Puck, and had to force down a hysterical giggle.

"Tristan? Are you still there?"

"Y-yes, Father."

"Good. That's settled, then. End of August. I'm relying on you, Tristan. Don't let me down." He hung up, the unspoken *again* echoing through the years of mutual incomprehension that lay between them.

Tristan slumped to Nanna Geary's kitchen floor, making sure to do it with grace and drama to obfuscate the fact that his knees were, in fact, a tad on the wobbly side. Everything was collapsing around him like a poorly anchored backdrop. Two months had dwindled into one, and that one month turned from *Dream* to nightmare. He'd have to tell Heather he couldn't play Puck. He'd have to tell Con he couldn't coach him to the end.

If the play would even, in the face of this latest setback, go on. No, how could it? Heather had called him her only hope. She'd have to cancel.

Tristan would have to let *everyone* down.

But at least there was one good thing—possibly—he could do before he left.

"Yes?"

An elderly lady less like Nanna Geary it was hard to imagine. Nanna Geary had exuded a sort of safe, solid competence, whereas Miss Wellbeck had a distinctly fragile air.

Tristan gave her his most trustworthy smile. "My name's Tristan Goldsmith. You don't know me but—"

"I'm sorry," she said, starting to close the door. "I don't buy anything at the doorstep."

"I'm not selling," Tristan said quickly. "I was just hoping you might be able to talk to me about life in the village during the war." Given her age, there was no need to specify which one. "I'm Jewish," he added, which as he'd hoped seemed to justify his interest, in her eyes.

"Oh. Well, I suppose you could . . . I shouldn't really let people in I don't know, though."

On impulse, Tristan pulled out his Equity card. It didn't have his picture on, but it did look vaguely official. "And I live at number twenty-two Valley Crescent," he added. "I don't suppose you knew Mrs. Geary, whom I inherited it from?"

Her anxious face cleared. "Oh—you're Alice's Tristan!"

Tristan blinked. Of course he'd been aware that Nanna Geary *had* a first name, and must even have used it at some point—say around seventy or eighty years ago when she'd been in pigtails, and ye gods, that wasn't an image that would leave him anytime soon—but to hear it bandied about like that was unnerving to say the least. "Ah, yes."

"Oh, you must come in, then. Alice was *so* proud of you, you know." She fluttered ahead of him into a tiny sitting room that faced out onto the children's playground behind the church. Faint shrieks from the throats of brightly clad toddlers filtered through the double-glazing. "I do love to watch them play," Miss Wellbeck added, proving she had at least some of her marbles. "I never married, you see. Do sit down. Would you like some tea? I always have a cup around this time of day."

"That would be lovely," Tristan said, hoping she was equal to the task. He was somewhat concerned that if she filled the kettle too full, she'd be in danger of buckling under its weight.

He sat upon the tiny sofa and occupied himself with looking around the room. As regarded furniture, it was a curious mix of the new and the old. Tristan imagined she'd previously inhabited a larger place and had, on retirement, been forced to quite literally downsize a fair number of her possessions. The overlarge armchair, which was where Miss Wellbeck liked to sit if the handily placed side table and the indentation in the seat were any guide, looked to be an old favourite, but the sofa had quite clearly been bought to fit the smaller living space and had an almost showroom-fresh air about its aggressively stuffed cushions.

Miss Wellbeck reappeared with a dainty tray, bearing tea in two china cups, milk in a jug and sugar in a bowl, which she placed carefully on the side table before sitting down. "Milk? Sugar?"

Tristan said *yes, please* to the one, and *no, thank you* to the other, and sat back with his cup and a smile.

"Now, what was it you wanted to talk about?" Miss Wellbeck asked. She didn't take sugar with her tea either. Nor were there any biscuits on offer—Tristan suspected she didn't have any in the house.

Or any other food, for that matter, from the size of her. "Oh yes, the War. Of course, I was only a little girl when that happened, and a lot of it passed me by. It didn't seem very real, you understand. We heard the news on the wireless, and of course we prayed every week for the young men who went off to fight. I do remember being very cross when there wasn't enough sugar to ice my birthday cake one year."

"Did you have older brothers and sisters?"

There was a pause. Tristan hadn't expected that to be a difficult question. He waited politely while Miss Wellbeck took a sip of tea, the cup rattling a little in its saucer.

She put it down on the side table and folded her hands in her lap before she looked at him once more. "No. There was only me. They wanted more, I think, but God decided otherwise."

There was something there. Tristan was *sure* of it. He backed off, all the better to execute a flanking manoeuvre. "I suppose living in the country, rationing wasn't too bad a problem, in general?"

"No, we always had meat on the table. And I was rather pleased, than otherwise, to have Mother cut down her old dresses for me. Made me feel so grown-up." She smiled. "Not that the boys thought so, of course. To them I was just a nuisance of a little girl."

The boys? It sounded oddly specific, the way she said it. But softly, softly . . . "Children's games must have been very different in those days."

"Oh yes. We had so much more imagination, I've always thought. Nowadays people just buy a child a toy or one of those electronic gadgets, but when you don't have much, you make up your own games." She dimpled. "To a fault, sometimes. I remember the boys getting into a great deal of trouble for some of the things they did."

And there it was again. Yes, Tristan was certain she had some very specific boys in mind. But it wouldn't do to be too direct. "Did boys *really* use to sneak into orchards to go apple-scrumping?" he asked artlessly. "One reads about it in old books, but it seems such an innocent crime these days."

"Oh, but you'd get a thrashing for it back then! And it wasn't just boys who did it, let me tell you." She gave him a mischievous look, and Tristan could suddenly see her as the girl she'd been. He'd be willing to bet she could wind the boys around her finger, once they'd reached an age to be susceptible to feminine wiles.

"Miss Wellbeck, I'm sure *you'd* never have done any such thing," he said with his most charming smile.

"Oh, but I did. I'm afraid Bill wasn't a very good influence on me," she said, her smile vanishing to leave a look of such sadness Tristan feared to prod even as he mentally punched the air.

But, damn it, what was he here for? "Bill?" he asked, as gently as he could.

She looked down at her folded hands for such a long time, Tristan began to fear she wouldn't answer. "So strange . . . I met Bill's grandson the other day, and I'm afraid I was terribly rude. It was the shock, you see. I suppose, after all this time, it shouldn't really matter—but you see, *I* never married."

Yes! This was the heart of it, Tristan was certain. "Bill was . . . your sweetheart?" he guessed aloud, keeping his tone soft.

She seemed to crumple. Alarmed, Tristan leapt to her side and took her tiny, cool hands in his. "I'm so sorry. I've upset you. There's no need to answer. Please don't try. Can I get you some more tea? A . . . a handkerchief?"

That seemed to animate her, at least. She pulled a tiny, lacy scrap from one sleeve and dabbed at her eyes, then put it to her nose and gave a delicate little blow. "No, I'm quite well. Silly of me, really. After all this time . . . No. Bill was . . . Bill was my brother. Half brother, I'm afraid. So you see, there could never have been anything between us."

A jolt shot through Tristan. Her *brother*? "Wasn't Bill the name of the baby your father found in the churchyard? Bill Izzard, named for a gravestone?"

She nodded and didn't seem surprised that he'd heard the story. Then again, it had probably been all over the district when she was a child. "Although of course it wasn't true at all, about finding him there. It was before my parents married. The mother was one of the women in the village. A married woman, but her husband was working away at the time. Father was a young man, just out of the curacy, and very handsome. Well, I always thought so."

And, apparently, she hadn't been the only one. "When did you find out about Bill being your brother? Was it when he stayed with you during the war?"

"Oh no. It wasn't until much later. He came back a few years after the end of the war, looking for work in the area, and asked if he might stay at the vicarage again, as my father had always been kind to him. He was quite disappointed to find Alf Smith was off doing his National Service at the time. They were such good friends as boys, you see. So Bill and I spent a good deal of time together."

It wasn't hard to read between the lines. "You must have been, what, fifteen? Sixteen?" She nodded. "Was Bill a good-looking man, like your father?"

"Oh, he was very handsome, but not at all like Father. His grandson has quite the look of him. I think that was why . . ." She trailed off, then looked up at him with a determined set to her jaw. "That was when Father confessed all to us, and . . . it was thought best that Bill should move away. I never saw him again, after that."

God, Tristan could see it now—the unacknowledged son caught stealing a kiss from the acknowledged daughter. The horror—the outburst—the terror of scandal. The tears, as the would-be incestuous couple were parted forever. "It must have been terrible," he said, stroking her hands once more, "to be parted from a brother you loved so much."

She nodded once. "Would you be so kind as to pour me another cup of tea? The pot's in the kitchen."

"Of course." Tristan scrambled to his feet and tried to think what on earth to do now. Should he mention he knew Con? Suggest bringing him round? He still hadn't come to a decision when he returned to the living room, cup in hand.

"Thank you, dear." She didn't take a sip of tea, seeming steadied by its mere presence in her hands. "You know, Alice would have been so pleased to know you've settled in the village. It's what she always wanted for you."

Tristan stilled, arrested in the very motion of applying bum to sofa. "It . . . is?"

"Oh yes," Miss Wellbeck went on, her expression happier now. "You know, some people were surprised when she got another cat at her age. But she always knew you'd look after Meggie for her." The dimples made a faint reappearance. "Now, I know you young people think old ladies don't know about such things, but I happen to know there's a young man in the village she had her eye on for you."

"There . . . is?"

"Oh yes. She wouldn't tell me who it was, but she left his number in her address book for you to find."

Tristan left Miss Wellbeck's flat feeling lower than a mouse's arse. To think he'd neglected the very animal it had been Nanna Geary's dying wish for him to look after. At least he'd *tried* to make amends, even if it *had* met with a singular lack of success.

He also had a new appreciation for Nanna Geary's deviousness. And a fierce desire to know just whose phone number he was supposed to ring. He knew very well the address book in question. It was a stiff, black, leather-bound monstrosity with a clasp. He hadn't even opened it, thinking it unlikely to contain anything of relevance to him.

God, he could have thrown it in the *dustbin*.

Looking neither right nor left—except when crossing the road, because dying at this juncture would be rather pointlessly ironic—he hurried home, where he opened the address book with a trembling hand. It couldn't be . . . Could it?

Yes. On a slip of paper pinned to the very first page—Nanna Geary had possibly been the last person on Earth to use pins to attach pieces of paper—was a note, carefully written in block capitals. *FOR ALL WORK CALL:*

There followed a number. One Tristan knew very well, and which he read now with a strong surge of emotion, yet with a total lack of surprise.

It was Con's number.

CHAPTER TWENTY-FOUR
WHAT FOOLS

Con was driving back to the village from a job when his phone rang. As he wasn't in a hurry and there was a convenient lay-by, he pulled over to answer it. When he saw it was Tristan, though, Con almost didn't bother. What was the point? Did he really want to feel even *worse*?

But he had to make the effort, didn't he? Had to get them back on, well, businesslike terms at least. They had a play to do.

"Yeah?" he answered cautiously.

"I've got some news for you. About Bill Izzard."

Okay, so *that* wasn't what he'd expected. "What do you mean?"

"Can you come here? I don't really want to tell you over the phone. Or I could come to your flat, of course."

"Uh . . . I'm out at the mo. I'll come to yours." The flat was in a right state at the moment anyway—that was the trouble with only having one room. Didn't take a lot of carelessness to turn it into a pigsty.

And, yeah, maybe Con had been a bit more careless than usual the last couple of days.

What the hell could Tristan have to tell him about Bill Izzard? Had he . . . what, found some old love letters between Grandad and Mrs. Geary? Or maybe Grandad had been her secret love child? Con tried to work out if it was possible—how old had Mrs. Geary even been?—but he couldn't do that and drive at the same time. Not if he didn't want to have an accident.

He found a parking spot a few doors down from Tristan's and jogged back up the road, hoping he wouldn't bump into Mr. Onslow again.

It was weird, knocking on Tristan's door after what had happened last time he'd been there. From the look of the bloke when he opened the door, Tristan felt it too. He seemed, well, smaller than he usually did, and sort of tense.

"I . . . ah . . . should apologise. For my behaviour last time you were here. And, well, certain things may have been said that shouldn't have."

Con swallowed. "'S all right." He didn't like seeing Tristan like this. Tristan was meant to be all confident and happy and stuff.

"There . . . Well. There may have been an element of sour grapes in— But, anyway, come in. Not really the sort of subject one wants to broach upon the doorstep, ahaha."

Okay, *now* Tristan was just being weird. "Uh, no," Con agreed cautiously, stepping inside, although he wasn't all that sure what the subject even *was*. Was Tristan talking about Bill Izzard? Or was he still on about all that business of, well, not actually fancying Con at all? Con swallowed. He *really* hoped it was about Bill Izzard.

"I went to see Miss Wellbeck," Tristan said abruptly, shifting from foot to foot in the middle of the room. Con had been about to sit on the sofa, but he froze at Tristan's words.

"Yeah?" he said after a moment, when Tristan didn't say anything more.

"She . . . I think she'd be ready to talk to you now. But there's something you should know." Tristan stopped again and looked Con in the eye, making him wish the bloke would bloody well get on with it. "Your grandfather," Tristan finally continued, "was her brother. Half brother. Illegitimate half brother."

Con did sit down then. "She told you that?"

Tristan nodded. "Apparently—and I'm reading very much between the lines here, but I think it's the truth—they became rather close in their late teens. Too close, if you get my drift. At least for that degree of consanguinity. It's actually quite a fascinating subject, genetic sexual attraction . . . But anyway, the vicar was forced, in something of a turnabout for the priesthood, to confess his sins. The lovers were parted, and that was the last poor Miss Wellbeck ever saw of Bill Izzard. She said you look very much like him, actually."

Tristan perched on the other end of the sofa, his legs drawn up and his arms around his knees. "All rather tragic. She never married after that."

"Grandad didn't either," Con said slowly. "I mean, yeah, he did, but not for years. He was forty or something when he married my gran. Only lived a couple of years after that."

Neither of them said anything for a bit. Con was just thinking how bloody sad life could be when Tristan spoke up again. "It's actually rather inspiring, in a melancholy way, isn't it?"

Con stared at him in surprise. "Inspiring?"

"Well, to think that two people could find a love so passionate, so all-encompassing, that even though they couldn't be together, they still forsook all others. For the rest of her life, in Miss Wellbeck's case, and for most of it, in your grandfather's." He smiled, but it looked sad. "I'm not sure if it gives me hope, or merely provides an impossible standard to live up to."

Uncertain, Con hesitated, then said it anyway. "Didn't think you cared about that sort of stuff."

"Love?" Tristan gave a gentle laugh. "'If you prick me, do I not bleed?'"

Con frowned. He'd heard that before—it'd been quoted on one of the websites he'd found on Jewish history, talking about Elizabethans getting their hate on—and he knew it was about Jewish people being the same as Christians. Except he had a feeling that wasn't how Tristan meant it. Wasn't Tristan just saying he had feelings, same as anyone else?

But then . . . "Why did you say all that stuff? Last time I was here. About . . . about all this flirting and stuff just being you having a laugh. Did you mean it?"

Tristan hugged his knees in tighter. It made Con want to put his arms around him, give him a proper hug. "It's all a touch moot, really, isn't it?" Tristan said at last, staring into the fireplace. "As my attentions were so unwelcome to you."

Con's mouth was dry. Tristan sounded so . . . so sad. So alone. And it was just *wrong*, and it wasn't fair. Not after everything Tristan had done for him—all the help with the acting, and, God, going to see Miss Wellbeck. He hadn't had to do any of that. And . . . and maybe he'd *said* he didn't care about Con, but if you looked at what he'd *done*... "What..." Con cleared his throat. "What if they weren't? You know. Unwelcome."

Tristan looked at him then. His eyes were huge and dark, with shadows underneath like he hadn't slept well last night. Con could sympathise with that. "They weren't?"

"No—well—it's just..." Con fought the urge to thump the arm of the sofa. Christ, when had *spoken* words started to fail him too? "If it's just sex, yeah, I don't wanna know, all right? But if it means something..."

Suddenly, Con had a lapful of Tristan.

"It means something," Tristan breathed, his hands cupping Con's face. "More than it should, for my sanity at least. Yes, it means something." And then his lips were on Con's.

Con was frozen. But only for a moment, thank God. Then he came to himself and kissed back, his arms wrapping around Tristan's slender body and pulling him close.

It felt like . . . It felt like that time he'd agreed to change old Mrs. Sealy's bathroom light fitting, which he didn't do, normally, cos you had to be safe with electrics, but she'd been so worried about *Mr.* Sealy falling down in the dark when he got up in the night to use the loo, which was a several-times-a-night thing, him having an eighty-three-year-old prostate, plus there was the risk he'd try to change the fitting himself, and fall off the chair and basically die, so Con had said he'd do it in the end, and she'd said *bless you*, and went to turn off the mains, except she'd flipped the wrong switch in the fuse box by mistake and Con had touched the live wire and then he'd fallen off the chair but being twenty-three and not eighty-three, he'd escaped with just a few bruises and a weird feeling right through his body for hours afterwards.

Yeah. It was something like that.

Only not.

And yeah, he knew Tristan was still going to be leaving at the end of September. He *knew* that. But, well, maybe it wouldn't have to end then? They could . . . They could work something out. So Patrick reckoned long-distance things didn't work—what made him the world expert on relationships? He hadn't even *had* a relationship since Con had known him. They could Skype and stuff, and . . . Or . . . Or maybe Con could even go over there with him, like Heather said? They could *do* this. If, well, they both felt strongly enough about each other—and Con *did*, he knew that now. What was the point in pretending he didn't?

And he was starting to hope Tristan felt the same.

Shit, they were too far apart. *Way* too far apart. Con tightened his arms around Tristan, who took the hint and shifted until he was kneeling astride Con's lap. Fuck, that felt good. So good. His tongue was in Tristan's mouth, and it tasted bloody gorgeous. Like cinnamon and like salt, but mostly like he really, *really* wanted to get naked. Preferably now. Or sooner. That would work.

Tristan was wearing a tight black T-shirt that made him look like sex on legs. That had *got* to go. Con pushed it up to his armpits and waited impatiently until Tristan broke the kiss and put his arms up. Yep, that T-shirt was history. Tristan's chest was golden-tan and completely hairless. Did he wax? Con didn't care. It was all good. He couldn't resist running his hands up and down those smooth pecs and watching those little brown nipples perk up.

"Tit for tat," Tristan said pointedly.

"Uh?" Con blinked.

"I mean, I've shown you mine, so you show me yours. Come on, off with it." He tugged ineffectually at Con's T-shirt until Con yanked it over his head.

"Mmm, Daddy Bear. This is *just right*," Tristan purred and buried both hands in Con's chest hair.

Con would probably have been embarrassed if he hadn't been so bloody turned on. He covered his confusion by shoving his hands down the back of Tristan's jeans. Well, trying to. "Bloody hell, did you spray these on?"

"No, but I'll be happy to peel them off for you." Tristan got off Con's lap and yanked open the fastenings, then stripped off his jeans in one smooth motion.

Con had been planning to ask if they'd taught him that in drama school, but he sort of got distracted by the fact Tristan hadn't been wearing any underwear. And his stiff cock was now bobbing only inches from Con's face.

It was long, thick—and circumcised. Con couldn't help letting out an "Oh" of surprise.

Tristan frowned. "What do you mean, *oh*? I'm fairly certain you've seen a penis before, so I take it you're referring to my lack of foreskin."

Con blushed. "Sorry—it's just, you said you weren't religious."

"I may not be devout, but I'm still Jewish."

"Right. Sorry. Um ... What's it like, being circumcised?"

"For God's sake, I was eight days old at the time! Forgive me for not taking notes."

Con tried to focus on what he'd asked. It wasn't easy, what with the seven or eight inches of distraction jigging about right in front of his nose, plus the way his own dick was jammed up uncomfortably against the zip in his jeans. "I mean, what's it like, not having a foreskin?"

"Oh. That. Well, pretty dreadful, actually." Tristan sighed.

Con looked up at his face in alarm. "Yeah?"

Tristan nodded sadly. "I don't suppose there's a day that goes by without me mourning my lack."

He'd have felt better if Tristan had just kicked him in the stomach. Why the bloody hell had Con been so fucking stupid as to ask something like that? "Shit. I'm sorry. It's really that bad?" He reached out to draw Tristan close.

Tristan gave an exaggerated eye roll. "No, of course it's bloody well not! *Honestly*. How would I mourn the lack of something I don't ever remember having in the first place?" He smirked, his erect dick still bobbing in Con's face. "And on a side note, were you aware that the latest edition of the Oxford English Dictionary managed to omit the word *gullible*?"

See, this was how Con knew he had it bad for Tristan—instead of feeling pissed off, he was just relieved the bloke wasn't unhappy like he'd been pretending. Con still stuck his middle finger up at him, though.

Then he grabbed the bastard by the arse and plunged his mouth down over Tristan's dick.

God, that tasted good. The explosion of salt when he tongued the head was even better. Tristan gasped, spurring Con on to suck him hard. Tristan's hands were on his head, alternately clenching in his hair and then releasing, as if worried they'd gone too far. Con pulled off. "I don't mind a bit of hair pulling, all right?"

Tristan looked well out of it. He blinked a few times, then shook his head. "I . . . This is . . . Damn it. Jeans. Off."

Con gave him a look. "Sure?" he said and got his lips around Tristan's dick again.

Tristan squeaked. "Damn it! I'm sure. I think."

Con pulled off slowly, ending with a swirl of his tongue that made Tristan whimper. "All right, then," he said, standing up. He couldn't do the dramatic flourish like Tristan could—*and* he was wearing underpants—so he made it slow instead, enjoying the half-starved look on Tristan's face as he stripped.

"Ye. *Gods*," Tristan breathed, when Con stood in front of him, naked as the day he was born. "'O! It is excellent to have a giant's . . . strength.'"

Uh? Con didn't bother asking, just grabbed Tristan with both hands and pulled their bodies together. Bloody hell, that was amazing. Tiny fireworks were going off everywhere their skin touched. Con's prick rubbed against Tristan's smooth, flat belly, and Tristan's was jabbing him in the hip. Con didn't know what to do next because fuck, it was *all* good. "What d'you wanna do?" he asked roughly, kneading Tristan's arse with both hands.

Tristan moaned. "Dyscalculia," he gasped. "Is it a problem?"

"Uh?"

"Because I would very much like to explore the possibilities of the number sixty-nine," Tristan finished.

"You know *your* problem?" Con asked, lifting Tristan bodily and depositing him on the sofa. "Too many words."

Tristan *oofed* in reply, and Con got himself into position, making sure he didn't accidentally crush his—fuck—his lover. Then he got his lips around Tristan's dick again.

"Oh God," Tristan gasped—and then there was heat and pressure on Con's prick, sending electric shocks up his spine and down into his balls.

God, it was almost too much already. Con tried to concentrate on what he was doing with his mouth, but it was fucking impossible.

Tristan's tongue was sodding *lethal*, and shit, he was going to come . . . Con tried to think of anything he could that'd stave it off. Being back at school getting a bollocking from his teachers, that was his usual go-to, but now *teacher* had turned into *Tristan*, and oh, fuck, Con was coming, helplessly spurting into Tristan's mouth in a haze of ecstasy. Con's vision went black and sparkly, and it took him a moment to realise he'd totally dropped the ball when it came to Tristan's dick.

"S-sorry," he gasped, panting. "Just gimme a mo."

"No hurry," Tristan drawled. His voice was languid, like he'd come already, which Con was pretty bloody certain he hadn't. "Come and kiss me first."

Humans, Con decided, had *way* too many limbs. At least, it seemed to take forever for him to get his four to do what he wanted them to. He'd only just got himself turned around when Tristan pulled him down for a salty, come-flavoured kiss. "What d'you need?" Con asked hoarsely.

"Just you," Tristan said, rutting up against him. Con managed to manoeuvre a hand between them and wrap it around Tristan's dick. "Yesss," Tristan hissed.

God, he was hot. Even a head shorter than Con, he was all man. Con loved the feel of his dick, so different without a foreskin. He rubbed his thumb over the slick head, and Tristan bucked in his arms, his body jerking against Con's.

"More," Tristan begged, so Con did it again and again, until Tristan was shuddering and spurting waves of come against their bellies.

Con stroked him through it until Tristan subsided, panting, and muttered, "Stop."

They lay there, bound together with sweat and come, for a long moment. Tristan's hair was all over the place, his lips were swollen, and he had stubble burn on his chin.

He looked fucking gorgeous. Even when he frowned.

"What?" Con asked, stroking his face. "Oi, not regretting this, are you?" Wasn't that Con's job? One he was being utter crap at right now.

"God, no. A thousand times no. But I can't believe I just let you shag me on Nanna Geary's sofa." He laughed, and Con joined him. "Then again," Tristan continued, "I do have at least circumstantial evidence that she'd actually have approved."

It was Con's turn to frown. "Yeah? What do you mean?"

"Nanna Geary, dear boy, appears to have turned matchmaker in her old age. Apparently it was her dearest wish that we get together. Well, that, and that I look after her cat, at which I seem to have failed abysmally. Still, one out of two ain't bad."

Con raised himself up off Tristan's chest. There was a lead weight in his stomach. "Is that why you did all this? Cos your Gran—or whatever—wanted you to?" Like Con needed looking after, or something. Like the *cat*.

Tristan's eyes widened. "No! God, no. Actually I didn't find out about it all until I went to see Miss Wellbeck. Rather missed my cue there, in fact." He laughed. "No, if it hadn't been for that bet with Amanda—"

It was the way Tristan suddenly stopped talking, more than his words, that punched Con in the gut. "What bet?" he asked, his voice sounding a bit funny.

"Ah. Forget the bet. Silly thing, not worthy of mention. *Moving on now*—"

"What bet?"

"It wasn't really a bet *per se*. Not originally. And fifty pounds is *nothing* between friends—"

"You bet a mate fifty quid you could get me into bed?"

"Well, *technically*, yes . . . But listen—"

Con didn't want to listen. He'd thought . . . He'd been so fucking *stupid*. When had Tristan ever given him any reason to think he actually gave a shit? Even all that stuff he'd done, going round to see Miss Wellbeck and that . . .

Yeah, well. Some people'd do *anything* to win a bet.

God, he was stupid. Why the bloody hell would Tristan *ever* give a shit about a bloke like Con? Someone who could barely even fucking *read*? Con scrambled off Tristan, grabbed for his jeans, and yanked them on.

"Con, please . . ."

He shrugged Tristan's hand off his shoulder. "Gotta go," he said roughly. There was that sharp, hot feeling in his eyes that meant he was about to cry. And, fuck, that'd just be fucking *brilliant*, wouldn't it? Crying in front of Tristan.

He couldn't. He just *couldn't*. He pulled on his shirt, shoved his feet in his trainers, and got out of there.

CHAPTER TWENTY-FIVE
A MINCED MAN

Tristan pulled a cushion over his face and howled into it, long and loud. Oh *God*. It had been like some kind of nightmare. As if he'd been on stage and had inexplicably forgotten his lines, and each effort at improvisation had merely driven one more nail into his self-constructed coffin.

Worse than a nightmare. At least if you die on stage, you come back to life when the curtain falls. What had he been *thinking* of? Well, that was easily answered. He hadn't been thinking at all. It was debatable, on current evidence, if he *ever*, in fact, thought.

How could he have been so irredeemably, utterly *stupid* as to mention the bet? Of *course* Con had been upset. Who wouldn't be upon discovering they'd just shagged a base, imbecilic *turd*? Tristan was a flesh-monger, a fool, and a coward. And that was the *best* that could be said of him. He lay there, the cushion still over his face in the vague hope he might manage to smother himself, until an odd sensation at his naked hip caused him to freeze in alarm.

It happened again. There was something smooth and warm brushing against his skin, soft yet hard, like an iron fist in a furry glove. And there was the definite suggestion of whiskers.

Slowly, Tristan removed the cushion from his face, and looked down to where a small black-and-white cat was rubbing its cheek on his hip. "Meggie?"

Meggie, for it must be she, stopped and looked at him. Moving cautiously, he reached down to fondle her head. She seemed to approve, putting a paw up as if exploring the notion of jumping on his lap.

Tristan was just trying to work out how to explain to her that, while he had nothing against that idea in principle, he'd really prefer said lap to be clothed at the time, when they both stilled at a knock on the back door.

A male voice shouted, "Hello? Everything all right in there? I heard shouting."

Onslow. Bloody buggering bigoted Onslow. Oh, what the hell. Grabbing the cushion once more, Tristan placed it strategically over his groin and padded into the kitchen. "Can I help you?" he enquired politely through the glass of the door.

His neighbour paled. "Er. Yes. Just a little concerned . . ." His gaze dropped, and Tristan realised Meggie had followed him out here. She wound herself around Tristan's naked leg, showing no inclination to leap through the cat flap and join her erstwhile foster father.

Tristan smiled. "Nothing to worry about. I was just enjoying a little quality time with my pussy. Weren't we, Meggie?" he added, bending down to stroke her furry little head and, incidentally, giving his neighbour a perfect view of the naked Goldsmith arse.

Really, he thought, for a man of his age and weight it was astonishing how quickly Onslow could move.

Late that evening, now fully clothed and with a purring cat warming his lap, Tristan stared at the mantelpiece with its picture of Nanna Geary and the infant Tristan in what was probably his last blameless hour, and thought. If Meggie could forgive him, perhaps Con could? After all, it was just a silly misunderstanding. Yes, that was it. All he needed to do was tell Con he lo—was fond of him, and all would be forgiven.

It would, wouldn't it? Of course, it might take a little time . . .

Time. The one thing he didn't have, not after Father's bloody bombshell.

Oh God. An icy pit opened up inside Tristan's stomach. And he hadn't even told Con about that. Had utterly failed to even hint that he'd be buggering off to New York next month, leaving the

Sham-Drams high and dry, and letting all Con's efforts—all he'd achieved—come to naught.

Oh yes. Of *course* all would be forgiven when he mentioned *that* little matter. The thought left a bitter taste in Tristan's mouth.

But, God, what could he do?

Desperate, Tristan reached for his laptop. What time was it in Hong Kong? Just about morning, he thought. And in any case, this was an emergency. And come to think of it, he hadn't heard from Amanda for *days*. He should probably be getting concerned about her. Yes, calling her was the only possible act of a true friend.

And it would be an excellent opportunity for Amanda to prove *herself* a true friend. After all, anything Suki said about her had to be taken with an ocean of salt, and vice versa. They simply brought out the worst in each other.

But to him, Amanda had always been a true comrade.

He made the call.

"What?" she demanded, her more-than-somewhat tousled head coming into view. Apparently he'd reached her in bed again.

"Shouldn't you be up already?" Tristan asked, concerned at her potential tardiness in the workplace.

"I'm taking a day off. I was *trying* to have a lie-in."

He sighed in relief. "Perfect. I need you, darling. Things have gone horribly wrong with Con."

"Oh, for God's sake, you're not *still* harping on about the local yokel, are you? Just forget it. I won't ask you for the fifty pounds. You can just buy me something nice for Christmas."

"I don't owe you fifty pounds. That's the whole point. *You* owe *me*. And he knows you do."

"What? How could he possibly . . . You know what, don't tell me. I'm *busy*, Tristan. I've got things to do today. Your existential crisis will have to wait."

"What things? What could possibly be more important—"

"I've met someone. He's here now, actually." She gave a smug little smile. "He works in futures—doing *very* well at it too. Making an absolute packet. *And* he has contacts in films. He's going to get me a screen test."

Tristan blinked. "Well, best of British, my dear. But, darling, I do need your help. How can I convince Con—"

She cut him off with an exaggerated eye roll and a noise of exasperation. "What does it even *matter*? He's nobody, Tristan. It's absolutely ridiculous to be so worked up about someone like that."

"He's actually a very competent actor," Tristan corrected her stiffly. "And one of the kindest, most genuine people I know."

"Oh, *whatever*. Look, just sort your own problems out, for God's sake. Call me when you've got something *interesting* to talk about."

Tristan's view of her tilted and disappeared as she closed up her laptop.

He sat there for a long moment, staring at but not seeing his dim reflection in the black screen of his computer.

CHAPTER TWENTY-SIX
SO OFT BEGUILED

"**H**e said *what*?" Heather looked like one of the lions off the pub sign come to life and about to gut someone with its claws.

"What a fucking tosser," Chris agreed. "Pint?"

Con nodded sadly. As Chris stood, Sean patted Con on the shoulder. "Can't believe it, mate. He seemed all right. You know, when you got to know him."

"Are you *positive* there was no misunderstanding?" Robert asked.

Sean gave him a disbelieving look. "Yeah, right. Like there's so many possible interpretations of *Thanks, mate, you just won me fifty quid.*"

"He didn't say it like that." Con wasn't sure why he felt he had to defend Tristan. Just . . . maybe he'd got it all wrong? Got the hump when it wasn't anything anyone ought to get upset about?

'Cept Heather and the rest had been even more pissed off about it than he had. Well, maybe not, but they'd said a lot of stuff that made Con think it might not be such a good idea for Tristan to cross their path anytime soon.

'Specially Heather. "'*Though she be but little, she is fierce,*'" Tristan had said. And, Christ, why did it have to hurt so fucking much to think about him?

"What's it gonna mean for the play?" Sean asked.

Shit. Con hadn't even thought about that.

"Might have to cancel," Heather said, like it didn't mean a thing to her either way.

Which was total bollocks. Con lifted his head to look at her. "You can't do that."

"If I gotta, I gotta. I mean it. I'm not making you go on stage with someone who's treated you like shit. A cast's a team, and if you can't trust your team members, it's not gonna work." Heather's gaze was determined. "I know he was helping you with lines and stuff, and that's not the issue—we can all chip in and help, can't we, lads?" There was a lot of nodding from Sean and Rob. "But I'm not making you work with that bastard if you don't wanna. I mean it." She gave him a wobbly smile. "It's just a play, innit? There'll be others."

Not with the Sham-Drams, there wouldn't be. Not with her directing, not if this one never got off the ground. And what were the chances Con would ever have the nerve to even consider going for a part in anything else?

It was well after closing time when Con finally got back to his flat. Head down, he didn't realise at first that there was somebody sitting on the stairs just outside his front door.

It was Tristan.

"Ah," he said, his voice cracking. He cleared his throat. "Can we talk?"

Con looked at him for a long moment. He looked . . . He looked good, like he always did. And part of Con—and not just *that* part, *Jesus*—wanted to say yes, and to take him inside. But he knew what would happen if he did. Tristan would break out the smiles and the smooth words, cos that was what actors *did*, and they'd end up in bed again—or for the first time, seeing as it'd been a sofa back at Tristan's—and then in the morning nothing would've changed. Tristan would still be the shit who made a bet about getting off with Con.

And he'd still be buggering off to New York in a couple of months. And what was worse, Con didn't even know which one he most was upset about, really.

"Look, about the bet—it's all just a silly misunderstanding. Yes, that was how it started. But that's not how I feel now. I, well." Tristan cleared his throat. "I've become rather attached to you."

He said it like Con should be pleased, and for a moment he kind of was, despite himself. But then it really sank in, and all he could feel was a knife twisting in his gut. "Yeah? So that makes it all right, does it?"

"Yes?" Tristan sounded hopeful.

Con sighed. Fuck, he was tired. "Look, let's say I believe you. That doesn't change what you did."

"Enjoyed a rather pleasant shag on the sofa?" Tristan's laugh sounded nervous, but it still rubbed Con up the wrong way.

His fists clenched at his sides. The staircase outside his flat probably wasn't the best place to have this conversation, but sod it. "You— Look, what if you hadn't *become attached*, yeah? Imagine that. What if we were here now, everything the same, but you actually didn't give a shit about me. *Hypothetically speaking*."

Tristan winced. "Well, hypothetically speaking, I suppose . . . Oh." Tristan flushed, like maybe the penny had finally dropped.

"You . . . you did stuff. Stuff that made me . . ." *Love you.* Con turned away. He just couldn't look at him any longer. "And then I find out it's all about winning a fucking bet. Look, I know you're fucking off to New York in a month or two. I *know* that. But you made me think . . . I dunno. That maybe we could've managed, somehow. Or . . . or I could've gone with you, even." Christ, it hurt to say it.

"You'd have done that? For me?" Tristan's brown eyes were wider than Con had ever seen them.

He shrugged. "Yeah, well. 'S all bollocks, innit?" He stepped round Tristan to let himself in and shut the door.

Then he went to wash his face because he wasn't fucking crying, all right?

He wasn't.

CHAPTER TWENTY-SEVEN
JOY'S SOUL

Con had looked . . . awful. Tired, and sad, and *hurt*.

God, Tristan was *far* lower than a mouse's arse. Geological strata and millennia of evolution separated him from the hindquarters of *mus musculus*. Vile, loathsome creatures such as Tristan *dreamed* of one day building up enough positive karma to be reincarnated as a mouse's arse.

Tristan lay on the floor of Nanna Geary's living room, a cat upon his chest, her solid weight now heavier by half a can of hastily purchased sardines. Her breath, Tristan had decided, would serve admirably as the beginnings of penance for his sins. Had she been Meggie the First, said penance would also have included his suffering *la peine forte et dure*, but apparently cat manufacturers went in for more lightweight models these days. Perhaps, later, he could persuade her to slice through his jugular with a playful bat of a claw? At any rate, the floor was all he was fit for. He *certainly* didn't deserve the sofa.

"You're all I have left," he told Meggie in a piteous tone. "Here I lie, alone, friendless . . ." No, wait, there was Suki, wasn't there? She'd undoubtedly still be up. Of course, how to reach her was something of a problem, given the aforementioned cat of penance on his chest.

Discarding the idea of performing a sort of feline bench press, he eventually went for the gradual approach, levering himself up on one elbow and slowly tilting his torso until she got the message and scrambled off with a reproachful mew. "Terribly sorry, old thing," he murmured and got to his feet to pad wearily into the kitchen. Perhaps it *was* about time he charged his phone again.

Suki answered on the seventeenth ring. "Tristan, darling, you're coming back?"

"Ah. Not as *such*. I called for some advice." Tristan cut to the chase. "You're a woman of the world. Say your young man had completely ballsed things up with you, how might you best be placated and won round again?"

"Wouldn't happen, darling. Life's too short for second chances."

"*Not* helping."

"Well, what did you do? Confess all, and I *may* be able to come up with a plan for you."

"Do? Did I say we were talking about me? I might be writing a play. A novel, even. It could be purely hypothetical."

"Darling, you wouldn't be ringing me at one o'clock in the morning for a hypothesis."

"I *might*." Tristan sighed. "Hypothetically speaking. Very well. I may have let on that my motives for pursuing a certain young man were—initially, only initially—less than pure."

"And he was disappointed? Good Lord, Tristan, have you developed a passion for a priest?"

"Not *that* sort of impure. There, ah, may have been a bet involved."

"Let me guess—with your little BFF? Which is not, by the way, supposed to stand for *best frenemy forever*."

"Amanda's not—" Tristan cut off his impassioned defence of her before it had even started, no longer entirely certain why he was bothering. "It's come to my attention that you may, just *may* have had an inkling of the truth when you warned me she didn't have my best interests at heart."

"If—and I doubt this most sincerely, darling—Amanda has a heart, the only best interests contained within that shrivelled little remnant are her own. Of course she didn't, darling. She couldn't *stand* you doing well in the profession while she languished on the sidelines in bit parts."

Tristan was silent a moment. "*Was* I doing well in the profession? I don't mean to be rude, but, well, performing with the Players, one doesn't exactly rake it in."

"Neither did Van Gogh, but he seems passably well regarded for his art these days."

"Canvas lasts for centuries. Our art is rather more ephemeral than that."

"Oh, how silly of me. Of course, no one's ever *heard* of Henry Irving, Laurence Olivier, Ellen Terry . . . Need I go on?"

"I'm not sure the average man in the street"—in Tristan's head, the man in question bore a striking resemblance to Con—"has heard of more than one in three of that little lot."

"So? Try asking that same man to name a painting by Van Gogh that *isn't* about sunflowers."

"Look, we're going *completely* off script here," Tristan protested. "You're supposed to be helping me with my romantic woes."

"Hypothetically?"

"No, curse it all. *Really.* I've cocked it all up, Suki. He isn't even *speaking* to me."

"Let me guess—he somehow found out about that bet you mentioned? How, by the way, did that happen? Given your toxic little chum is on another continent."

"I . . . Well. I may have, ah, alluded to it. In bed."

"You know, it really is the supreme irony that you get to utter Puck's famous line about mortals being fools."

"Yes, thank you, I'm *quite* aware of that. Now come on, darling. *Help* meee."

There was a pause. "But aren't you going to be leaving him behind in a couple of months in any case?"

"One month, if Father has his way. But . . ." Tristan's heart clenched at the thought of it. "He said he'd considered going to New York with me. Con, that is. Not Father, thank God."

There was a silence, although if Tristan imagined hard, he could hear her drawing in a drag from her cigarette and then blowing it out again through pursed lips. "Darling. I really don't think he'll do that *now*."

"No. No, I don't suppose he will." Oh God, he could have had his cake and eaten it. Except . . . was that really the sort of cake he wanted in any case? Did he really want to force down baked cheesecake, when he could have a nice slice of Victoria sponge? Or, for that matter, Bakewell tart, or scones with jam and cream . . .

Suki was speaking again. "Then you'll just have to forget New York and join us again, won't you?"

"And how will that solve matters? I still won't be *here*."

"Damn. I was hoping that wouldn't occur to you."

"Your opinion of my intelligence is touching, my sweet. As is your incorrigible self-interest."

"Well, if you really *won't* come back to us, London's only a short train ride away from you, and I do seem to recall there being one or two theatres there."

"Where I can fight tooth and nail for every part, and even if I should prove successful, take home barely more than minimum wage for my pains?"

"Well, it's your choice, darling. Do you want to spend your life as a highly remunerated, mediocre, depressed financier, or a poorly paid but fulfilled, excellent actor? With, I might add, the man you love by your side?"

Tristan's heart clenched painfully. Oh God. When she put it like that . . . "I don't recall telling you I love him," he said at last.

"Oh, darling. You don't have to *tell* me these things."

There was a faint click as she hung up.

Tristan was on his own.

He padded back into the living room, where Meggie showed she hadn't quite forgiven him by sticking one leg in the air and starting to lick an area a true lady, he felt, would have attended to in private. Tristan sat on the floor beside her, and stroked her head absently.

Could he do it? Could he really go against Father's wishes, and remain in this green and pleasant land?

It might mean a fatal breach between them. He'd almost certainly have to give up the BMW. And, obviously, all hope of ever gaining paternal approval. His insides roiled at the very thought, as if a modern-day Prospero were exercising his art to raise up a very localised tempest.

But weren't Nanna Geary's wishes worth as much as Father's? True, she was no blood relation—but every fibre of Tristan's being cried out that she was family, for all that. Perhaps even more so than Father, given how many more hours he'd spent in her company as a child. And she'd wanted him to settle in the village. With Con.

"Oh, Nanna Geary," he sighed, gazing up at her stern, beloved visage in the photo on the mantelpiece. "Couldn't you have given me just a *little* more in the way of stage directions?"

Tristan felt torn in two—unable to appease one parental figure without disappointing the other, even if posthumously. "To act, or not to act—that bloody well is the question, isn't it, Meggie? Whether 'tis nobler in the mind—" He broke off as, having concluded her X-rated ablutions, she jumped back on his lap. "I see you decided comfort was more important than injured dignity. It must be nice to have to consult no one's feelings but your own."

God, how could he decide between Father and Nanna Geary?

Tristan groaned in despair—a rather pleasing, hollow sound— and then sat up straight, causing Meggie to mew in irritation and dig in her claws so as not to be dislodged. Tristan welcomed the pain as well-deserved punishment for his failings. He was an idiot. Father and Nanna Geary weren't the only ones with speaking roles in this little drama that was his life.

There was Con too, could Tristan but persuade the man to hear him out—and damn it, there was Tristan himself. Did his own wishes count for nothing?

Fired with new resolve, Tristan lifted Meggie gently off his lap and got to his feet. The blast of war was blowing in his ears, and he was about to imitate the actions of the tiger. Or, at the very least, those of a small, black-and-white cat.

Then he paused. Probably, in the long run, it wouldn't have a great deal of effect on how things played out. But Tristan couldn't help feeling it might not help his case if he were to ring Father to discuss his future in the wee small hours of the morning. Sighing, he took himself to bed. But it was a long time before nature's soft nurse could be persuaded to weigh his eyelids down and steep his senses in forgetfulness.

If it hadn't been for Meggie's soft purrs in his ear, he doubted he'd have got to sleep at all.

CHAPTER TWENTY-EIGHT
LOVE'S LABOUR'S WON

Con wasn't too chuffed to get back to his front door the next night—late, cos he'd popped round to Alf's for tea again and they'd got talking—and find Tristan camped out on the doorstep.

Again.

He sighed. "Look, I've had a hard day, all right? Spent all afternoon digging out ivy. I'm covered in dirt and cobwebs and probably bugs as well, and I'm knackered. Can we not do this?" *Ever*, he added internally.

Tristan stood up. "I'm not going to New York. I rang Father and told him I wasn't going to let him dictate my life. And I refuse to eat cheesecake. I'm staying in Shamwell." He stopped and just stood there, looking small, and pale, and determined.

Con was struggling to make sense of it all. Especially the cheesecake. Tristan wasn't leaving? "What . . . what about your job?"

"I'll get another one. Try, anyway. I'm going to start auditioning. We're in easy reach of London here, so there are lots of opportunities."

"You're gonna stay in acting?"

Tristan nodded.

"What about money?" Cos Con was pretty sure it wasn't just a matter of wandering along to an audition and then landing a cushy job, for most actors.

Tristan shrugged. "Well, it's not like I've a mortgage to pay. And there's some money in trust. Not a lot, but, well, I'm still a lot better placed than most actors trying to make a go of it. If needs must, I'm sure I can talk my way into *some* kind of job. And I'll be here for *Dream*, of course." He sent Con a shaky smile that was miles away from his usual confident, I-own-the-world smirk.

Con was still trying to get his head round all this. "How'd your dad take it?"

Tristan's smile turned into a grimace. "Remember I told you about the first time I ever acted? Well, rather like that. Only with more fireworks." He paused. "I came here to . . . well, to tell you all this, obviously, but also to say I'm sorry. Truly. I should never have treated gaining your affections like some kind of game. If it's any consolation, I've been pretty thoroughly hoist by my own petard. And the friend I made the . . . the bet with? I don't think we're going to be speaking anymore."

"Oh." Con knew he probably ought to say something a bit more meaningful than *oh*, but there was so much going on inside his head, it was bloody impossible to separate it out into words.

Tristan's face fell. "I realise you've got no reason whatsoever to even consider giving me a second chance," he went on. "I know I don't deserve one. I just . . . I just want you to know that if you ever thought you could, well, I'd do my utmost to be worthy of it." He took a deep breath. "And just so you know, I'll be forsaking all others in the meantime. I'll . . . I'll let you get in, now. Sorry to have disturbed."

He was halfway down the stairs before Con could get his scrambled thoughts together. "Wait," he called.

Tristan looked up at him, his expression a mix of fear and hope that caught at Con's insides.

"You're not going to New York? Like, at all?" Con asked, cos he really, *really* wanted to be certain on that bit.

"Both boats and bridges thoroughly burned." Tristan paused, then seemed to come to a decision. "And . . . I realise there may be a degree of self-sabotage in telling you this, but it's not just for you. I'd have been making a terrible mistake. Nanna Geary knew it long before I did. A high-flying financial career? I'd have crashed within months. And, well, I like England, with its history and its traditions and even its bloody awful summers. I like it *here*, in the village, with all the people I've got to know. None of whom, I imagine, are currently speaking to me after the appalling way I treated you, but there you go. One makes one's bed, et cetera."

Con felt suddenly ashamed. He hadn't given Tristan a chance to explain himself—hadn't even given it a bit of cooling-off time, just dashed up to the pub to slag the poor bloke off to everyone. "Sorry," he said, though it didn't feel like nearly enough.

Tristan stared at him. "What the bloody hell for? *You* haven't done anything wrong. Anyway, I should—"

"No," Con cut him off, surprising himself. "Look, come in for a bit, yeah? This is all . . . It's just a lot to take in. But don't go." He fumbled with his key to open the door, then looked back over his shoulder to make sure Tristan was still there. "Come in," he said again.

When the door closed behind them both, Con had a brief moment of elation—then uncertainty closed in again. Were they gonna talk? Cuddle? Shag? Right now, option number two sounded best to Con, but would that just be putting stuff off?

Plus, well, he really was covered in crap from work. Shit. "Look, um, sorry, but I really gotta shower. You'll wait, yeah? I won't be long."

Tristan nodded. It made Con feel better to find even he'd run out of words.

Con legged it to the bathroom and showered as quickly as he could, realising too late he hadn't taken any clean clothes in. Walking back into the living room, towel around his waist, the empty sofa hit him like a punch to the gut. Tristan hadn't waited.

Then he realised Tristan was in his bed. His dark hair lay tousled on the pillow, one bare shoulder was showing above the duvet, and he was fast asleep.

Con's heart melted. He turned off the light, dropped the towel to the floor, and slipped into bed beside him. Tristan stirred but didn't wake, even when Con wrapped his arms around him and pulled him close. He just mumbled something that didn't even sound like English and drifted back into deep sleep again.

Con smiled. Yeah. This was way better than talking.

CHAPTER TWENTY-NINE
FOLLOWING DARKNESS
LIKE A DREAM

Tristan struggled awake from confused and vaguely horrifying dreams of his father dressed as Oberon, ordering him to give up Con, who was improbably attired in an oriental pageboy outfit several sizes too small. Relief washed over him as he opened his eyes to Con's handsome face, the rugged jawline softened by sleep, on the pillow next to him.

"'Oh thou, my lovely boy,'" he murmured, enchanted by the view. Con snuffled in response, his stubble rasping almost inaudibly on the pillow.

Tristan would have been quite content to feast his eyes for, oh, the foreseeable future, but then Con stirred and blinked awake, and other ideas came irresistibly to mind. He snuggled up to Con and, to forestall any possible problems with reeking breath, kissed him thoroughly on the neck.

Con rolled over and pulled him close, his hardness pressing against Tristan's hip. "Mm. Mornin.'"

They frotted gently together, Con's hands on Tristan's arse. One of Tristan's arms had somehow got trapped under Con's not inconsiderable weight and was going to sleep. Con's chest hair was tickling his nose. Tristan's head felt muzzy and thick, and he desperately needed to pee.

It was perfect. He came with a groan and flopped, boneless, as Con carried on rutting against him until he, too, climaxed between them, his whole body tensing with it. They lay entwined, panting, for a moment.

But Tristan really *did* have to pee, and besides . . . "Ugh. Gross," he muttered, looking down at the slimy mess on Con's hirsute stomach. "Shower? Together?"

"Uh . . . It'll be a bit of a squeeze."

"Then you'll just have to hold me *very* close," Tristan told him, getting up. His face felt funny, as if stretched into a besotted, lovesick smile, which closer inspection in the bathroom mirror revealed was, in fact, the case. It was a touch unnerving to find his face doing things like that without consulting him first, but Tristan found he couldn't bring himself to care overmuch.

The shower was, indeed, a tight squeeze. Tristan loved it.

"Any plans for the day?" he asked as he towelled himself off and enjoyed the view of Con standing there naked and dripping, as they'd neglected to bring in another towel. "I was thinking straight back to bed."

"Um. We probably ought to call Heather at some point."

"Kinky. Not really my thing, but I suppose you could persuade me—" Tristan yelped as Con snatched the towel out of his hands. "I was still using that."

Con grinned. "You were taking too long. And I meant she might want to know her play's still on."

"God, she's going to kill me, isn't she?"

Con shrugged, halfway through drying his hair. The vigorous rubbing motion made things lower down jiggle distractingly. "Maybe. But I reckon you're safe until after the final performance, at least."

"*I can see the headlines now.* 'Tragic epilogue to virtuoso performance; England's most promising young actor cut down in his prime.'"

"'England's most promising'? Who says?" Holding the towel in both hands, Con threw it over Tristan's head and drew him in for a damp embrace.

"Nanna Geary, chiefly, and I'm quite certain it's disrespectful to be remembering her while you're doing *that*."

Con grinned and did it again.

EPILOGUE
ALL IS MENDED

The Shamwell Amateur Dramatics Society production of *A Midsummer Night's Dream* by William Shakespeare took place during the last weekend of September. The weather was still warm during the day, but the nights had started to turn chilly and the first leaves were beginning to fall from village trees. The performances were, over the three nights, increasingly well attended, and some of the audience were even below retirement age—in fact, Heather had exclaimed excitedly that she'd never seen so many young people come to a production.

Tristan's ego might have started to get a trifle inflated were it not for the gang of giggling teenage girls who'd accosted Con after the second night and asked him, blushing, to sign their programs. Con's embarrassment hadn't eased when Heather told him that nobody, in the entire history of the Sham-Drams, had *ever* been asked for an autograph before.

Con's performance had been a triumph. As had Tristan's, of course, and the rest of the cast had made a creditable attempt to keep up with them. The audience had laughed, clapped, and generally declared this to be the best performance of *A Midsummer Night's Dream* ever seen in the village. Tristan was reliably informed (by Heather) that they actually meant it as a sincere compliment, and weren't just damning them with faint praise.

She even gave him a hug after the last curtain call. "I *knew* we were right, not hacking you to pieces with a spoon and burying you on the common in an unmarked grave."

"I'd only have come back to haunt you." Still high on performance adrenaline, Tristan laughed as a thought struck him. "Imagine that: you'd have been able to put on *Hamlet* with the late king played by a real ghost."

"Yeah, I think we're gonna give Shakespeare a rest for a bit after this. Do something with a few less characters, for a start. *And* a lot less men."

"*The Vagina Monologues*?" Tristan suggested drily.

"God, no. In Shamwell? They'd run me outta town. Nah, I was thinking a farce, maybe." She grinned. "Con'd be good in a farce."

"*Con*, dear child, is going to be busy with his evening classes—remember?" Tristan couldn't keep the pride from his voice, not that he tried all that hard. Con had signed up for courses in English and Maths *and* a carpentry and joinery course, the college having agreed to allow him to obtain the entry requirements concurrently. "And don't pull that face. From what I hear, *you* were the one who got him thinking about education in the first place."

She smirked. "Yeah, well. Sorry to ruin your sex life."

"Oh, *please*. You're only jealous. My sex life, darling, is *magnificent*. My sex life—" Tristan broke off with a *mummph* sound as a large hand clapped over his mouth from behind.

"Is something I'd prefer kept between the two of us, all right?" Con finished for him. Then he took his hand away and gave Tristan a proper hug. "You were brilliant tonight. Absolutely bloody brilliant."

Tristan felt lighter than air wrapped in his arms. "We were *all* brilliant. Teamwork at its finest."

"Oi, no feeling up the fairies!" Chris yelled out from across the stage, bursting Tristan's bubble nicely.

"Keep it down, you prat," Heather snapped back at him in a stage whisper. "People are only just leaving."

Tristan tiptoed with comically exaggerated care to the edge of the curtain, and Chris laughed. Con, because he was far smarter than most people gave him credit for, followed him and soon guessed why Tristan was scanning the audience as they filed out.

"Did you think your dad might have turned up?" he asked gently, his arm around Tristan's shoulders.

Tristan sighed. "No, not really. But one always hopes, doesn't one?"

"Yeah, well, he's probably just holding out for when you're topping the bill at Her Majesty's," Con said loyally.

Con's friend Alf had been there the previous evening—and leaning on his arm, the former Miss Wellbeck, now known by her own request as Auntie Mary. Well, technically she was *still* Miss Wellbeck, but Tristan expected that to change with very little notice. He could only hope the stress of wedding bells wouldn't prove too much for geriatric hearts. Then again, she was looking noticeably less fragile these days, probably because both Alf and Con seemed to think some kind of edible gift *de rigueur* every time they visited her.

The ill-fated Patrick had turned up on crutches for closing night and stayed to have drinks with the cast after the audience had departed. Con insisted on dragging Tristan over to introduce him. "Patrick? You never met Tristan, did you?"

Patrick held out a genial hand, but his gaze was cool as it met Tristan's. "Nah, but I've heard a lot about you."

"All good, I hope?" Tristan returned politely.

Patrick's expression didn't waver. "That'd be telling, wouldn't it? Anyway, good to meet you. Great performance," he added, then got his crutches back into position to hobble away.

"I don't think he likes me," Tristan muttered to Con.

"Yeah . . ." Con rubbed the back of his neck. "Don't worry about it."

Tristan gave him a sharp look, but Con's expression betrayed nothing. "What? Is he worried I'm going to snatch all the best roles from now on? Perhaps someone should tell him about *Electra*." Suki, bless her, had finally given up on trying to persuade Tristan back to the Players and put in a good word for him with *Electra*'s casting director, who was an old friend and, Tristan thought privately, ex-lover. Tristan's role would call for him to murder a parental figure, which he expected to find nicely cathartic.

"Nah, it's not that."

"Oh? *Oh*. Well, I'll be damned if I'm letting go of the best *man* around. I hope you've told him I'm here for good and that you, dear boy, are mine for even longer," Tristan added. He looked up at Con to find him staring down with a strange expression in his eyes. "What?"

"Just . . . You're amazing, you know that?" Cupping Tristan's face with both hands, Con leaned down to kiss him thoroughly.

Fortunately, being actors, everyone was far too superstitious to wolf whistle.

The following day was all hands on deck for clearing up. There was scenery to be dismantled and props to be put away.

Con's eerie forest, clothed in moody tones pulled from the lower end of the spectrum, was now just boards. The ass's head—or, more properly, hood—was now just a scrap of fur fabric. Even Puck's horns seemed no more significant than any supermarket Halloween prop.

"It's a bit sad, this bit, innit," Con said in Tristan's ear when they stole a moment's break together.

Tristan smiled as well-muscled arms wrapped around his waist, and Con's chin came to rest lightly upon the top of his head. "I've always thought so. The theatre, without the magic. Our insubstantial pageant faded, leaving not a rack behind. Funny, though—it doesn't feel so much like an ending, this time."

"No?" Con's deep voice rumbled through Tristan.

"No. More like a beginning. I'm entering a new stage of life. No more mewling infant, nor whining schoolboy—would you like a ballad to your eyebrows? No? Ah, well. As you like it."

Con chuckled. "You know what your problem is?"

"Let me guess—too many words?"

"Well, that too. No. Your problem is, you don't realise the effect you have on people."

"Intense irritation?"

This time, Con laughed out loud. "Well, yeah. That too. Again. But what I *meant* is, you don't realise how inspiring you can be. How . . . People are gonna remember your performance in *Dream*. And me, and Hev, and all the others? We're gonna remember all that stuff you taught us about putting on the play, making it funny. Making it real. So I might not know what a rack is, but I do know it's bollocks that you're not leaving anything behind. You're leaving stuff. Good stuff. So yeah, it's a bit sad, but like you said, it's not an ending. It's a beginning. And it's gonna be great."

Tristan turned in Con's arms, his heart melting with happiness so sharp it hurt. "You . . . 'I am amazed and know not what to say.'" He laughed, shaking his head ruefully. "'The eye of man hath not heard, the ear of man hath not seen, man's hand is not able to taste, his tongue to conceive, nor his heart to report, how I feel about you. And I am but a patched fool if I try.'"

Con smiled that adorable, lopsided smile of his. "Me too. You know that, don't you? You're the best thing that ever happened to me. Oh, and you know what else?"

Tristan gazed mistily up at the man of his dreams. "Go on."

Soulful brown eyes looked deep into Tristan's, and Con stroked his cheek with a tender hand. "I always thought you were a bit of an ass."

Tristan stared—then burst out in helpless laughter. Heads, he was dimly aware, turned. Eyes, he was fairly certain, rolled.

He couldn't care less.

The course of true love, for him at least, finally ran smooth.

Chapter Twenty:
    "After life's fitful fever he sleeps well." —*Macbeth* (The Scottish Play), act 3, scene 2
Chapter Twenty-one:
    "Oh, I am fortune's fool!" —Romeo, *Romeo & Juliet*, act 3, scene 1
Chapter Twenty-two:
    "Misery acquaints a man with strange bedfellows"
    —Trinculo, *The Tempest*, act 2, scene 2
Chapter Twenty-three:
    "Of charity, what kin are you to me?" —Sebastian, *Twelfth Night*, act 5, scene 1
Chapter Twenty-four:
    "Lord, what fools these mortals be" —Puck, *A Midsummer Night's Dream*, act 3, scene 2
Chapter Twenty-five:
    "Ay, a minced man: and then to be baked with no date
    "in the pie, for then the man's date's out." —Cressida, *Troilus and Cressida*, act 1, scene 2
Chapter Twenty-six:
    "And therefore is Love said to be a child,
    "Because in choice he is so oft beguiled." —Helena, *A Midsummer Night's Dream*, act 1 scene 1
Chapter Twenty-seven:
    "Joy's soul lies in doing" —Cressida, *Troilus and Cressida*, act 1, scene 2
Chapter Twenty-eight:
    Love's Labour's Won — "lost" play by William Shakespeare
Chapter Twenty-nine:
    "And we fairies, that do run
    "By the triple Hecate's team,
    "From the presence of the sun,
    "Following darkness like a dream,
    "Now are frolic" —Puck, *A Midsummer Night's Dream,* act 5, scene 1
Epilogue:
    "If we shadows have offended,
    "Think but this, and all is mended—

"That you have but slumbered here
"While these visions did appear." —*Puck, A Midsummer Night's Dream*, act 5, scene 1

In the course of the novel, Tristan (mis)quotes many works by William Shakespeare, the Bard of Avon, including several of his sonnets. Other works scurrilously abused include but are not necessarily limited to:

Pygmalion, George Bernard Shaw
Withnail & I (1987, wr. & dir. Bruce Robinson)
The Discworld novels of Sir Terry Pratchett
The novels of P.G. Wodehouse
Blackadder the Third, "Duel and Duality," Ben Elton & Richard Curtis
Mansfield Park, Jane Austen

Explore more of *The Shamwell Tales* at:
riptidepublishing.com/titles/universe/shamwell-tales

Dear Reader,

Thank you for reading JL Merrow's *Played!*

We know your time is precious and you have many, many entertainment options, so it means a lot that you've chosen to spend your time reading. We really hope you enjoyed it.

We'd be honored if you'd consider posting a review—good or bad—on sites like **Amazon, Barnes & Noble, Kobo, Goodreads, Twitter, Facebook, Tumblr,** and your blog or website. We'd also be honored if you told your friends and family about this book. Word of mouth is a book's lifeblood!

For more information on upcoming releases, author interviews, blog tours, contests, giveaways, and more, please sign up for our weekly, spam-free newsletter and visit us around the web:

Newsletter: tinyurl.com/RiptideSignup
Twitter: twitter.com/RiptideBooks
Facebook: facebook.com/RiptidePublishing
Goodreads: tinyurl.com/RiptideOnGoodreads
Tumblr: riptidepublishing.tumblr.com

Thank you so much for Reading the Rainbow!

RiptidePublishing.com

ALSO BY JL MERROW

The Shamwell Tales
Caught!
Out!
Spun!

Porthkennack
Wake Up Call
One Under (coming March 2018)

The Plumber's Mate Mysteries
Pressure Head
Relief Valve
Heat Trap
Blow Down

The Midwinter Manor Series
Poacher's Fall
Keeper's Pledge

Southampton Stories
Pricks and Pragmatism
Hard Tail

Lovers Leap
It's All Geek to Me
Damned If You Do
Camwolf
Muscling Through
Wight Mischief
Midnight in Berlin
Slam!
Fall Hard
Raising the Rent
To Love a Traitor
Trick of Time
Snared
A Flirty Dozen

ABOUT THE AUTHOR

JL Merrow is that rare beast, an English person who refuses to drink tea. She read Natural Sciences at Cambridge, where she learned many things, chief amongst which was that she never wanted to see the inside of a lab ever again. Her one regret is that she never mastered the ability of punting one-handed whilst holding a glass of champagne.

She writes (mostly) contemporary gay romance and mysteries, and is frequently accused of humour. Her novel *Slam!* won the 2013 Rainbow Award for Best LGBT Romantic Comedy, and several of her books have been EPIC Awards finalists, including *Muscling Through*, *Relief Valve* (the Plumber's Mate Mysteries), and *To Love a Traitor*.

JL Merrow is a member of the Romantic Novelists' Association, International Thriller Writers, Verulam Writers and the UK GLBTQ Fiction Meet organising team.

Find JL Merrow on Twitter as @jlmerrow, and on Facebook at facebook.com/jl.merrow

For a full list of books available, see: jlmerrow.com   or JL Merrow's Amazon author page: viewauthor.at/JLMerrow.

Enjoy more stories like
Played
at RiptidePublishing.com!

Hotline
ISBN: 978-1-62649-486-2

Summer Stock
ISBN: 978-1-62649-569-2

Earn Bonus Bucks!

Earn 1 Bonus Buck for each dollar you spend. Find out how at
RiptidePublishing.com/news/bonus-bucks.

Win Free Ebooks for a Year!

Pre-order coming soon titles directly through our site and you'll
receive one entry into a drawing for a chance to win free books for
a year! Get the details at RiptidePublishing.com/contests.